Eden Valley Editions. *Son.*

In my teens I refused to app
places were elitist. I was mo
government and liberating a
London.

During this period I learnt to dress fabulously from shops like Cornucopia, second hand and charity shops.

After 3 years peeling potatoes and doing care work I was getting nowhere. My parents, becoming desperate, tricked me into going to America (carrying an urgent parcel). I stayed for several years with a family who rescued me from myself and talked me into going to Hunter College in New York. There I studied Drama and English and graduated Summa Cum Laude.

I returned to England, worked for 2 years as a journalist, married and had 4 children. With the third child sitting on my knee I hammered away till late at night at this book. Rejected by one publisher the script sat in a bottom drawer for 10 years.

When I was told I had terminal cancer I took it out and dusted it, thinking, "Sod it. If not now, when?" and here it is.

SOMEONE LIKE ME

SOMEONE LIKE ME

A NOVEL

Emily Smith

Redemption is hell when you'd prefer to stay a sinner

EVE – Eden Valley Editions

First published in Great Britain in 2014

Copyright © Emily Smith 2014

The moral right of the author has been asserted

A CIP catalogue record for this book is available from the British Library.

ISBN: **978-1500413965**

Styled by Marie-Louise Avery

Cover design by Ellen Deakin

Printed and bound in USA

1 Fircroft Way, Edenbridge, Kent TN8 6EL

www.evebooks.co.uk

DEDICATION

For my parents

CHAPTER ONE

I have an allergy to my sister's boyfriend. It's not just a personality thing, it's his beard. The night I shagged him it brought me out in hives all over my face. I have low tolerance to my sister, also. She makes me puke.

It's fortunate, then, that I so rarely bump into Amanda. In fact, I go to great lengths to avoid bumping into her. Even a trace element – the smell of patchouli, the brush of a woollen shawl – makes me feel giddy and sick. But there's always the odd occasion, isn't there? A wedding that your mum says you have to go to or no more high teas until the Second Coming; a funeral that you are forced to attend because you are the beneficiary of a Will. It's only good manners, after all, to show up under those circumstances.

And I look brilliant in black.

The last time but one I saw Amanda, she skipped up to me at my cousin Caroline's white wedding six months ago. I blame myself – I heard her ankle bells a mile away but paused to quaff my Pimm's before running for it in my brand new killer heel Christian Louboutin sandals and I was too late to escape.

"Becky! Hi! How are you! I haven't seen you for a billion years! You look fantastic! Thin as a rail! Too thin! Sooooo - guess what. I've got a new boyfriend. How's your love-life?"

"Oh, fine."

"Great! Is your boyfriend here?"

"Ah... no."

"Oh! Too bad. Well, Mike's over there. Look!" She gestured lovingly at a bearded chap in baggy, striped trousers, a kind of smock and a necklace who was pinned in a corner by my barking mad Auntie Dodie. "Dear old Auntie Dodie! She's telling him all about the universal causal process."

"What's that?"

"Oh, one of the main things about Buddhism."

"Oh right. Buddhism." I thought this Mike looked under pressure. Without doubt his house and garden are clanking with statues of the Buddha, wreathed in the smoke of joss sticks, but for some reason Auntie Dodie is a bit of an expert when it comes to near Eastern philosophy and I was sure he had been flushed out as an ignoramus. They're like that, these hippies. All talk and no Tantras.

"Mike's wonderful, Becky!" enthused my sister. "He's absolutely fabulous! He's the nicest, most loving, kindest, most peaceful, most centred person I know. He's not just a man. He's more of a feminist than I am. He really is a person in his own right. I just love him. And he absolutely adores me. I'm happy, happy, happy. I'm moving in to his house in Hackney next week. Guess what! It's called 'Bird Calls!' Isn't that a cool name? Oh, it's such a cool house. My goodness, though, it's chaotic!"

Of course, she meant by that 'a loveable muddle'. But I know, I just know it's covered with piles of paper, heaps of abandoned knitting projects and dog hairs. Sooner her than me. Still, one has to observe the decencies and show polite interest. Family small talk is a bit beyond me, but I stroked my perfectly cut skirt lovingly over my slim hips and stuck to the clichés. "When did you meet him?" I asked.

"A month ago at a gathering of the Natural Nurturing Network."

"And what on earth is that?"

"It's this amazing, supportive network for parents to nurture their children naturally."

"Sounds ghastly."

"You're such a tease! No really, we all gather to support each other and our own needs while caring for our kids."

"Correct me if I'm wrong, but the last I heard, you don't have any children, Amanda."

"Well, no, not exactly – but Mike has."

"Really? How many?"

"Three. They're fabulous."

"But are they natural?"

"What?"

"Let it go."

"So, where's your boyfriend?"

"Somewhere else. Now if you'll excuse me, Amanda, I must be off to think about him in a corner, all by myself. I'll see you around."

"Oh. Okay. Bye, Becky! Love you!"

"Right. Goodbye."

Meanwhile, our mother was making a big effort, although almost invisible under a hat in shape and colour exactly resembling a three-day-old field mushroom. She joined Mike and Dodie, and I could hear her from afar asking Mike some difficult questions about crystal therapy and ley lines. Yeah, yeah – plenty of time to chat up my sister's hairy beau, but she didn't have any time for me, of course. Mother's always very busy making sure that Amanda's feeling all right when I'm around. It's some crazy idea she has that I make my sister feel insecure. For God's sake. Why doesn't Amanda do therapy like normal people?

Mind you, Mum's been a lot worse about other people's insecurities since Dad slung his hook. He ran off with the next-door neighbour – a raddled, chain-smoking alcoholic called Lorraine – two years ago. But give him credit, he did it properly. They eloped all the way to Brisbane, Australia where Quiche Lorraine's brother has a business printing car stickers (My Other One's a Porsche, that kind of thing). And now my Dad's thinking up unfunny things with which to annoy the driver behind, while my Mum phones him up about once a month to ask him when he's coming home and to complain about me. I don't know why she bothers. As far as I'm concerned, he might as well be dead. He sent a photo once. He was wearing a really horrible shirt and holding a surfboard, and La Quiche was grinning like a great white shark in a neon bikini. Let's hope he nicks himself shaving and she savages him in the water.

In this instance, Mum was annoyed because due to oversleeping I had made my grand entrance in the church just as the vows were being taken. How petty can you get? She totally ignored me at the reception, so after I had got rid of Amanda, I concentrated on chatting up the best man. He consented to accompany me home before his speech, which, I discovered afterwards in a letter from cousin Caroline, had caused rather a sensation. Something I specialise in.

So that was the first time I met Mike. Then about three weeks ago, Amanda had him in tow once more at the handily pre-Christmas funeral of my Great Uncle Patrick. Trailing behind them, trying to fend off Mum who was trying – as ever – too hard, were two incredibly unpleasant teenagers, Mike's children from his previous relationship. To everybody's surprise, his ex was there too. What a disaster. As far as I could tell from a distance, she looked about as poisonous a character as ever noshed a nut roast.

This time, I made a determined try for the door but was tackled by the hippy scrum and against my will, presented to the foul family. The girl – a chubby number with the standard pierced eyebrow, pierced nose and dreadlocks – was introduced as Honeybee, which I naturally thought was a joke, but while I politely tittered the boy was pushed forward and identified as A Robin's Nest. "Pardon?" I said. "Excuse me? Did you say, 'A Robin's Nest?' Is that a name? Seriously?" While I stared, Mike attempted to introduce me to his former squeeze; her name appeared to be Midge but she had nailed my second cousin Bernie to the drinks table and seemed far too busy flapping her kimono around to come and shake hands. Then a toddler appeared, waving a spoon of beige gloop dangerously close to my skirt and losing his nappy down his legs. This, it appeared, was Pumpkin. "You have named your child after a Halloween vegetable that nobody can bear to eat, even in soup?" I inquired. It seemed that this was so. I hastened to excuse myself on the grounds of inconsolable grief over poor old Great Uncle Patrick, and shot off to get pissed.

I wasn't alone at the bar, but sadly there are no well-endowed best men at the funerals of eighty six-year-old accountants. Like a swarm of maddened bees, aunts, uncles and cousins buzzed in from far and wide to ask about my career in concerned tones.

Bernie set the pace, waving a lager in one hand, a sausage roll in the other and spitting bits of beer-soaked pastry dangerously close to my face. "So how's the newspaper industry?" he barked. "Not doing too well, I hear! See your column's at the back these days. Too bad."

"Shut up, Bern!" snapped his mother, Auntie Alice. "Becky's doing very well. Very well indeed. I mean, my next-door neighbour's youngest daughter's best friend's boyfriend's mum always reads her stuff! Gives her a good laugh! It's hard enough being a cartoonist without people like you putting her down, Bernie. So behave yourself or I'll take you home."

"Thanks, Aunt Alice," I said, draining my fourth double vodka tonic and fantasising that I had an Uzi in my handbag. "I'm not a cartoonist, actually. My column's Hey Good Cooking. It's about celebrity eateries. Nothing to do with cartoons at all. Nothing. Nada. Niente. Niet."

"Oooh! I'll have to tell Doreen next door. She'll have to spread the news. What's an eatery, anyhow?"

I preserve a stony silence.

"Well dear, whatever it is, it's very good. A very nice column. Say sorry, Bernie."

"Sorry," mumbled Bernie, who is aged approximately 44. He thrusts the remainder of the sausage roll in his mouth and chews with his jaws dangling open. It's a vision of hell.

"Are you going home for Christmas, dear?"

"Absolutely not."

14

"Oh! Don't you like Christmas, dear?"

"A bit too... what's the word? Festive for me, thanks. I can't stand a thing about it, actually. Everybody sitting around pretending they like each other and opening presents they don't want. Besides, the food's crap. Give me Italian any day."

A stray uncle lurched to my side. "Haw haw haw!" he croaks. "I like a bit of meat on the bones. Nothing like meat on the bones. What you need is a good turkey roast, my girl. A few floury potatoes. Some nice bread sauce. Haw haw haw! That'll put some meat..."

"Stop it, Billy!" interrupted Aunt Alice. "Don't tease this lovely young girl. Being slim is the fashion. Even if she does look anorexic. Lovely clothes, though."

"Thanks."

"So, dear, is the money good at the London Star? Even if you're not a cartoonist?"

"Good enough to buy a gorgeous flat and justify not going to university. And to dress in such a way that Bernie here – forgive me for being frank – couldn't even scrape the shit from my shoes I'm so out of his price range. Not bad, eh? Hey. Another vodka tonic please. Make it a triple. And served sometime before the end of the century? I want to get pissed before picking up my bus pass."

I turned away from the bar to discover that Bernie, Billy and Alice have scuttled away, clucking like a flock of offended old hens, and that they have been replaced in the queue for lukewarm drinks by a complete retard in baggy trousers. Ah yes. Amanda's ghastly boyfriend. What's his name?

Mike.

15

Now, my behaviour from now on has to be judged on the basis that I was very drunk, very angry with my mum, very irritated by Amanda and very, very bored of people like my cousin Bernie. And Mike's behaviour has to be judged on the basis that he's a spineless idiot with beans for brains and a cucumber in his trousers just waiting to be peeled.

Reader, I shagged him.

In a Portaloo. I didn't think I could sink so low, but that's what a collection of my relatives drives me to. It's everybody's fault but my own. I filled him up with vodka tonic, chatted for forty-five minutes about the Buddha, led him outside and did the dirty just for a laugh.

And check it out. I went through all that – funeral bender, sex in a Portaloo, colossal hangover – for nothing. I mean, nothing! Great Uncle Patrick left me a token ten thousand pounds. Honestly. That isn't enough to keep me in stockings and sunglasses.

The very next day, the phone calls started. Even at the time, Mike had been groaning "what about Amanda! What about Amanda!" like a scratched CD, but the situation developed horribly. I was lying on my custom-made black leather sofa watching Desperate Housewives when my phone rang. I have a machine that can screen messages, and this is what I heard.

"Hi! Becky! Mike here! Wow! Hey! You're not in. Just thought I'd give you a call. I love you. Call me. Bye."

"I love you?" I thought, turning the sound of the television up with my remote control with one hand and deleting the message with the other. Christ. It's the male equivalent of the all-star Bunny Boiler. The phone rang again just as I'd got comfortable.

"Hi! Becky! Me again! Hey! I forgot to leave my phone number!" He left it. I deleted the message.

The phone rang.

"Hi! Becky! It's me again, Mike. I just called again to hear your voice on the answer machine. And I thought you'd like to hear mine. Hey! It'd be great to see you again. I can't wait. Wow! Yeah. Bye. Oh, I love you. Bye."

Evening after evening it was the same. He didn't get my message, but boy, did I get his. All twenty-two of them.

Today is the last straw. I'm at the office on a Friday afternoon, and he's on the phone absolutely insisting on a cosy chat. Naturally, I don't mind my colleagues hearing me rejecting suitors, but to be frank, I've had a warning about personal telephone calls. I lower my head so that my hair swings over my face and mutter into the receiver: "Okay. We'll talk. Call me on my mobile," and I give him the number and repair to the ladies. En route I give sexy Simon, our handsome young editor one of my steamier glances through lowered eyelashes, but he doesn't respond. There's no doubt about it – he must be gay.

As I swing through the desks, Marlene Anderson, the fashion editor, calls my name. She starts saying something but I can't concentrate. As usual, I can focus on nothing but her face. To be honest with you, it looks like a great big bum. Really. Two wobbly cheeks and a round hole in the middle. She even wears brown lipstick. I believe sincerely that people who have faces closely resembling a large bottom should be sacked on principle. Plus, at thirty-two years of age she's five years older than me – a tired old has-been stuck on the shelf and totally out of touch with hip happenings.

"Rebecca? Rebecca?"

"Oh, sorry, Marlene. Got distracted. What were you saying?"

Big sigh. "Rebecca, I was saying that Steve from accounts was looking for you earlier. Apparently he's been emailing you but you haven't replied. And he really, really, needs to speak to you."

"Oh, sure. Steve. Of course." I know what that's all about – my expenses. Well, they're high! So what! I'm a high profile hack!

"Listen Marlene," I breathe, bending down over her desk and ignoring the fact that she leans back so far in her chair she almost goes over into the wastepaper basket. "You've just got to tell me. Have you been thinking about a career move? I was chatting to Simon the other day over lunch and he sort of hinted about it. Anything exciting?"

Marlene cheeks begin to wobble. "No, I'm not, actually. Why, what did Simon say?"

I snap bolt upright and whack my hand over my mouth. "Oh God! Sorry! Perhaps I spoke out of turn. Better zip the lip. Old blabbermouth me! Well, see you later!" And off I spin, chuckling to myself. It's so easy to get a rise out of the old hen. And if she ever did have a career move – in other words, start ordering the sandwiches as is her natural role – guess who'd walk straight into her job. That's right. Me.

For some time I have been aware that the fashion pages of the London Star would profit from my energy and genius as I told Simon just the other day in the bar round the corner after work. I sashayed over with my Voddie on the rocks and had a good go at him about Bumface – she's hopeless, I told him, appalling. I could do the job standing on my head waving my Jimmy Choos in the air.

18

Just as I had finished telling him all this, Marlene came out of the loo and joined us, which was opportune. I asked her where she had got her jacket (box shoulders, I mean, please!) and when she told me, couldn't restrain a delicate shudder. Perfect. Simon saw my point proven.

My column, Hey Good Cooking, is brilliant, as I say, but really I am stuck with doing a great job on a tired concept. Basically, I chuck in a bit of stuff about where the bright and beautiful are to be seen wielding their knives and forks, and pop in a few details about celebrity chefs. The good news is that I get to visit all the trendiest restaurants in town; the bad news is that because of my 24-7, 365 days a year no-fat diet, I don't get to eat much. But hey. A moment on the lips, a lifetime on the hips...

So to cut a long story short, I hit the ladies, check the cubicles and when I'm sure I'm alone, do a quick hoover, sort my nose out and switch my mobile on. Sure enough, it rings almost immediately.

"Rebecca Crisis," I say curtly.

"Hi! Becky! It's Mike! We talk at last! It was too bad you were just going out the other night. It would have been great to hang out..."

"Can I help you with anything specific, Mike? I'm rather busy."

"Oh! Got it. Is somebody there?"

"I repeat, can I help you?"

"Right! Someone is there. I'll just keep talking shall I? All you have to do is say 'yes' and 'no'. It's just... since the other day... I've been thinking about you a lot. You're so like Amanda – but you're so different. Becky, I think you're the one for me. Does that shock you?"

"No."

19

"We have to be honest with Amanda. What are we going to tell her? I'm dreading it, aren't you?"

"No."

"You're so brave. Wow. Wowee. I mean, I owe her a decent explanation, but it's a heavy scene, isn't it, Becky?"

"Rebecca."

"You do my head in. You are amazing. You are fantastic. I think I've been waiting for you all my life. I'll never forget what it was like at the funeral – that passion, that energy..."

He pauses to gather breath, and I can tell that it's high time for that old standby – the fading mobile.

"Hello? Hello? Can you hear me? Mike? Mike?"

"Yes, I can hear you..."

"Mike? Hello? I can't hear you."

"I CAN HEAR YOU!"

"Hello? It's no good. I've lost you."

And I press the red button, apply fresh lipstick, smooth my hair, straighten my skirt, check my nose once more and stride confidently back to my desk. When Simon comes over – he may be gay, but he can't keep away – I am deep in the midst of my column. It was rather lucky, I was at Eat It Up last Tuesday lunchtime, and Somebody Famous came in with a couple of her kids and I was able to overhear their food order.

"Hi Simon! Looking sexy!" I say. "Hey. Good news. I had lunch with Sadie and the kids the other day at Eat It Up."

"What's that?"

"Oh you know. The new kiddie eatery all the stars are taking their spawn too. So I had a yummy nosh up with my mate Sadie and her little darlings. In fact, Simon, I'm working to a deadline now. Can I help you?"

20

I say this because it's always important to be in control of an encounter, but at the same time I look up at him through my lashes and hitch my skirt up a bit.

"Oh, ah, yes, Rebecca. Hum. Hum. Actually, can you come to my office around three tomorrow? You are coming in, aren't you?"

"You know I always work on Saturdays, Simon. I am devoted to the cause of your mighty organ."

"Ah! Yes. Thank you. Well, to be honest, I want to discuss the future of Hey Good Cooking. You might come prepared with a few ideas."

I smile as he departs, but I'm thinking, Bastard! He has to say that about the good ideas, so that he can pretend he's giving me a chance to build readership. I'm sure he's planning on axing my column. What a... Hey. Maybe he's planning on promoting me to Fashion Editor after all. That's it! He wants me to come up with some spicy ideas for the column for my successor, then I'm going over to the glamour pages. How exciting. How – just right.

I'm just fantasising about this when my mobile starts vibrating and, in the name of no personal calls, I bolt back into the ladies with a turn of speed more impressive than a new season's filly at Epsom Park. Goddamn. It's Amanda. And not calling for a soup recipe either – in her own wet way, she's madder than a hornet with its sting up its arse. So shrill are her Tinkerbell tones that I have to hold the handset a few feet from my shell-like.

"Becka! You know why I'm calling!"

"What? You tell me. And it's Rebecca, please."

"Okay. Mike just... Mike just..." She hiccoughs for a bit.

"Well, what?"

"He's just told me... about you. About you and him. That you're... you're..."

21

"What?"

"In love."

"What!"

"Oh, Rebecca, I'm devastated. I can't believe this is happening. Tell me this is all a crazy dream. Is it a throwback to when you made me eat that magic mushroom when we were twelve?"

"What?"

"It must be some sort of hallucination. I mean, Mike just called me from a patient's house – I mean, that's so unprofessional in itself, and he told me that you two are in love and going to live together..."

"WHAT?"

"... and I'm in chaos here. I mean, I'm in the middle of an aromatherapy session, and Nancy is trying to calm me down with rescue oils, but I'm all over the place, Becka. Is this really true?"

"Completely and totally, one hundred per cent, not true."

"I knew it! It's a magic mushroom throwback!"

"Mike and I are not going to live together. Ever. Ever. Ever."

"What a relief!"

"But we did have a shag. Sorry."

There are choking, gurgling noises on the other end of the line and a faint sound of breaking glass. Clearly a few bottles of essential oil have bitten the dust.

"Look, I said sorry. Now, I've got a lot to get on with. Do you mind if we talk about it another time? If you need to, that is? I have a deadline."

"Talk about it some other time? Talk about it... not now, Nancy. I've got to sit up. No, no more oil, thank you."

"Goodbye, Amanda."

"No! Don't go. I'm still here. I'm in shock, Rebecca. I'm confused. I've broken a bottle of essential oil of root ginger and the fumes are making me dizzy. Did you just say what I think you said?"

"Afraid so."

"Well. Well. I'm at a loss for words."

"Bye, then."

"No. For once, you are going to have to listen to me. Hold on a mini-mo. Let me find my centre. Nancy, do you have essential oil of lavender to hand? Can I just have a whiff? It might clear my head and calm me down. Ah. That's better. Okay. Now. Let me explain, because you've ruined my life, Becka, you really have. No really. We were moving to the country next week. Making a fresh start in the fields and valleys. The children were going to this great school and everything. It's so important for Honeybee to abandon her coursework halfway through sixth form in order to explore her creativity – she couldn't pass the exams anyhow, she's been so traumatised by I don't know what really - and I was going to really tackle her weight problem, and Λ Robin's Nest's acne, and his shyness, and Pumpkin's potty training and I don't know what else. We were going to make a happy home – a family, all together."

"Great! When do you go?"

"Oh, I'm not going now, Becka. Are you mad? I couldn't live with a man who betrayed me. And with my own sister. I can't believe he would do this to me – and to the kids, I'm practically their stepmother now. But you, Becka, you... I know you hate me..."

"Oh, don't exaggerate."

"You do! You do! You've always hated me! I should have expected that one day you'd steal my boyfriend from me. The first one you fancied, you took him. Just like that."

"Give me a break."

"No breaks. You've always hated me, and if it hadn't been for Mummy standing up for me, you'd have ruined my life long before this."

"That's right. She always takes your side."

"Are you surprised? The things you do. The things you say. You don't care about anybody but yourself."

"That's rubbish."

"Rubbish is a case in point. Do you recycle? Do you care about Gaia?"

"Gaia? Who's Gaia?"

"Mother Earth, dumb-dumb. Well, do you? Recycle?"

"That's for me to know and you not to find out."

"I bet you a thousand million trillion pounds you don't. And do you have any friends?"

"A thousand million trillion."

"No you don't. I bet you don't have one. And how many family members are on speaking terms with you?"

"All of them."

"One of them. Me. But not any more. You've done it now, Rebecca. That's IT between us. You are quite simply out of touch with karma. The most out of touch person I have ever known, in fact. I can't cope any more with your hostility and antagonism. I just hope you're happy with yourself. You've ruined my life, taken Mike and stopped me moving to the country. I'll just have to move in with one of my friends for now. At least I do have friends. Kind people who love me. Unlike you. In fact, I'll tell you what: If you had nowhere to go, nobody would want you. You'd be homeless, Becka. Homeless."

"Is that a fact?"

"And Mike's children will be devastated, of course. From what he said I thought you'd be moving in, but from what you've said, I guess not."

"Not. I wouldn't live with that hairy piece of cheese for all the marching powder in Bolivia."

"So there'll be nobody to look after them, poor loves. Well, they only have their father to blame. And you. I'll never forgive you for this, Rebecca, never."

"I'm scared. I'm trembling in my Agent Provocateur crotchless panties."

"Don't push me too far, I'm warning you!"

"Look, Amanda. You are the wettest piece of crap I have ever known. No wonder your boyfriend fancied a bit of somebody else. Have you looked in the mirror lately? Did it crack? Your sandals alone would scare the birds from the trees. You are a complete and utter loser, going nowhere."

"You can't say these things to me!"

"Yeah, I can. You make me sick. I've been waiting for years to tell you exactly how I feel about you. You drive me crazy. No wonder you're Mummy's little favourite – somebody has to like you. You're stupid, useless, boring, self-centred, hypocritical and ugly. You're fat. You have terrible dress sense. You talk a load of old cobblers about crystals and shamans and fuck knows what else. Everybody is totally bored by you. People run screaming at parties when you come in the door. Who wants to shag you? Only a bunch of losers with beards. I hate you and I always have."

"All right, Rebecca. All right. You don't need to say any more. Now I know where I am in life. Now I know – I really do know - what to do."

And she puts the phone down, without saying goodbye. I have to admit, I feel a little perturbed after this somewhat heated exchange, and my hand is actually shaking as I switch off my mobile. So to cheer myself up, I look at myself in the mirror. Stunning. That's the only word for me. I try a smile. No. Not a look that suits me. Just as I am leering at myself in this experimental way, a loo flushes, the cubicle door opens and pa-da! It's Bumface. She comes to wash her hands without looking at me and hastens for the door. Whoops! Oh, who gives a fuck.

What is Amanda getting her manky old Marks and Spencer's knickers in a twist about? Mike's all right, but he looks like what he is – a man who leaps at the chance to do a bit of wood whittling and cleans up the sawdust afterwards without being asked. Oh, I know that her sobs and wails should move me, but they don't. Quite the opposite. When God was decanting the milk of human kindness into the fruit of my mother's womb, he had an unsteady hand with Amanda. I got the dregs, and not many of them either. And that's good! If you don't care about anybody, you can really enjoy not sharing your life.

I wend my way back to my desk, shooting a few torrid glances to the left and right as I go. And I can't miss seeing Bumface in Simon's office. We work in an open plan environment, but Simon has a sort of glass cube in the middle. He piles his papers all around the outside, so that you can actually only see him when he stands on tippy-toe, and that's just what he and Bumface are doing – staring at me. I give them a little wave and sit down at my desk. Okay, she's telling him that I had a somewhat heated personal phone call. It was in the loo, wasn't it? I can be private in the loo can't I? Fuck off to the pair of them. Oh fuck it. It's five o'clock. I'm going home. It hasn't been a good day. I switch off my computer, gather up my handbag and coat and make for the door, Simon and Bumface still looking. They duck down when they see me glancing over. How pathetic can you get?

I swing out of the building with a sexy, "hey, Dave!" to the head of security (he's a pile of flesh with no brain, but you never know when you might need a tame minder) and pop round the corner for a quick drink. There are a few people I know in the bar, but they all jump up to leave as I come in. Apparently there's a press party somewhere, or something. Thanks for asking me too, guys. Oh who cares. I slurp a quick double gin and tonic or few while chatting to the bartender, then slip outside and hail a cab. No nonsense about public transport for me. I'm above that. I have my image to support – and it's rather expensive. Spending money is a real pleasure to me. It's what you might call my hobby. But hey. Don't get me wrong, I'm not fussy. I like spending other people's money too.

As my cab chugs at walking pace through the mean streets of London town, I muse contentedly on my glammy flat, with its shining floors, ultra modern furniture, sweeping views and state-of-the-art galley kitchen. In my mind's eye, it looks wonderfully, deliciously, refreshingly free of men with beards and sisters in Indian skirts with jangly tie details. I like it at my place. I like the way that when I am not there, nothing happens. It's not like a house. Houses are subject to the wicked ways of floods, rodents and burglars. A luxury, high-storey apartment in a smart, modern block overlooking the Thames complete with shared gym and doorman has that isolationist quality I value so much.

Unusually for a Friday night I have nothing on and work tomorrow, so I am looking forward to a DVD, a bottle of fizz all to myself, some excellent olives and a few snorts of the scrumptious cocaine, which I have left at the ready on the coffee table. The cab stops, I disembark, pay up and enter the building. It's eight o'clock. A mere three hours since Amanda slammed the phone down on me.

I am mildly surprised when the doorman reacts to my presence as he buzzes me in. Let me explain. We have a right to a doorman, also to a boy to operate the lift. It's in our service contract. But what I cannot understand is why we have to employ a contract firm that supplies us with an ever-changing rota of complete retards who can't speak English. I want a doorman who I have met more than once, who is capable of addressing me by name, who knows who I am, who has more than fourteen brain cells cluttering up the cranial cavity and who can speak to me in my own language. Same counts for the lift boy. Is that too much to ask? Is it?

Anyway, on the way in, I usually say something like, 'Up your bum' to the doorman, and 'Suck on this, Sunshine' to the lift boy in the full knowledge that neither can understand a word I say, that neither has seen me before and that if the future resembles the past, neither will see me again. But on this occasion, I am pleased to note that both of the dumb muppets have registered my presence. Usually, they just look at the floor and grunt. But now, they are exchanging glances, looking at me, then each other and – in short – I have created rather a stir. I get in the lift and start flicking through my copy of the London Star while lift boy prods nervously at the buttons. We fly up to the 14th floor and I stroll down the corridor to my own front door and insert my key.

Make that, try to insert my key. It does not insert. I jiggle it, cursing soundly, for a few seconds and then realise that I am not alone. Somebody is breathing heavily on the other side of the door, and my guess is, that this person has inserted another key into the lock so that my entrance would be fatally impeded.

Someone has broken in! How annoying is that? I consider racing downstairs to alert the doorman, but decide against it – he won't understand a word I say. I get out my mobile to call the cops myself, when there is a hissing sound and to my utmost amazement I recognise the tones of my sister.

"Bitch!"

"What?"

"Bitch!"

"Amanda? Amanda?"

"Yes it's me, BITCH!"

"Oh for God's sake. Let me in."

"No."

"Please let me in."

"No. Forget it. Sit on my finger and swivel."

"You don't know enough insults to be credible. Now, I'm standing out here shouting at you through a door. It's embarrassing. Let me in, you stupid cow."

"No."

"Okay. Fuck it. Let's talk."

"There will be no talking. You are not coming in. I've left Mike – but it didn't take me long to pack. Oh no. I've got all the clothes I need here, thanks."

"What are you talking about?"

29

"It came to me in a blinding flash – it must have been the root ginger. I've got a little plan for both of us – I think I'll enjoy my part. Having nowhere to go because of your treachery, I've decided to stay here for a little while. It's lovely, your flat! Just super! But you weren't in when I called an hour ago, so I had to get the spare key off the doorman. It's in the lock now, and you can't get in. Poor baby. Never mind. In the meantime, you know where you can go, don't you?"

"To hell? What a cliché."

"Well, it might just be hell to you. How about moving in with Mike?"

"Are you crazy?"

"Not as crazy as Mike is about you. I'm sure he'd love to sweep you off your feet and take you with him to the countryside. Remember he's moving on Monday? Well, I would certainly feel happier if you were a million miles away from me. So I suggest that you move with him. Meanwhile, I'll just hang out here. I'll be fine. I shall luxuriate in wearing your clothes, and I'll try to spend as much of your money as I can. You'll be very happy at Mike's I'm sure, unless you can find anywhere else to stay. One of your thousand billion trillion friends might just give you a roof over your head. But if they don't, I shall really enjoy thinking about you having to move Mike's stuff and his fat, zitty kids and his ex-girlfriend and God help you his DOG to Sussex. Don't worry about little old me. I am going to stay here and put my feet up and drink all the white wine you have in your fridge and I am going to eat all your olives and sleep in your bed. Tomorrow I am going to your GLAMMY newspaper office and do your GLAMMY job and when your FAT pay cheque comes in I am going to spend it on designer clothes and Vidal Sassoon hairstylists."

Misinterpreting my mocking snort (I mean really! Vidal Sassoon!), Amanda continues: "Yes, you may well gasp in horror. Your life here is over for good. When you walk away, you walk away for ever. You can't ruin my life and get away with it. All this time you have been sneering at me, and despising me, don't deny it! Now, I will have my revenge. You, Rebecca, are going to live my life and I, Amanda, am going to live yours."

"Amanda," I say, attempting to sound friendly, "you are bonkers. Let me in right now, or I shall call the police." She ignores me and carries on.

"You want Mike? You have Mike. You want my life? You can have my life. Just now, I am FUCKING FED UP and you can have the lot. You can find Mike at 'Bird Calls', 17 Arcadia Terrace, Hackney. Have a good trip."

There is a thud of footsteps, the distant slam of a door and I swear I can hear the hiss of an opening fridge, the slosh of fine wine and a sigh from the leather sofa. Certainly I hear the sound of the television as the remote control is wielded to good effect. I didn't even know she could push the right buttons. Right, that's it. I'm calling the police.

More footsteps. She's back. "By the way, Rebecca, don't even think about calling the police. That's quite a little stash of what I assume is cocaine or worse that I've found on the coffee table."

"Rubbish. It's... it's... baking soda."

"Do you think I was born yesterday? Most people store their baking soda in the kitchen cabinet. Anyway, what would you want with baking soda? You've never baked a cake in your life. No, it's hard drugs, Becka, and enough

31

to deal in, I'll wager. I'll have it handy just in case the boys in blue stop by. They'd be interested, I'm sure. Bye now!" And she stumps off once more.

I stand in the hall, irresolute. I must admit that calling the police seems like a non-starter. And I can perfectly understand how she got in. No wonder the doorman and liftboy were puzzled when they saw me. I haven't bothered mentioning it before, but Amanda and I have the misfortune to be identical twins and look, really, well, identical. The only way you can tell the difference is that she has terribly split ends while my hair is in marvellous condition. Then of course there are the clothes (mine, designer; hers, charity shop) and the general aura. Amanda dances on the lawn before breakfast and thinks that every dew drop is a fairy's tear; I like six-inch killer heels and Sky television. But facially, at least, we are really very, very alike. So no wonder the trogs in charge of door and lift were puzzled. First, they would have observed Amanda enter in quest of a key, wreathed in shawls and eau de Glastonbury. An hour later, they would have seen what to them was the same person coming in once more, dressed in a white, Alexander McQueen suit as if nothing was unusual.

The doorman wouldn't know that I had an identical twin. It's not something I might tell a doorman about. And of course, Amanda has never been to my flat before this. Absolutely NOT invited. Ever. But long ago I had been pressurised into revealing my address so that she could send me her weedy birthday presents (I forget her birthday, of course, every year). That was a mistake. Memo: never give anybody, even your sibling, your address. They will use it against you.

Baffled and grinding my teeth with rage, I call the lift once more and am whisked by a nervous looking lift boy downstairs. I approach the doorman, who is glowering into the pages of the London Star.

"Excuse me," I snap. "There is somebody in my apartment." He looks at me blankly, leaving the paper open on his desk. That's so rude! I reach across and crunch it up between my trembling hands.

"There is somebody in my apartment," I repe

at... then stop in despair. It's quite clear that he doesn't have a clue what I'm going on about. He's just confused. And he couldn't let me in if he tried. He's already given Amanda the spare key. There's nothing he can do except call the police for me. And Amanda's quite right. I don't want to call the police. And it's at this ghastly moment that I realise a stunning loss. My Prada bag. I dropped it at the door when I was talking to my demented sister, and forgot to pick it up when I got back into the lift. With a howl of anguish, I leap back into the lift and beg the boy to press his buttons pronto. We hit the 14th floor – I pound to the door – and it's gone. Now I'm mad. I hammer frantically on the door and hear Amanda's footsteps approaching.

"Looking for something, Rebecca?" she cackles. "I thought you'd be back for your bag. Too bad! Ha ha! Finders keepers, losers totally screwed. Tell you what though, I'm not all bad. You can keep your mobile phone. Oh, and twenty pounds. That'll keep you going until you hit the soup kitchen. I believe that hostels for the homeless are quite comfortable these days, with regular checks for fleas. Now, just piss off. Okay?"

There are no letterboxes, of course, in flats like these, but the last owner had installed a cat flap for reasons known only to himself. With a thud, my Motorola and a folded twenty pound note shoot through it. I grab them.

"You'll never get away with this, Amanda."

"Oh, I think I will."

"You won't!"

"I will!"

"You fucking won't!"

"Bye, bye, you foul-mouthed harlot!"

And she's gone again. I press the lift button with a trembling hand. Okay. There is no way in, and with twenty pounds in my pocket, a limited range of ways out. Who can I call on for help? Friends? Well, Amanda's right on that one. Mine aren't the sort of friends you can go and stay with unexpectedly. Or even expectedly, come to that. I have purely social friends. We meet in bars. We share details of our sexual experiences, but we don't talk seriously on any subject. If any of them dropped off the face of the earth I wouldn't notice for months, I'd just assume they'd run out of talk time. I'm sure they feel the same about me. Relations? I can't stand the sight of any of them and the idea of asking for help gives me hives. Colleagues? Certainly not. Keep work and social life strictly separate has always been my golden rule. My Mum? Last resort only. Pleeeeze. My Dad? He'll be too busy choosing floral shirts and polishing his surf board to give me a hand. Anyway, he's there and I'm here.

Lift boy, who is beginning to enjoy himself, escorts me down once more and I stand in the foyer for a moment, baffled. I really and truly don't know what to do, or where to go. A hotel is out of the question in my cashless state. The doorman is staring at me, fascinated and I begin to feel uneasy. I move out into the street. Fine. I'm homeless. Lots of people are homeless, I've read about it in the paper. Once I even gave a homeless person some change. Well, it was bagging out the pocket of my new Stella McCartney coat. I trail off down the embankment feeling sorry for myself and I spend quite a long time just walking around looking at things and thinking it all over. There is no way on earth I am going to go to Mike's house and throw myself on his mercy. I'd rather eat glass. Luckily, I'm respectably dressed – more than that, I look glamorous. Nobody is going to mistake me for a homeless person, so as long as I don't have to pay anything to get in anywhere, I will have a roof over my head all night. It's just a question of switching venues. To cut a long story short, I kick off by going to the café at the National Film Theatre and pretending I'm waiting for somebody until it closes. Then I go to a bar and pretend I'm waiting for somebody until last orders is well and truly over. Then I go to a drinking club I have patronised in the past and pretend I'm waiting for somebody until it closes. Then I go to Victoria Coach Station and hang around pretending I'm waiting for somebody to get off a coach. Finally, unable to stand up one more minute in my high heels, I creep into a corner, pray that nobody attacks me, and fall heavily asleep.

CHAPTER TWO

Waking is horrible. For one moment I think I'm in my bed, but after an earthquake. I seem to be welded to the mattress with fallen rubble, and there is a frightful noise. It takes me some time to realise that I can't move because I am so stiff, and that the noise is a million tramping feet at the level of my nose. The clock tells me it's ten o'clock. I'm amazed that I wasn't moved on, but then, I am still – in a way – smartly dressed. Staggering to a hot drinks outlet, I sacrifice a significant proportion of my funds to buy a lifesaving cup of tea. Let me tell you honestly, I have not enjoyed this experience. And I feel like shit. I'm exhausted. Grey with exhaustion. My teeth are as furry as a 1976 Womble suit. My hair is all over the place. My feet ache, my head aches and my whole body is screaming in protest. I'm starving hungry. I'm desperate for another cup of tea, but I'm too scared to spend the money. This is crap. And to cap it all, I have to go to work. Just have to. For one thing, I've nowhere else to go, and for another, I can't miss Simon's meeting at three o'clock. All right, I won't be my normal, poised self, but I'll be able to tidy myself up a bit in the loos.

I'll be safe in the office. Somebody will lend me some money. Perhaps I'll be able to scrounge a go in someone's makeup bag. First I buy a packet of cigarettes – reduced to asking for the cheapest brand – then trickle out another few coins for my tube fare. Bollocks. Wouldn't you know it? I fall asleep again in the warmth of the train, miss my stop by miles and have to struggle back again. What a waste of time. All in all, I don't hit the office until around twelve. And I don't go in right away, for I have had a terrible thought. A memory has come back to me. Didn't Amanda say that she was going to take over my job, as well as my home? Might she be there now? With a horrible sinking feeling, I extract my mobile and caring nothing for the disapproving frowns of those forced to swerve round me on the pavement, I dial my desk number – the phone is picked up on the first ring.

"Rebecca Crisis!"

Oh my God. She's here. I press the red button slowly. What am I going to do? I'll tell you what I'm going to do. Chuck her off my desk pronto, that's what. It shouldn't be a problem. Big Dave from security is my main man, he's fancied me for months. I'll get him to kick her arse into the middle of next week. Hey! This could be a story! I like it. Identical twin tries to take over sister's life. Jealous, deranged twin attempts character heist. I'll be famous.

I'm instantly energized. This is the plan. I'll ring Quentin, our staff photographer, with a tip-off and have the whole thing splashed across page three. "It Girl's Evil Twin..." I can see the headlines now. Goddammit, I'm a columnist! I'll write the story myself. The fact that I have never mentioned my identical twin at office get-togethers will only add spice to the situation. I can just see myself in my admittedly very grubby Alexander McQueen suit posing stylishly by the door while sexy Simon and all the staff watch with their jaws dropping. With elegantly turned sentences I will strip Amanda's soul bare as if with vitriol

38

and she will have to go to a spa hotel for a month to recover. If she could afford it – so not likely.

Simon will approach me afterwards – his blue eyes sexily gleaming – and invite me out to dinner to celebrate. Or, no - perhaps after Amanda has slung her hook and the tension is over, I'll totter to my desk and break down a bit. Yes! Then he will approach me with his eyes swimming with pity and invite me out to dinner to cheer me up. God, yes!

I jab in the main switchboard number and ask for Quentin. Every minute's delay is making my hair curl. I haven't got unlimited talk time, after all. He's on. I make my voice sound low and interesting. To his gruff "Yeah, Quentin here", I reply: "This is a tip off. Wait outside the London Star building for a photo opportunity in approximately fifteen minutes. This is not a hoax." I press the red button. Great! Quentin's up for anything. He'll think it's worth a fag break just to see if it's a hoax or not – and he'll get a brilliant pic of Dave chucking Amanda out on her fat arse, which will make my story sing.

I was right. Five minutes later, approaching the building, I can plainly see Quentin lurking over the road. With all the panache I can muster, I swagger up to the front desk, casually picking up a freebie London Star from the coffee table as I go. If push comes to shove, I can biff Amanda on the head with it. My buddy Big Dave bends his eye on me. "Hi, Dave," I say confidently. The man's been in love with me for months.

"Can I help you?"

"I just said, 'Hi Dave'."

"Do I know you?"

"Of course you do. I'm Rebecca. Rebecca Crisis."

"I've got down here, that Miss Crisis has already entered the office today," he rumbles annoyingly, swivelling his Ins and Outs book towards him on the counter.

"Yes! I just popped out for a minute."

"Then you've changed your clothes and taken your make up off and done something funny with your hair is for sure."

How impertinent! My personal appearance is my business! Smoothing my hair and batting my naked eyelashes, I coo: "Yes, that's why I popped out. To change into something more comfortable. Just my little joke! Actually Dave, there is a problem..."

"I got you marked in, but not out here, lady," is his only reply and he eyes me with both gloom and suspicion. One hand, I note is moving to the part of the counter, which lifts up so that his massive person can proceed into the foyer.

"Let me explain," I start. But he doesn't listen. Those cauliflower ears are not bending my way. In fact, he's looking rather aggressive and – what a cheek! – he's grabbing at my arm.

"I don't know who you are," he says ponderously. "But you ain't marked in and you ain't marked out and you ain't Miss Crisis. We'll have to see what the police make of this."

The police? The POLICE?

"And first I'll have to detain you in my back room and search you for offensive weapons. Miss Crisis is by way of being a friend of mine and I would hate for her to get hurt in any way. Step this way please."

I attempt to wriggle out of his iron hold. "This is ridiculous. You know who I am! Look. Okay. I'll explain. I know I came in already today, but it wasn't me. The woman up on my desk is somebody else. She is my twin sister."

"Tell that to the marines, girl."

"For God's sake! Can't you see? It's me! I'm Rebecca! She's Amanda! We look exactly alike. She's my twin sister masquerading as me for her own sick fun and I want to throw her out."

40

"Oh yeah?"

"Yeah! So let me in right now you meat loaf."

And with that, I give him a hefty dig in the stomach. Useless. The iron bands of his fingers never falter.

"I'll buzz up. Don't move."

Well, I *can't* move, so I sigh histrionically while he calls up.

"Hello? Miss Crisis? Dave at reception here. I've got someone here claims she's your twin sister. You don't have a twin sister? You know who I'm talking about? I see. I SEE. Do you want to come down? You're too scared? I'll handle it. Yeah. Yeah. Don't worry. Don't be frightened."

"Pardon me while I throw up."

"Shut up you. Yeah. Yeah. Thanks Miss Crisis. I'll deal with the situation. Goodbye now."

The receiver is replaced, and he turns back to me with a truly evil gleam in his piggy eyes. I wail with all my heart, "Shit on a stick! She's lying! She is my twin. Of course she is. We look exactly alike!"

"Not to me you don't. Miss Crisis is one very smart lady. You is a mess."

"I'm Rebecca I tell you!"

"So prove it."

And he had me with that one. Amanda has all my ID and the staff here clearly believe that she is me. In a flash, the future flashes before my eyes. Nobody here knows that I have a twin sister. I have no way of proving that I have one, or even that I am me. This isn't good. I could end up in the incident room here.

Dave is on the move. Despite my struggles, he is dragging me to his back room and let me tell you, that's a place I don't want to go. Suddenly I wrench my head round and shriek, "Rebecca! Thank God you're here!" Oldest trick in the book, but Dave swings slowly round and his hand relaxes slightly. I knee him in the groin, rip my arm away and head for the door at a million miles an hour.

41

He's hard on my heels, and before I know where I am, he's tugging on the sleeve of my suit jacket. Screaming at the top of my voice, I wrench myself out of his grasp, but the seam goes and with a horrible tearing noise the entire sleeve parts company with its mother ship. I hurtle to the ground, and Dave stumbles, not, I am glad to say landing on top of me or this story would be ending at the next full stop. I leap to my feet and with one arm bare, flee up Fleet Street like an arrow from a bow, neither turning nor pausing until I have reached Tony's Coffee Haven where I duck in to regroup.

Call me a coward, but strip searches, backrooms, ju-jitsu sessions on the pavement and sooner rather than later the cops is not part of my plan. I was looking forward to something decidedly more sophisticated. It is clear to me that getting Amanda out of the London Star building is not going to the pushover I planned. But why was Dave so suspicious? He has a brain approximately, and I may be exaggerating here, the size of a microchip but with none of the information and I am frankly amazed that he didn't just wave me in with a lechy leer. What's going on?

Tony, ordinarily a cheery soul but today very dour, serves me coffee and a doughnut. I sit down, and while I am shaking out my paper, he is muttering with Maria and shooting me dirty looks. Really! Does one missing sleeve mean so much to the hot drinks vendors of this world? It could be a simple fashion statement for God's sake. I light a soothing cigarette and leaf through to (let's face it) page 48 to check up on my column. I always like to check for typos.

AARGH!

Coffee splurges all over what is left of my extremely expensive jacket and puts out my cigarette with a hiss.

MY STALKER HELL by Rebecca Crisis.

Ever seen Single White Female? This is the nightmare that I am living.

A woman, I don't know her name, has been reading my column since I joined the London Star. So obsessed is she that she refers to herself as my 'twin sister'. Through skilful manipulation of make-up, hairstyles, even wigs this madwoman has managed to twist her tortured features into a face that remarkably, if superficially, resembles my own.

She comes to my London flat and lurks near the door, waiting to talk to me. I've changed the locks, but still I just can't feel safe.

She attempts to bribe the doorman and porter in frantic efforts to get into my home, using implausible excuses such as "I've lost my key" and "don't you know who I am".

She has even threatened to brave the portals of this fine organ, the London Star. If she does, she will find a rough reception from Security. Dave – thanks! I owe you one.

Madonna, Queen Elizabeth, Posh... I salute you. It's hard to keep a smile on your face when you are being pursued by that most deadly fan, the Celebrity Stalker.

No way. No way! Somehow, somehow, that woman my sister has managed to axe my Sadie and the kids story and run her own instead. It can't be possible! But it's right here! I must be dreaming! But I'm not! Mopping coffee from my top and gathering up my change I flee Tony's just in time – I've got a feeling he's about to call the cops. This is like a bad film. He's definitely fingering a London Star behind the counter.

How could this possibly have happened? I stop in the street and rub my eyes with both hands. The only way she could possibly have done this was to phone in a story change before they rolled the presses. That is what she must have done. My God. I always thought my sister was as limp as a stale biscuit with the get up and go of an eighty-year-old with a heart condition. Turns out that she is a hyperactive criminal mastermind with sadistic tendencies. I almost feel a grudging respect for her – and a lot of self-pity for myself. But one thing I've learned from life is that you should never give up. I must keep thinking. Okay, she's at work. So I have a key to my flat, don't I? I'll simply go and let myself in. Or... possibly not. I scrabble frantically through the column once more. As I thought. She's changed the locks, she says. Of course. With shaking fingers I extract my key from my pocket and drop it in the gutter. So that's that.

This is incredible. I'm hungry, cold, aching all over. My beautiful white suit is torn and soaked with coffee. My feet ache, I'm damp and shivery. I've broken two nails, my hair is a mess and I haven't got my makeup bag with me. My God, I haven't even got a toothbrush! I'm just musing on the fact that it's the first time in my life that I haven't brushed my teeth three times a day, when a kindly-looking middle aged woman in a Marks and Spencer's suit and fake-leather handbag puts her hand on my arm.

"Are you all right, dear?" she asks.

"Sorry?"

"Are you all right? You look a bit under the weather. Has somebody hurt you?"

It's a terrible shock. I stare into her concerned eyes, and for the first time since I was a small child I feel like having a good cry. In fact, I could just fling myself onto her shoulder and go boo hoo hoo. It would be a blessed relief. I could tell her all about it. She could lend me her hankie and makeup bag and take me home with her and be my new mum. Then I pull myself together.

"I don't know what you mean."

"Your suit jacket – it's badly torn and stained. And you've lost your bag. Have you been mugged?"

"Certainly not. This is a couture suit as it happens. It's meant to look like this. In fact, it was very expensive. And

44

who needs a bag? This is the twenty-first century, for Christ's sake."

"Sorry dear. I'm sorry. I'm not very with it with the fashions. I just felt a bit worried, that's all. Sorry."

"So you should be. What a nerve."

"Goodbye, then."

"Goodbye..." I watch her walk off with an odd mixture of triumph and dismay. Someone offered me help – I should have taken it. She was nice. Sod it. I wander off once more, a ghost in the crowds. People are marching from their nice safe offices to the shops or cafes, then returning with bulging carrier bags. The boutique shops are full of people whipping out the plastic. There's somebody talking on their mobile every three steps I take. Nobody looks at me but following my encounter with the Nice Lady I know perfectly well that they've all clocked me as a lunatic, drunk, mugging victim or worse. Every now and then I try walking with more purpose, but I feel so exhausted and ill that there seems no point. I just can't make up my mind what to do or where to go. I'm on the point of throwing myself on the mercy of the police, when suddenly, there's a change. Everybody has been walking purposefully all afternoon in various directions, now they're all being sucked into the underground as if by a giant vacuum cleaner. They're going home. Home! What a word. I feel I have never appreciated any home I ever lived in until now. Soon Amanda will be home too, in my home. My own home. It's unbearable.

Then a brainwave penetrates my sodden brain. One of real genius. What if I pretend to be somebody that Amanda would like to see? Somebody like an aromatherapist, for example, somebody like her friend Nancy? What if I pretended that I was an aromatherapist coming by appointment to see me – Rebecca –after work? She'd buy it. I know she would. All I would need is for her to get the doorman to send me up and open the door

45

when I get there. I'd be able to burst in, taking her by surprise. Then let battle commence – and I'd back me and my nine inch nails any day. One problem I can foresee. The doorman may well have read the London Star and be on the alert for evil lookalikes, so I will need some form of rudimentary disguise. My apathy vanishes. It's great having a plan. After some thought, I pop into Boots and invest in an alice band and the largest, cheapest pair of sunglasses available. I also buy a white face flannel and a packet of safety pins with which I contrive a sort of sleeve to replace the one Big Dave tore off my jacket. With the other sleeve rolled up, it's not so bad from a distance. And with my hair scraped back severely and the glasses obscuring a goodish portion of my face, I am confident of being unrecognisable – at least, to the doorman, who may never have seen me or Amanda before anyway.

Once again, me, my ruined suit and my high heels tramp off through the streets to my block. The pain of my blisters adds to my rage with every step. My God, if I could just get through the door, I'd sort her out. If she even opened the door a tiny crack, I'd throw myself at it and hurl her to the ground. If she called the cops, I'd find a way to prove I am genuinely Rebecca. But my guess is, Amanda would crumple as soon as I was in the flat.

I approach the building with caution, peering around the corner and extending my gaze upwards. I can see an open window, glimpse a figure moving around – result! She's on the balcony. Now for it. I approach the doorman – another complete stranger, of course but I'm not complaining this time - and say in fluting tones, "Top floor, please. Miss Crisis is expecting me." He backs away giving me many a queer glance, and telephones up. Then looks at me. "Wat eez sor noime?" "Sue... er... Smith. I am a masseuse. Miss Crisis has booked this appointment weeks ago. She has probably forgotten!" and I add a light laugh by way of entertainment. He mumbles into the telephone once more and my hopes are high. Then the doorman speaks the words of doom. "See's comink doine." What a cow! What a mean, suspicious mind! Of course the game's up. I unleash an histrionic cry of horror. "Oh my gracious! I have suddenly remembered a most urgent appointment on the other side of town! Please give Miss Crisis my apologies, but I really must go..."

Then I have a brilliant idea. She'll have left the door on the latch. People like Amanda always leave their doors on the latch. I flash the doorman a radiant smile, and head for the stairs. With an airy, "Actually, I'll go on up! No need for her to come down", I vanish through the doors as the elevator pings, and stampede up the first flight of stairs. Not so fast that I don't hear Amanda's cry of "It's her! The Stalker!" and the thud of flat feet in hot pursuit, but fast enough that I stand a chance.

I puff and pant my way up, the doorman lurching along behind but just too slowly to catch me. At about the third flight I begin to regret that I hadn't invested in something simple on the second floor. At the sixth flight I wish that I had given up smoking long ago. At the tenth floor I wish that I'd snorted loads of cocaine for the energy. At the twelfth floor I wish that I was dead – and I nearly am. But blood will out. Despite the fact that a stitch is crippling me and my head feels as if it is about to explode, I make it to the top, leaving the doorman a flight behind. I hurl myself at the familiar door and bruise my shoulder rather painfully. It is locked. Falling to the floor, I whip the cat flap open and peer inside. There are Amanda's feet clad in my beautiful Russell and Bromley stiletto boots. With a moan of anguish, I stick my head inside as far as it will go and rather painfully twist it sideways so that I can look up – thereby risking a kick in the eye, but I only thought about that later. Her eyes meet mine.

"Really, Rebecca," she purrs. "You are out of breath aren't you? It's all those silly, silly cigarettes. Did you enjoy your run up the stairs? I came back up in the lift. It's so much easier."

"Let me in."

"No. I think you'd better wait for Dmitri – he's had *such* a time trying to catch up with you." And she walks away down the hall, twiddling the key most provocatively in her hand and wriggling her fat bum around in my favourite, absolutely perfectly cut black trousers and a Nicole Farhi top. Who is Dmitri for fuck's sake? Oh! He must be the doorman – God knows how she knows his name – and he's nearly at the top of the stairs. With a strangled snarl, I extract my head from the cat flap, whip round and race into the lift. Lift boy cowers terrified against the wall, unable to perform his duties. With a crisp curse I grab his wrist so that he can't ring the alarm bell and press the button myself. A few more frenzied seconds... and freedom. As I leave I glance up at the balcony. Amanda raises a glass of champagne and blows me a kiss as the rain begins to fall. I grit my teeth and hobble away into the night.

Round a few corners, leaning against a wall with streams of happy, motivated people flowing past me, I face facts. There's only one solution. Only one person who can prove who I am to Simon, my doorman, Big Dave, Tony and Maria, everybody. I've got to call my mum. I whip out my trusty mobile and after lighting a cigarette dial the number. There is a God! She answers.

"Hello, Mum?"

"Who's that?"

"Me, of course."

"Who's 'me'?"

"Rebecca."

"I'm very well, thank you Rebecca, and how are you?"

Oh for God's sake. "Fine, fine. Mum..."

"What can I do for you, Rebecca?"

"Mum..."

"Rebecca. Are you smoking?"

How can she tell? I took one puff! I stub it out with a sigh of irritation that should have shaken the streets all the way to Surrey, where in my mind's eye Mum is standing in the hall of the Tudor-style des res in which I was raised.

"Listen Mum..."

"No, you listen to me young lady. I've got my London Star here, Amanda sent it to me via a little man this morning and we've had quite a chat about it, I can tell you. I know all about it and I know why she wrote that article and let me tell you, I one hundred and fifty percent approve of Amanda's actions. I think she's been very clever, and very brave. That poor girl. Not content with torturing her when you were kiddies, you've put her out of house and home."

"No! She's put me out of my house and home!"

"You took that rat of a man away from her, Rebecca, as you know full well, and it's perfectly unforgivable. I've contacted your father in Brisbane. He and I consider that Amanda has a perfect right to your life, and we wish you the very best of luck with hers. That'll teach you a lesson you'll never forget. He's a vegetarian, I believe."

"For God's sake, Mum, I'm standing here in half a suit bereft of everything in this world. Amanda's fine. Why do you always take her side?"

"Don't take the Lord's name in vain, Rebecca. You talk of having nothing. Well, when you have learned that what is yours is yours, however little it is, and what is somebody else's is theirs, I can talk to you again. Until then, you will get no help from me. And don't think about contacting your father, either. He says they've just had a new deck put in, whatever that is, and he's very short of money. So don't try transferring the charges – he won't pay."

"But Mum! You're the only ones who can prove who I am!"

"And that's just what we're not going to do."

This is it. I'm facing a personal crisis of the utmost intensity. I'm going to have to do what I swore I would never do – go to Mike's. But this is his fault, after all. He'll just have to bale me out. It's strange really, having made this decision I feel a tremendous sense of relief. Fuck the tube. Mike can pay for a cab. I step out into the road and throw my hand up like a Roman empress summoning a eunuch. Instantly, a taxi stops, despite my extremely dishevelled appearance.

"Take me to Hackney," I rasp, leaping in before the cabbie has a chance to change his mind. "A please wouldn't hurt you," he mutters. All I can see are his baleful eyes staring at me in the mirror. What an old git. I light a cigarette with a delicious sense of luxury. But these days there is always some arsehole prepared to rain on my parade.

"See the sign?" He's pointing out a 'please don't smoke' sticker and fidgeting ostentatiously with an air freshener shaped like a Christmas tree. Really. These evangelical anti-smokers are genuine, slice–it–anyway–you–like fascists. They just don't want anybody to have a life. They should be grateful for a bit of passive smoking free of charge, cigarettes being the price they are. They should be thanking me on their knees instead of wasting nicotine by forcing me to throw my fags out of the window.

Still – back to reality. The important thing is definitely to keep calm and examine my options and situation generally. Regarding assets: I have an Alexander McQueen suit, no longer in good shape, a pair of high heeled shoes, ditto, my mobile phone (no charger), some worn underwear, the alice band and sunglasses and not a lot of money. Regarding items stolen from me under my very nose and currently unavailable: My cash, credit and debit cards, my entire wardrobe, my job and my home.

I am musing on this when the cab screeches to a halt. The driver appears to have lost his rag for reasons mysterious. "I'm going to have to ask you to leave my cab," he is saying.

"Why? What are you talking about? What's going on?"

"I have asked you to stop smoking. You have not stopped smoking and I must ask you to get out of my cab. You owe me four pounds and fifty seven pence."

"You have no right to do this. I'm calling the police."

"Call them all you like. Four pounds and fifty seven pence, PLEASE," he repeats.

"Look, I'm sorry. Okay? I didn't even know I was smoking."

"You look like a tramp, and you smoked in my cab. Now pay up and fuck off out of it."

"There's no need for that. Oh, take your fucking money." I count out the last of my cash. It doesn't cover the fare.

"That's all I've got. If you take me to where I'm going, they'll pay when I get there."

"Yeah, right. Now *I'm* going to call the police. Unpaid fare – that's very serious."

"Call them all you like. I'll report you for abusing me."

"Oh for fuck's sake. Keep your fucking money for the hostel."

And with a quick "fuck you too" I am ejected into the rain. I stand there and my shoulders slump. It's pissing down and the only place I've got left to go in the world is Mike's. And I'll have to get back there by bus. I've never taken a bus in my life, and it takes me ages to find one that will convey me to Hackney. I mean, I'd hardly *heard* of Hackney before all this. Now it's my home – for one night, anyway. Because unless I can think of something clever quick, I'm going to be moving to the country very shortly. And the country really is somewhere I know nothing about.

Musing on this, and after many ghastly mistakes involving my last few pence, double decker buses and asking directions, I arrive at 'Bird Calls', 17 Arcadia Terrace, Hackney. I fight through the macramé pot holders and windchimes and hammer on the front door until Mike appears. He tries to speak but without a word I thrust him aside and totter into what I assume is the sitting room. There is a squelch and a yelp as I tread on a shady looking dog of mixed breed, but the sound of its suffering is mercifully drowned by a general gasp as the assembled company take in that Amanda's evil twin has arrived. After all, they've met me once, and once bitten, twice shy. Mike ahemed from the doorway where he was hovering anxiously.

"Hey, everybody, this is Rebecca, Amanda's twin sister! You've met before, of course, but Rebecca, this is A Robin's Nest, Honeybee is right there and Pumpkin's here. The pooch is Pepys. Come here Pepys! What's wrong with the dog? He doesn't usually hide under the sofa like that... Sorry, Rebecca, would you like a cup of something? Tea? Coffee? Something decaffeinated? Herbal anything? No? Yes? Come into the kitchen. Please. Kids, watch Pumpkin for a second, okay?"

I sneer at the teenagers, lower my eyebrows in Pumpkin's general direction and follow Mike through to the kitchen.

I look around the room with appalled disbelief. Nothing, and I mean nothing, could be more different from my clean, modern, gadget-based arrangements. The pine (oh, please, how yesterday) table is cluttered with earthenware crockery, there is a dresser crowded with 'amusing' mugs and piles of paper. Behind the sink, as predicted, lurk various pots of herbs – both living and dead by the looks of things. There's an armchair in the corner with a suspiciously dog-shaped dent in the patchwork cushion. The wooden floor is liberally encrusted with grain-based foodstuffs. It is all absolutely revolting.

I turn around to Mike and open my mouth to speak, and would you believe it? The guy tries to stick his tongue in it! Clasps me in his arms! Actually hugs me! With an outraged howl I spring away, nearly taking his tongue with me between my teeth, which clamp together in a nervous reaction to his outrageous lunge.

"What are you on? Fuck off!" I screech, when I can get the breath.

Mike is bent double, clutching at his mouth and spluttering. After a while, he straightens up, extends his tongue, and checks for blood with a finger tip. What a fuss for a grown man to make. There are only a few drops. Even a shark wouldn't get its teeth in a twist about that little bit.

Finally, he can speak although with a bit of a lisp. "Ow! Rebecca! Sorry! Ow! Wow! I assumed you're here because, because you want to be with me? Now that Amanda's left. Am I wrong?" His voice tails off and I feel no pity at all. He'd cheated on someone, not me.

The thing is to be clear as crystal from the outset, and so I tell it to him straight. "Mike," I say. "Quite honestly, what happened between us was a deed I could never repeat without a date rape drug being added to my vodka tonic. You are absolutely, one hundred percent the kind of man I could never, never be with under any circumstances bar total anaesthesia. I find you repellent in almost every respect, and am only sorry that you have lost the love of my sister, a manic macramé-maker of high renown and perfect for a man like you. Of course you're very nice... it's not you it's me... well, anyway, I wouldn't be here at all if I had anywhere else to go. The fact is that Amanda's moved into my flat, locked me out and nicked all my stuff. I've got nothing but what I'm wearing. No money, no clothes, no nothing. And nowhere to go but here. It's all your bloody fault, I'm afraid. You didn't have to tell her but you did. And as a result, you are going to have to sort this mess out."

Mike is looking far from amorous now. The idea that I am not here for romance has definitely sunk in. In a sort of shimmy which we may call, The Adjustment Of Ideas, he dabs at his tongue once more, brushes back his hair, scrapes his chin with a gnarly nail, rubs his eyes, folds his

53

arms and comes back with, "How? What can I do? I'm sorry about it, but what can I do?"

"Talk to her. Get her out of my flat."

"Talk to her? That won't be possible, Rebecca. I'm really sorry, but the last time I talked to Amanda it was a bit of a disaster. She won't listen to me. What a character transformation!"

I insist that Mike comes with me to force Amanda to open my front door. It takes some time before Mike succeeds in persuading me that he is the very last person on God's earth except for myself to persuade Amanda to open so much as a can of lager, but eventually I have to give up on that one. Moodily, I explain that if that is indeed the case, Mike will simply have to put me up at a hotel until Amanda gives up on all this revenge rubbish. He looks perfectly aghast.

"I can't possibly afford to put you up at a hotel. I couldn't put you up at a bed and breakfast! All the money I've got is going on this move. And the school fees of course."

"Oh, yeah. I'd forgotten about the move. Well, I can't move out of London. I have to stay here."

"Okay, well, I'm moving, that's all I've got to say. And you're welcome to come too if you need a place to crash. As I said, I can't afford to pay for you to stay anywhere."

"Okay, okay. What do you *do*, Mike?"

"Do?"

"Your weekly pay cheque. From what profession does it stem? Amanda may have told me, but I have forgotten. Perhaps mercifully. But your earning potential now matters to me. What, I repeat, do you do?"

"Oh right. Yeah. I'm a freelance doula."

"A do what?"

"Well, a doula helps a woman throughout the birthing process, both pre and post partum. We..."

"You are a male midwife."

54

"No, a doula is much more than that. We are part of the entire birthing experience."

"So your earning potential…"

"Is more spiritual than material. Sorry."

"Just thought I'd ask. Well Mike, there's only one thing to be done. I'll have to move in with you, first here and if I can't sort Amanda out, at the new house. Don't get any ideas, it's purely for my current convenience and I'll be out of your life as soon as I possibly can. You will also have to lend me some money on a regular basis until I get sorted."

Mike looks shifty. "Like, how much? And how long for?"

"How the big fat F word should I know? For as long as it takes your foul ex-girlfriend to get the hell out of my flat, that's how long for."

"Because we could cut a deal."

"For instance?"

"Well, you could help me out with the move, and when we get there, helping with the kids. Stuff like that."

"I am not a bloody nanny."

"Oh I know! I know. It's just that with Amanda gone, and Midge is a bit upset by the whole move thing, and I've got work to go to and to be honest, Rebecca, it could be a bit of a godsend having you around. I'd pay you, of course."

"How much?"

"Well, how about fifty quid a week plus room and board? That's what my mate's au pair gets. What do you think?"

Great. I have gone from It Girl to Clean-Up-The-Shit Girl in the space of a few frenzied hours. Fifty pounds doesn't even pay for a quarter of a pair of shoes. But – gritted teeth now – beggars (that's me) can't be choosers.

"All right. For now. And no funny business. No bed sharing, if I must spell it out."

Mike gives me a strange look. "You know, Rebecca, I do see now that we shouldn't be together. Don't worry."

"And I'd like my first week's salary in advance. Come on, ante up. Fifty quid right now." I practically have to hold him upside down and shake, but he coughs up. While he's counting out the notes, Honeybee comes in with a plate of sandwiches. It's very public spirited of her, but I have to pick out something called mung sprouts by hand. While I am doing so, I fake a polite interest in my future.

"You'd better tell me where we are moving and why," I say.

Mike suddenly comes over all animated. "It's a place in Sussex called Much Jenner. A really cool village with the greatest school. Holt Park, it's called. A really beautiful house set in the most amazing grounds in the rolling countryside. Wow! I went to see it with Amanda. It's really cool. No uniform, no exams, no pressure..."

"No education?"

"Yeah! Of course there's an education. The kids learn to learn for themselves, you know? They learn to stand on their own two feet. They go camping and learn farming and building and stuff. They built some of the school buildings themselves! And they learn to really appreciate their surroundings. For example, they actually clean their own classrooms and stuff!"

"Sounds like the school's onto a winner there. Don't they make the parents pay fees as well as getting the kids to do the maintenance?"

"Yes – there's no state funding. Unbelievable."

"But I thought you had no money, being, as you are, a lowly freelance spoola or moola..."

"Doula. Dee oh you el ay."

"Doula. How can you afford to send them there, let alone sling me fifty quid a week?"

Mike looks a bit shifty. "Oh, we scrimp and save. We mix and mend. Actually, my parents have offered to pay."

"Oh. I see. Standing on your own two feet, eh?"

"I'm excited about this move, Becky. The school is something else. The kids learn everything through artistic and musical mediums. It's so great. A Robin's Nest and Honeybee will be so much happier than at the local comp here. And Much Jenner is brilliant. The school attracts people from all over the world, you know. It's a really cosmopolitan atmosphere. You'll love it."

"Sure I will."

"You will! And you'll love where we are living. Cobweb Cottage. It's really rural and down to earth. Nothing fancy. A real breath of fresh air. It's back to basics. No television..."

"What the fer fer fer?"

"Simple organic wholefoods..."

"No!"

"Plenty of country walks, quiet family fun..."

"Absolutely no way!"

"No stereo..."

"You must be joking!"

"I'm even considering giving up the phone and electricity. What do you think?"

"Oh, I think *that* one is a really *great* idea."

"Good to have your support! Of course, Cobweb Cottage is quite small. We're going to have to leave quite a bit of this furniture behind. The sofa in the sitting room for instance. And the dining table and chairs. We'll all eat together still, but on the floor. I think of us as the village Bedouin. We'll all eat sitting together on a carpet."

"I'll look forward to it."

"Now. We mustn't hide away here in the kitchen any longer. You must get to know the family, Rebecca. I know they'll love you... A Robin's Nest, Honeybee and Pumpkin – I'd like you all to meet Rebecca!"

Poor bloke, as he ushers me back into the sitting room he's beaming like a lighthouse but no grin is big enough to shoehorn me in without a struggle. Honeybee – a vision in hair extensions and pierced eyebrows - is frankly sneering, and A Robin's Nest is scratching his head in confusion – either that or it's head lice.

"Hi Rebecca. Dad?"

"Yes, son?"

Do people really say things like, 'yes, son?' I wish they'd warned me.

"Where's Amanda?"

Honeybee gets up and stretches, showing off a most unpleasant and bulging midriff, then has her little say. "Amanda's fucked off because Dad bonked Rebecca. She told me before she left and I don't blame her. I don't know where she is now, but if I knew I'd go with her rather than stay here with you pair of losers. Well done, Dad. Rebecca, I assume that you are moving in to be our evil step mummy now? Or have you just come for a quick shag before tea?"

"I don't think that silly little girls should be told about their fathers' sex lives. You'll just have to guess, won't you? You'll have to listen at night for grunts and groans. But that might just be your brother picking his spots."

"Okay, okay, okay, okay, okay!" Mike sings out. "Kids. Here's the deal. Becky is, out of the goodness of her heart..."

"Ha!"

"...joining our family to help out for a while. So, hey. Let's put the past behind us, and move forward in a spirit of positivism. Come on Honeybee. Give Becky a hug."

"Dad! No!" shrieks Honeybee.

"That won't be necessary," I add in alarm. It's more than likely that some part of her much pierced anatomy will entangle itself in my hair if physical contact is made. Hugs of all kinds must be strictly avoided.

Mike looks a tad disappointed but accepts defeat and suggests instead that we adjourn to the attic so that I can meet Midge.

"Must I?"

"She's such a sweet person," here he lowers his voice, "but just a wee bit upset by life." Mike fixes me with his large brown eyes. They positively brim over with soul. "We have to tread just a leetle bit carefully with Midge. She's very easily distressed."

Up a flight of stairs we go, and open a door. Immediately I am enveloped in a cloth of some description, hanging just inside the doorway and there is a powerful smell of joss sticks. Having fumbled with the fabric for some moments, Mike pokes his head inside to the strains of some kind of ethnic instrument.

"Yoo hoo Midge my love! I've bought a friend to meet you."

Honestly, it's like being at a hospital. I stride forward with a hand extended. It is taken and pressed by the limpest set of fingers I have ever encountered. If it wasn't for the multitude of rings, I reckon the whole hand would dissolve into the atmosphere. Two large green eyes regard me mournfully from under a drooping fringe with a mouth to match. The chin, what there is of it, trickles down into a caftan. Bare feet liberally adorned with toe rings and ankle chains with little bells attached complete the merry scene. Mike speaks slowly and rather loudly, as if explaining the increased price of cheese to his granny.

 "Midge my love, this isn't Amanda. Amanda has gone on a little holiday. This is Rebecca, her twin sister. Ha ha! Aren't they alike?"

"Yes," says Midge with a sigh. "Very alike. But of course I knew at once that this wasn't my darling Amanda. Amanda has a beautiful lilac aura, most soothing. This person has an acid green aura. I spotted it immediately. I felt it coming up the stairs. Are you in distress?"

"I wouldn't mind a quick pee thanks for asking, but other than that..."

"I can feel your distress." Another limp hand reaches out and adds itself to the clasp quota. "I can feel your distress, and please understand that it distresses me to feel your pain."

"A full bladder..."

"Your aura is speaking to me and I am listening. I am here for you, here in my eyrie. When you need to release your anger, release your pain, please come to me. I will be waiting."

"Ah. Yes. Erm... this is interesting music. What is it?"

"An Afro-Celtic fusion group. Truly wonderful. A linking of cultures totally physically and spiritually separated for so many years that their entwined roots had almost been forgotten by all humankind."

Mike sticks his oar in thank God. "Midge my love, did you remember that we are moving the day after tomorrow? You do remember that I asked you to start looking through your stuff? You don't seem to have made much of a start with your packing."

Midge retains my hand, but turns the headlights balefully onto Mike. "Packing? Packing? I will pack when the mood takes me, Mike darling. I will fill these few, poor boxes with the remnants of my life when I have the strength, my darling. Now. Please take your new friend downstairs. I have to meditate. Oh, and Mike, what day is it?"

"Saturday, my own love. Final packing day tomorrow. Moving first thing Monday morning."

"Ah! Thank you! Now, Rebecca... farewell. For now." She drops my hand and flutters her fingers sadly as I exit, pursued by an aura. "I see what you mean," I tell Mike on the second floor landing. "She's as nutty as a regifted fruit cake."

"Oh I wouldn't say that. She's really in touch with the life forces, that's all."

"I can see why she isn't in touch with her children."

"Ah now, Becky, don't be unkind. Midge just finds life a bit tough sometimes, that's all. She's a very sweet person."

"She's a very mad person."

"Well, let's get on, Rebecca. How about some supper? There's some bean curd in the fridge. It's fresh! Not from a packet. And, get this, organic. I've got a great source – the one thing I'll miss when we move."

I spend the next five minutes kicking Pepys off my leg. Honestly. Dogs are so oversexed. My suit is grotty enough as it is without being further soiled by a shagging dog.

After a perfectly putrid supper in company with the glowering teens and the mash-it-up manners of Pumpkin, I make Mike bed down on the sofa (after all, this situation is more his fault than mine. I'm known to be nasty, but he's supposed to be nice and should have just said no.) I repair to his room after a hot cup of something rather disgusting, and am annoyed to note that the door doesn't shut properly – it's warped, like everything else in this hell hole. And his bed is vile. I'm sure there are crumbs. I undress and rummage around in Mike's cupboard until I find a shirt and pull it on over my underwear. Then I get into the bed, wriggling my feet down cautiously among the debris, and turn out the bedside light.

I haven't had my eyes closed for more than ten minutes before the door is softly pushed open. I lie perfectly still. Someone pads softly towards the bed and sits down on it. Then suddenly, something warm and wet descends on my face just as I open my mouth to scream. There's a frenzied eruption of sound, and I launch myself back onto the bedside table, fumbling for the light. When I finally manage to switch it on with shaking hands, a horrible sight meets my eyes.

It's Pepys! He's on the bed looking completely terrified. For Christ's sake! First I have Mike trying to give me a frenchie, now his goddamn dog has stuck its tongue down my throat. I roar at Pepys: "Get the fuck out, you hound of

Hades!" and he nimbly leaps onto the floor and scuttles out. I spend a few minutes brushing dog hairs off the pillow, then climb back into bed, having wedged the door shut with a pile of washing. And believe it or not, just as I have my finger on the light to switch it off, the door is pushed open once more. Nothing daunted, and really losing my temper this time, I pick up the first book on the bedside table that comes to hand – it happens to be a hardback bumper edition, fully illustrated, of the Kama sutra – and hurl it with all my might at the door as it opens. There is a 'wumpf', a whirl of Indian cotton, and I perceive that I've hit Midge right on the solar plexus. Now, what the hell is *she* doing sneaking into my room after hours? This is outrageous.

She has collapsed onto the floor, gasping and choking, but I'm hardly going to leap out of bed and give her the kiss of life. For all I know, she's a rampant lesbian making a move on my body. Or after my precious cash. Anyway, I've a right to my privacy - people shouldn't sneak into other people's rooms for any reason. While I stare my nastiest stare, Midge manages to regain some breath. Then she heaves herself onto her hands and knees and crawls over the floor to the bed. Slowly, her head rises above the level of the blanket. We eyeball each other for what seems like a couple of hours before she breaks the silence.

"I came in here," she gasps, and breaks off to cough. I sigh histrionically and glance at my watch. Or where my watch would be if I had one – it's on my bedside table at home. I start tapping at my cigarette packet. That'll annoy her. After a short while, she pulls herself together.

"I came in here to find Mike," she resumes, "to discuss the situation with him. But I see that you are either waiting for him, or have usurped his position in this room. May I ask which?"

"He's on the sofa, if you must know. That's the *situation*, if that's the *situation* you wanted to discuss. Now why don't you just piss off and take the mongrel with you."

"I will stay no longer than necessary, but while I am here, I will make a simple request. Can you please not raise your voice when playing with Pepys. He's a very sensitive dog. He responds very badly to negative vibrations in the atmosphere. He is under the homeopath."

"How uncomfortable," I drawl, applying a match to my cigarette.

"He is also being treated by an aromatherapist. Therefore it is vital, *vital*, Rebecca, that you do not smoke in his vicinity. And as I have said, it is most important that you do not raise your voice when communicating with him. I am stunned. Stunned by your violence. May I ask why you threw the Kama Sutra at me?"

"I wasn't throwing it at you. I was throwing it at Pepys."

"Indeed? Why so?"

"Only to flatten him. Doing you a favour, actually. Saving you the vet's bill for putting him down."

"Heartless! Oh, heartless!"

I blow a puff of smoke in her face and she hisses like a cobra. "You will find me more difficult to deal with than you think, Rebecca. I will not tolerate cruelty to animals. I will not tolerate smoking in this house. You are welcome to do your own thing, of course, but if you want to be a part of this family, you must understand our philosophy of life..."

"And follow it to the letter? Now that's broadminded of you."

"I say, our philosophy of life, which is the only true way that life can be led in honesty and peace. We respect each other's space."

"Oh right. So if I have a hamburger in here, that's okay? But I can't have it in the kitchen?"

"This is a meat free house."

"All over?"

"All over."

"So where's my space to be free in?"

"Well, there's only one way to answer that, my dear. Not here. Elsewhere."

"Truly liberal. I'm sure you'd just love to see the back of me, but unfortunately I'm now Mike's paid employee – the au pair in fact. And I've had a week's money in advance. So if you don't want to get value for money I'll go... no? Okay. I'll stay. Now listen up, Midge. I must be getting some shuteye now. Would you kindly mind effing off? I'll see you tomorrow. Don't fall over the Karma Sutra on your way out – oh, too bad. Sweet dreams, cupcake!"

I toss and turn all night and under the circumstances, it's hardly surprising that I crawl out of my nest of crumbs and dog hairs at an early hour. I wander into the kitchen and search for teabags, which I eventually find nestling coyly in a forest of houseplants. Thoughtfully I make a cup of tea. The presence of Pumpkin banging a spoon at the table and shouting for porridge barely registers, until A Robin's Nest rolls in and begins to stuff food into his mouth. I cut off his attempts at conversation with a glare, and return to Mike's room sipping tea and feeling very depressed. There's no way round it. I've explored every avenue that I can think of, and it looks like I am going to have to move to Much Jenner with Mike and his repulsive family. Oh, and Pepys. Mike, his repulsive family *and* Pepys. But every cloud has a silver lining, and a comforting thought sustains me as I wearily sift through Amanda's clothes to find something halfway decent to wear. Most garden sheds contain weedkiller. I'm sure a dog is just as susceptible as a weed. Just let Pepys try to play tonsil tennis with me once more... and it's curtains.

CHAPTER THREE

Today is, of course, packing day at Beardy Towers and despite all my efforts, my doom is cast. I'm coming too. I'm not very happy about it in any respect, but the packing process is really getting my goat. I mean, it's hard enough when you're moving yourself and all your very own designer odds and sods, without moving a family of hippies to the sticks. The boxes in each room speak of a modicum of organisation, but I fear the worst. My personal luggage will be minimal of course as I intend to leave as much of Amanda's so-called wardrobe in bin bags outside Oxfam (hah! And you thought I didn't have a social conscience!). I'll have to pack a few things, though. And some supervision of the others may be required. I flop on the sofa until my need for coffee overcomes my fear of family life and tottering back into the kitchen, I behold a horrid scene. Pumpkin is penned in his sticky high chair, consuming the usual gloop. A Robin's Nest (what a name, what a name) and Honeybee are glaring at each other over the muesli and Mike is juicing carrots in an agitated manner.

"Rebecca! Hi! Want some breakfast?"

"Coffee please. Hold the lactose."

"Right! Coming right up! Rebecca..."

"Yes?"

"You couldn't help Pumpkin with his breakfast, could you?"

"Only if you promise one thing. Yesterday you were threatening life without electricity. But we must have electricity, Mike. I'm not coming otherwise."

"Why? It'll be cool, living without the trapping of capitalist commercialisation."

With nutters like this, you have to think on your feet. Feeling he would not be sympathetic, I forbore to mention electrical essentials such as epilators, mobile phone chargers and digital cameras. Instead, I honed in on his mania for the global market.

"Without electricity we can't have a computer, Mike. And without a telephone connection we can't go on-line."

"Who wants to be on-line?"

"If we are on-line, we can order all sorts of fabulous things, like organic cotton bed-linen from Kashmir. And special foldup bicycles from Germany. Stuff like that. It'll be a saving."

There are signs of intelligent life beneath Mike's beard which – if I may digress – wags up and down when he vigorously chews muesli, as he is doing now. I avert my eyes. Honeybee and A Robin's Nest, who, I wager, are on my side about this, hold their breaths. Eventually he bursts out with a resounding, "You're right! We will have electricity. But we won't sell out to the utility bosses. I'll get a second-hand generator. I've got a computer – I was going to put it on a ritual pile along with the telly on the skip. But now I'll keep it."

"Smart move."

While spooning Pumpkin's breakfast into his mouth, I fix A Robin's Nest and Honeybee with a beady eye.

"What are your responsibilities for today?" I ask.

Each with a moronic gape, making four in all if you count Mike and Pumpkin, the spotty teens indicate that they have no idea.

"Well if this move is going to take place, I suggest that each householder is assigned specific tasks," I say crisply.

"That's a great idea, Rebecca," cries Mike, handing me a steaming mug. "Hey everybody! Who volunteers for what?"

The teens gape harder. Well I could have told him. "It would be more effective if you assigned the tasks," I advise.

"Oh. Right. Right. Well, Honeybee, you pack up the… um… your room and um…"

I break in with a histrionic sigh. "Honeybee, A Robin's Nest, your task is to pack up the bedrooms. Boxes are ready and waiting. Used bed linen in bin bags please, ready to be washed on arrival. Mike, your task is to pack up and clean thoroughly both kitchen and bathroom. Please throw away as much as you can including that manky plate of sprouting somethings that I see there on the windowsill please if you expect me to accompany you."

"What are you going to do, Rebecca?"

"A surprisingly pertinent, if impertinent, question, A Robin's Nest. As your au pair, I shall naturally take charge of Pumpkin. Pumpkin and I are going to go to the park."

Obviously there is no reply to that one.

"Mike, I suggest that you go upstairs and sort Midge out," I say. "Honeybee, can you please prepare your baby brother for his outing. I am going out into the garden to consume a cup of the necessary and would be alone. A Robin's Nest, finish up that cereal and upstairs with you to commence operations."

Feeling really very efficient, and as if my fifty pounds has already been earned for week one, I grab my mug and proceed into the great outdoors. Dank patches of snow are fighting for supremacy of the lawn with the dog shit. The sky is glum and overcast and a bleak drizzle is beginning to mist the air. Perhaps moving to the country isn't such a bad idea after all. You never know, I might give up smoking. The thought gives me the creeps and I extract a cig and breathe the life restoring nicotine with a shudder. Turning towards the house, I note A Robin's Nest and Honeybee staring at me balefully through the window. For God's sake! Will that Pumpkin disaster ever be ready for me to take out to the park? I gesticulate impatiently and the teens disappear. Peace perfect peace.

It doesn't last, of course. Pumpkin emerges strapped into a buggy. I give him a quick curl of the upper lip, grind my cigarette stub into the ground, wave Honeybee back into the house and set off through the mean streets in quest of a playground.

Honestly!

Now I know how those tiresome people in wheelchairs feel. I always get annoyed when they are wheeling around in my way – I mean, why do they need to go out at all, poor things? Surely it's pointless. But for the first time, sympathy, even empathy, dawns. Far from gliding smoothly along, the buggy is constantly being stopped by kerbs with no flat bit, broken paving stones, heaps of dog shit and plain old holes in the road. More than a few incredibly selfish drivers have parked on the pavement, which means that I have to steer the thing into the road on a regular basis, there to run the risk of instant death.

Playgrounds... playgrounds... evidently playgrounds are few and far between in Hackney. I've been walking for miles with not a sniff of one. Don't the town planners think of people pushing their goddamn buggies? My feet are killing me. Fortunately Pumpkin isn't making a sound. With any luck, the straps have strangled him.

Ah! Behind a wooden fence with more than one slat missing I see signs of play equipment. With a great deal of troublesome work, I manage to wrestle the buggy off the road and to the gate, which, of course, opens outwards. This makes it very tricky to get the buggy through. Great design, guys!

The playground features some tawdry animals on springs, one swing, a damp slide and a dodgy looking climbing frame liberally daubed with spray painted phalluses. An unlovely sight, but it generates vital symptoms of life in the child.

There is a bench and I sit on it, having released Pumpkin to his fate. He doesn't move, but stands at my knee, staring.

"What? Go and play. What?"

"Whee."

"What?"

"Whee."

"You want to wee?"

He takes my hand and much against my better judgement, I am led to the swings.

"Oh, you want to swing? Well, swing."

"Pumpkin go whee. Pus, pees."

I've read about this. Children like adults to push them on the swings. And he did say please. With pursed lips I assist him onto the swing and push. He swings with no sign of pleasure, but as soon as I head back to the relative comfort of the bench, there are howls of protest. I go on pushing. And pushing. And pushing.

Do you know, I have been pushing this child for twenty minutes with no sign of him being satiated? It's insane. I am gradually becoming convinced that he would swing all day if I would push. Well, I won't. Who's in charge here, after all?

Okay, Pumpkin is in charge. There's something very disturbing about his wails when I sit down on the bench. I simply have to push, although much against my better judgement.

Eventually there is the blessed sound of Greensleeves and unlikely though it may seem in this freezing drizzle, an ice cream van hoves into view. Within minutes a collection of bovine mothers and their ill-clad spawn has gathered. Wrestling my way to the head of the queue I select a Mini-Milk for Pumpkin on the grounds that it is small, so won't be too messy, and is extremely economical. "Do your worst on that," I say indulgently, chucking the wrapper on the ground. Pumpkin eyes the Mini-Milk, then eyes me. He slowly begins to lick.

Three minutes later, Pumpkin is completely covered in ice cream. Soaked in the stuff. I had no idea that a Mini-Milk could contain so much fluid. His hands are sticky to a degree I would not have thought possible. He has Mini-Milk up his nose and in his hair. It is on his shoes. And he hasn't finished yet.

It seems like many hours have passed and I wish it were time to go home but the merry gang can't have finished doing all the dirty work yet. I suggest jettisoning the foul remains, but due to lack of cooperation, stuff him back in the pushchair still clutching the lolly stick. We trundle off through the empty streets and mercifully Pumpkin falls asleep. A cinema! I buy a ticket for the nearest thing to a romantic comedy and go in. The manager protests but I explain that my child is in his buggy, sound asleep, and I will take him out immediately if he cries. Plus, there is nobody in the cinema so nobody to care. Daytime stuff is weird. I haven't been to the movies in daylight for years – perhaps ever. The womb-like dark and warmth lulls me to sleep in seconds, and Pumpkin and I are both well rested by the time we emerge. I purchase some chocolate buttons and cram them into his hand the second he wakes. That'll hold him. Despite the movie stop, I am exhausted. I leave the buggy in the hall complete with sticky child munching chocolate and stagger into the sitting-room, where I drop into A Robin's Nest's lap, so silently is he lurking on the sofa.

With a cry of alarm I bounce off and, for the first time since arriving, take a long hard look at the young heir. At first I mean merely to frighten him. But as his appearance sinks in, I begin to feel a faint sensation of nausea. A Robin's Nest is a grisly sight. Starting at the bottom, he is wearing a pair of black gym shoes, Bob the Builder socks, grey trousers considerably too short and a rank maroon sweater which clashes miserably with his spots. He is gazing into the middle distance, gnawing damply on his knuckle. Oh dear oh dear.

"A Robin's Nest, my lad," I say briskly, "I wouldn't be seen dead in a ditch with you. We're going shopping." I quash his pretty enthusiasm with the news that far from taking to the town, we will be doing our purchases on the web. "We can't help the move, but in general I really would not be seen outside this house with someone looking like you," I tell him kindly. "When we reach Much Jenner, you'd better stay inside until we can get it sorted. Your spots are a disgrace, but new clothes and a decent pair of trainers will at least distract the eye."

"It doesn't matter what you look like, it matters what you're like inside," announces Honeybee from the doorway.

"In your case, I beg to differ."

"Why?"

"From what I've seen of your inside, you're better off relying on your outside. And frankly, that's a bit of a gamble. Most people think that pierced eyebrows are very last summer. I say this for your own good. And isn't your hair rather – ah – smelly?"

"Oh, get lost."

A Robin's Nest chimes in. "Actually, I would like some new clothes."

"Oh yeah? She's bought you then. The woman who stole Dad and wrecked her own twin sister's life has won you over with the promise of some lousy trainers. Right on, Robbo."

"Shut up, Honeybee."

"Both of you shut up," I roar suddenly, making them both jump. "Shut up and fuck off. I am in need of rest and repose. Leave me."

They slouch off and I put my feet up. I put my feet up, I say, which implies rest but far from it. My mind is as busy as maybe. If I am going to do this job, I am going to do it right. First off, Honeybee. Her attitude stinks. Her outlook on life is negative. She is rude and unpleasant. All that has to change. I'm not sure how, but it has to change. A Robin's Nest? The name for a start. It has to go. Clothes we are already working on. Spots? I was fourteen once myself. There are remedies. Pumpkin? The name again is a factor but we'll leave that one a while – he's not old enough to be mortified. Now. What else does one do with toddlers. They appear to do nothing but eat, sleep and play. Wait a minute – the grand opening of the bowels is surely a factor and I haven't seen anything of that yet. In fact, as far as I know, the nappies have been mercifully quiet since my arrival.

"A Robin's Nest!"

"Yeah?" He's in my midst, like a genie out of a bottle. Gives me quite a turn.

"What is the state of Pumpkin's bowels?"

"Uh?"

"Pumpkin's, ah, dirty nappies. How often?"

"Oh. I heard Dad telling Mum about that. Not often. He's bunged up."

Right. I thought as much. The child is bunged up. Now correct me if I am wrong, but I believe prunes are the answer to that one – prunes, and I have not so much as seen a prune for many, many years. When we get to

72

Cobweb Cottage, every olde worlde kitchen cupboard will be crammed with prunes and we will get that child's system rolling. Come to think of it, A Robin's Nest could do with a few prunes. I read somewhere that long ago smart ladies gave themselves enemas every morning to keep the complexion fresh.

"A Robin's Nest!"

"Yeah?" He's back instantly! Does he wait outside the door or something?

"Do you like prunes?"

"Uh?"

"Prunes. Ever eat them?"

"No."

"Right."

Mike slouches in. "Ever eat prunes, Mike?"

"Uh?" Honestly. Like father, like son.

"Never mind. What's up?"

"We're ready to roll first thing in the morning. Now. It's been a long day. What's for supper?"

"How should I know?"

"It's your job to cook it."

"Then we'll be calling the local takeaway."

We do just that and, after another ghastly night, this time thankfully without nocturnal visits from Pepys or Midge, whom I gather from the scratching sounds above are cowering together in the attic, we arose to a breakfast of leftover Chinese food. At least, the teenagers did. I felt I would rather starve and contented myself with nicotine.

And a mere ninety minutes after Mike announced that we are totally, completely and utterly ready to depart, we are all crammed crossly into what Mike sunnily calls the Mikemobile and anybody else would call a heap of rust that once was a VW camper van.

We exit London in a puff of smoke that trails for miles and are soon rumbling through the suburbs (three stops for minor repairs), the semi-rural outlands (one stop for a

73

puncture but handy pub nearby where I bolster my fading spirits with three double vodka tonics) and the bloody outright wilderness (countless stops for Midge to gather garlands and shove them in our faces).

On the way out of the aforementioned pub, I had spotted a grease-stained copy of today's London Star and grabbed it as we left. Now I flick through the pages to find my column as we chunter along, destroying the ozone layer with every press of Mike's sandaled foot on the accelerator. On finding the page, my frenzied howl of rage nearly results in a fatal accident. The van sways violently as Mike struggles to regain control, and there are some very satisfying screams of fear. Perhaps Midge has wet herself. I'm not cleaning it up.

"What's the matter Becky!" is the universal cry.

"Nothing. Nothing at all! Tra la la! A mere spot of tummy ache, that's all!" I say airily, folding my Star into a tight little baton, about the right size for shoving up my sister where the sun don't shine. I'm not going to let this bunch of hippies see the page my column is on. They don't need to see me in any other state but my best – or as best as I can be under the circumstances. They don't need to see the picture... they don't need to read the words...

The panic has died down and everybody is looking out of the windows, listening to Joni Mitchell. I surreptitiously unfold the relevant page, and sneak another horrified look at the Rebecca (read Amanda) column. It's the picture that dominates, but the words are juicy also. The picture is of me – me in my ruined suit, sprawling in the gutter, snarling at a bouncer recognisable as Big Dave. My nails look like claws, my eyes are frenziedly staring, my hair is on end and I can see foam on my lips, a straightforward manipulation of the image. I never actually foam, however angry I am. Superimposed on this is a little cameo of Amanda, looking very sad and soulful.

MY NIGHTMARE BECOMES REAL, by Rebecca Crisis

Today it happened.

The Single White Female who is stalking my every step arrived at the London Star building and attempted to gain admission, pretending to be me.

The smooth-talking maniac attempted to convince the London Star's top-flight security team that she was me – Rebecca Crisis – and that she had just popped out for a bite to eat, and, said Dave Coulson, head of security, "to change into something cooler."

Mr Coulson, known affectionately as Big Dave, was not fooled.

After close questioning, the sinister stalker insisted on entering the premises – and I was contacted at my desk.

I confirmed that I was upstairs, and not at the door.

When Mr Coulson, 43, volunteered to call the police, the demented female made a break for freedom. Risking life and limb, Big Dave attempted to stop her in her tracks but she made her getaway after a violent struggle.

"She was vicious, really vicious," recalled Big Dave. "I'm strong, but she felt stronger. Biting, scratching, punching – you name it. Not the sort of woman you want to meet while you're jogging in the park. I wouldn't put any act of violence past her. A very dangerous individual indeed. I wouldn't have been surprised if she'd had a knife, to be honest. I did think of my wife and kids. But it's my job, isn't it?"

Meanwhile, I sat trembling at my desk, my hands frozen over the computer keyboard, my eyes riveted to the lift door. Any moment, I thought, this crazed individual – probably heavily armed – would burst through them and attack me in my own office.

I was actually physically sick when I heard that she had made her escape. I feel safe nowhere. I am having to charter limousines around London to ensure that she does not approach me on the street.

The London Star has provided dedicated security at my top floor flat, so at least I can call my home my own.
But it's scary. Very very scary.
A horror movie – and I don't know the ending.
Watch this space...

It's outrageous. Absolutely outrageous. She's lying through her teeth to up the readership. Physically sick, my arse. And how can they use that photograph of me without permission! It's the most intrusive thing I've ever seen. And making the London Star pay for limousines and private security – I mean, that's downright fraudulent. I've a strong mind to send an anonymous letter. Or not anonymous. Except that they'd think that either letter came from me – the evil bitch single white female stalker, that is, not the real me. The real, sensitive, suffering, kindly me.

I crush the paper viciously in my hands, vowing to destroy it the second we hit civilization. The rest of the journey flashes past – for every cloud has a silver lining, does it not – as I muse on Amanda's perfidy, grinding my teeth so much that several times, A Robin's Nest asks innocently if the van is running okay. Of course, the answer to that is uncertain at the best of times.

Before I know it, we are trundling into Much Jenner. For some bizarre reason, the village is not shy of announcing its presence although I would advise it to keep its head down, and there's a sign, Much Jenner, twin town La Petite Malaise. And at the sign, a ragged cheer rises from the tousled occupants of the Mikemobile. Myself excepted, of course. I'm too busy tightening my lips with scorn to ejaculate any sound.

We follow an arrow indicating a car park, and on arrival a health food shop is spotted, nestling coyly by the public toilets. "Aha! Ideal! Let's stock up on a few supplies," says

Mike cheerily, and the van creaks to a halt in a shower of rust.

"Don't forget prunes," I say, darkly.

"Prunes?"

"Yes, and lots of them."

Honeybee and A Robin's Nest topple out of the VW and trail over to a wall on which they sit, gawping at nothing. Pepys squats in a corner with an embarrassed look on his shaggy face. Hey, there's hope for it's a car park. He may get run over. Midge lies back in her seat, nostrils aquiver. Pumpkin, bless his woolly socks, is fast asleep in a sea of rice cake crumbs so I can afford to relax for a moment. I draw out the ciggies and after a disapproving intake of breath from an otherwise moribund Midge exit the van and wander around the car park. But not aimlessly. I am never aimless. I am checking out Much Jenner, and from what I can see, my checking out options are strictly limited.

We are in a fairly standard car park with the health food shop on the left – I can see Mike's bobble hat nodding above a pile of turnips or some such wholesome vegetable – and a bakery on the right. A fairly sub-standard pub lurks on the corner and moving on into the high street, I see a mini-mart (useful for fags and milk), a gifte shoppe full of jewelled lampshades and strange things to put candles on, and a crystal emporium among other undistinguished stores. The customers to view are a mixture of elderly women who look like they play golf and middle-aged mothers with spreading hips and home-knitted sweaters.

Other than the pub, I see nothing to amuse or stimulate. The best the town hall has to offer is a list of foreign films presented by the Much Jenner Motion Picture Club, not one title of which I have ever seen, or can even understand. Some are in another alphabet.

I wander sadly back to the Mikemobile, musing on my immediate future. Clearly, if I have to stay here for longer than 48 hours, I may as well kill myself now. But what choice do I have? No money, no home, no family, no job, no nothing but Mike and his wretched family until Amanda stops this lunatic revenge. A wave of rage breaks over me and I whip out my mobile and stab the number of my flat (MY FLAT!) in. No result. There is, of course, no signal in the fabulously interesting Much Jenner car park. I shove the mobile back into my bag with a curse.

"Hey, Becky! Becky! Bex! Are you coming?" calls Mike. I insert myself sulkily into my seat, treading hard on Honeybee's toes as I do so. I hope she has corns.

"My name is Rebecca," I say unpleasantly. "Not Becky, still less Becks. And if you're spelling it Bee Eee Ex, as I rather think you are, still less that. It's Rebecca. Okay?"

"Okay! Sorry! Don't get heavy! Come on guys, cheer up! We're nearly there. Cobweb Cottage here we come!" Mike tosses back a packet of prunes and I shoot a few Pumpkin's way. He busily munches while we swing through a most mediocre village centre.

"Lafyette, ve are ere!" sings Mike, sticking his arm out of the window. Did I mention that the indicators gave up the struggle some miles back?

The VW squeezes down an unfeasibly narrow lane and mounts the verge before coughing to a halt. There is a deep silence, broken only by the farting of Pepys, while we all gaze at Cobweb Cottage. Its fond creators all those years ago probably hesitated. "What shall we call it?" they may have mused. "Cobweb House? Cobweb Mansion? Chateau Cobweb? No. What about, Cobweb Wee Nook? Cobweb Nutshell? Cobweb Crappy Hole in the Ground? Describes it exactly... but Cobweb Cottage sounds bigger. Let's call it that."

If they had stuck to Nutshell, the estate agent would not have had to have lied in order to get Mike to take a look at it. The dwelling place masquerading as a cottage is tiny to an extreme. By the looks of things, it is a one up, one down and one teetering right at the top, squeezed in between two larger neighbours like a toddler squashed up with mummy and daddy on a train. There is no front garden, simply the verge on which we are parked and it is a dead end street, so all the cars in sight are parked like a demolition site on a rush day. Clearly, we are going to have to back the van out for half a mile in child-infested territory every time we want to go out.

The car doors creak open and we trail towards the door. Most of us are struck dumb with horror, but Midge is happily shrieking while a chuckling Mike attempts to carry her over the threshold. We file past him into the... well, it's not a hall. More a porch. Eyes left for... not a sitting room. More a closet. Eyes right, the kitchen. More of a larder, really. Up the rickety winding staircase – steps you might call them – to on the right what the estate agent presumably and now Mike refers to as the 'master bedroom' (need I say more) and on the left, the junior bedroom (look out if you're more than four feet tall in your cotton socks). Up a sort of ladder and Midge gives a squeak of horror. This is the 'lovely attic' – two rooms of such minuscule proportions that Tom Thumb would find either a squeeze. One is rather bigger than the other, but in neither could you swing a cat, proverbial or otherwise.

"Yeah! Midge in here I thought," barks Mike happily in the larger room, flinging a window open. Lacking a sash cord, it descends immediately and hard back onto his thumb, which renders him inactive for long enough for Midge to stage some kind of fit in peace, while Honeybee races (or rather shuffles at speed, there's no room for more than that) into the other room.

"Mine," she says, shooting A Robin's Nest a filthy look. "I'll stay up here next to Mum. There's more room downstairs, because you'll have to share with Pumpkin. Go on, Robs. You have the best room. I don't mind."

"Uh, I want to be up here. You share with Pumpkin."

"You're both boys. I need my girl space."

"Uh, okay, I suppose so. Come on, Pumpkin, let's go and have another look at our room." A Robin's Nest who, I might add, has been carrying Pumpkin around all this time – he's really rather useful – trots off downstairs. Then I hear him calling, "Hey Dad! Your room's good! It's got a fireplace!"

"Your room?" I say to Mike with a haughty air. "If that room is your room, then where am I staying. In the outdoor lav?"

"Oh no," Mike seems to be taking me seriously. For God's sake. "There would be no room for you out there."

"What? You mean there *is* an outdoor lav?" I suddenly realise that the grand tour, and you've probably noticed it too, has not featured a bathroom.

"Oh yes," grins Mike, the oaf. "It's great! There's a loo, and a sort of bath system..."

"Cistern?"

"System. A system of having a bath. I'll show you. It's cool. Anyhow, obviously there's no way you can have the outhouse for your room as we'll be needing it. No, I thought you could share this bigger room with Midge."

There's a big reaction to this one. Midge, who has roused herself enough to be drooping over the edge of the ladder and listening to Mike's explanation of the bathroom, lets out a piercing wail and I congeal into an icicle.

"Mike, my darling," Midge trills. "I don't need this great big room. Why don't I have the smaller one, and *Honeybee* can share with Rebecca?"

"No way, Mum. I've already bagged the little room."

The pair of them scramble for the smaller room, in order not to share the 'bigger' one with me. Really, if it weren't so pathetic, I'd take offence.

"I'm not in the market for a roommate myself, Mike," I drawl. "Midge and Honeybee are welcome to go single up here. I'll be quite happy on the first floor."

"But that room belongs to A Robin's Nest and Pumpkin," explains Mike.

"Not that room. The other one."

"But that's my room!"

"Let's be clear. The room with the original feature fireplace – although if you want my opinion this dump has far too many original features including rats – is mine, all mine, and if no other bedroom is available, you will have to bed down on the sofa."

"But there's no room for a sofa! We left it behind! We're having beanbags instead, one each."

"Nice idea. You can sleep on your own private beanbag and I hope you'll be very happy."

"*Can't* you share with Honeybee, Midge?" There's a pathetic note of pleading in his voice.

"No," is the unanimous answer from Midge and Honeybee.

This could go on for some time, so I take control with a brisk "Now. Shouldn't we be getting the place cleaned out? If I am not very much mistaken, the moving van will be arriving within the next couple of hours and we are not ready. I suggest that Midge takes Pepys for a very long walk while Honeybee and A Robin's Nest clean the bedrooms. I'd better cope with the kitchen and Mike can shift the rubbish in the back garden. Pumpkin can help A Robin's Nest hold the duster. There's a box of cleaning items in the back of the VW. Now – move!"

Such is the power of my personality, that slowly but surely the clan begins a diaspora and I can inspect the bathroom in peace. You cross a little yard, and there it is – a sort of shed plentifully supplied with all the spiders and woodlice one would need for a lifetime of nature study. There is a toilet and sink, but they do not arrest

81

the eye. Other things do. Item A is a water heating device, a sort of suspended barrel well endowed with perishing rubber tyres and ancient notices such as 'VERY HOT' and 'TAP TURNS ANTICLOCKWISE'. Item B, the bath itself, is an iron tank in which one would have to sit upright, possibly on a small stool. A large cork is plugged into a hole at the bottom. Sheer, unadulterated, four-star luxury.

With a shudder, I turn back to the house and revisit the kitchen which is empty of everything but a ratty piece of lino, which I take up – then hastily put back down – and an ancient range. At least, I believe that a range is what you would call it. A largish blackish stove with rings on top. An Aga it is not. I have clocked Agas in magazines. This is a range from the wrong side of the tracks. The Aga's embarrassing relation, its old aunt with bad breath and bits in its teeth. As I am staring at it in horror, Mike rolls in.

"Ah, Becky!"

"Rebecca."

"I see you've found the range! Isn't it great? I had them deliver coal ready for our arrival. I'll just..." he starts fiddling around "have a look..." bending over into the dark recesses "hmmm..." fiddle, fiddle "Aha!". There's a few clanks, a couple of clunks, the rattle of coal. Newspaper. Matches. Kindling. Grunts and groans. Swearing. I start cleaning the floor. Black smuts shoot out all over the place so I give up and leave the room to exercise a little quality control on the – to my surprise perfectly adequate – work that A Robin's Nest and Honeybee are doing upstairs.

The removal men arrive, explaining that there is no way they can get the lorry down the lane. They will have to carry everything. We will have to help. After a great deal of sighing, the teens depart up the road and begin hauling boxes, while I unpack them as they come in.

82

Looking back, I have to say, I was magnificent. While Pumpkin slept in his buggy and Mike wrestled with the range, I made beds, piled towels, threw ornaments in corners for picking over, hung curtains, threw down rugs, put up pictures and heaped clothes into drawers. In the kitchen, Mike's backside very much in the way, I dragged in a pine table and two cupboards followed by the relevant boxes. I unloaded all the ghastly earthenware crocks, huge pans, bent cutlery and foul foodstuffs. Finally – the kettle, and an impressively sized one it is too. Ho for a cup of tea. Where is the flex? Come to think of it, if there were a flex, where would it attach to the kettle?

"Mike – I know this seems ridiculous, but I can't work the kettle."

"Simple, Becky!"

"Rebecca."

"It goes on top of the range."

"What?"

"It's not an electric kettle. Literally, it goes on these rings. See?"

"Okay, but what good will that do? The range isn't working."

"Just where you're wrong! It's alight. Look."

He opens a small door and bids me peep inside, and, like the witch in Hansel and Gretel, I bend down for a look. And I have to admit (although never to Mike), I really did feel a primeval sense of satisfaction and excitement when I saw the flicker of flame deep inside the iron monster.

"Nought to tea in three hours. Not bad."

"Don't be so negative, Becky! It's alight. It'll be hot enough to boil the kettle before you can say Jack Robinson. Look, I'll fill the kettle now and put it on. Tea soon - you'll see!"

While the kettle has a think about things, I trail around exhaustedly checking up on the rest of the house and other than Midge's quarters – she has made a nest out of quilts and burrowed down among the boxes – all the rooms are basically ready for action. The hippies are milling around muttering about various lost possessions, and I head for the sitting room. Or sitting cupboard as it might be.

God, it's over! The move is over. I slump onto one of Mike's beanbags and close my eyes. Too weary even to haul myself to the kitchen for a quick cup of tea... too weary even to kick off my shoes... forty winks... blissful silence... thank the lord they must have all gone outside or something...

Suddenly I am aware of a very terrible pong. I open my eyes, and there is Pumpkin. He has clearly wrestled himself free of the buggy, removed his trousers and – good lord – what's that in his hand? Could it be... no...

"Poo. Guk. Poo. Guk. Guk. Guk. Poo."

Oh God. Pumpkin's hands are covered with poo. There is poo down his legs. He is thrusting a hand liberally spread with poo into my face. Help! He's had his hands in his poopy pants!

"HONEYBEE!"

Silence.

"MIKE!"

Silence.

"A ROBIN'S NEST!"

Silence.

"MIDGE!" (A long shot, but you never know.)

Utter silence. The Marie-Celeste was like a party boat on the Thames in comparison to Cobweb Cottage. Right. I stash Pumpkin under one arm, lug the lukewarm kettle off the stove with the other hand and carry him outside to the bathhouse. Problem number one is the nappy. I've never seen anything like it. Call me behind the times, but haven't disposables been invented? So what is this rank, sodden material wedged inside a pair of plastic pants?

I get it off and put the whole thing in a bin bag. Then I stand the frantic Pumpkin in the tub and rinse him while he screams. Then he stands on the bathmat while I decant the contents of the kettle and check the temperature. Then I soap and shampoo him from top to toe. I really throw myself into my work, and I have to say, derive some pleasure from it. When I have finished, Pumpkin looks quite a lot better than he has done ever since I first made his acquaintance. I find myself humming as I wrap him in a towel – thank goodness I unpacked them. I wedge a hand towel around his bottom to catch accidents, and give him a final polish.

Just as I finish, the house refills with human sounds. The wanderers have returned, just in time to give me no help whatsoever. Who cares? I didn't need it! Proudly I steer Pumpkin downstairs and present him to the assembled company. My back aches, my clothes are soaking, I have poo on my trousers. But Pumpkin – although naked under two towels - looks perfect.

Honeybee is the first to speak.

"Rebecca, are you all right? You look terrible!"

"Yes you do," chimes in Mike in worried tones. "What happened?"

A Robin's Nest gapes in a concerned manner the while.

"I gave Pumpkin a bath."

"Is that all?" cries Mike. "You look awful!"

"Thanks. You can do it next time."

"Hey, this'll cheer you up. Take out curry tonight. Special treat."

"Most generous," I say sarcastically, but it's lost on Mike. Honeybee and A Robin's Nest are looking vaguely animated so thank heavens for small mercies.

CHAPTER FOUR

For one wild moment, when I woke up and before I opened my eyes, I thought I was alone in my precious flat. Then a smell of burnt porridge wafts up the stairs, and with a shudder first my nose, then the rest of me, remembers the dreadful truth. I pull the duvet over my head and plunge into despair.

Here I am. In Cobweb Cottage. With my new family, Mike, Midge, Honeybee, A Robin's Nest, Pumpkin and Pepys the dog. It's not really *me*, is it? We haven't really delved into my past, but there's no doubt about it – I'm glamorous, and always have been. Also, passionate, tempestuous, fastidious, secretive and solitary. Even as a child, I hated my mother to embrace me. From the age of five, I preferred manicuring my nails even to brushing my Barbie doll's hair. My ideal room is a white cube with a black leather sofa, a mammoth television and a well-stocked drinks cabinet. My ideal man is sleek and sophisticated. My ideal children are safely locked away at boarding school. My favourite pet – oh forget it. I'd have all animals put down immediately if I ran the country. Except for those we need to eat, and I prefer not to see those. Nasty, smelly creatures.

Lying here, in an unfamiliar bed between flannel sheets, with an orange poncho spread over the blankets for extra warmth, a few bursting bin bags crammed with Amanda's clothes and ever-increasing sounds of family life swelling up the rickety stairs, I am frozen with horror. Perhaps if I don't move, the future will never happen. I can just lie here and...

"Yoo hoo! Here's a cup of tea, Becky. Rise and shine!" It's Mike. His smile alone makes my head ache. "Where shall I put it? Here on the floor? You take it with two sugars and milk, right?"

"Black."

"Whoops! Could have sworn you took milk and sugar."

"Sweet, milky tea is vulgar and working class. Only builders take milk *and* sugar."

"Aha! There's a treat to cheer you up, though. This is maple sugar. Three times the price and very gourmet."

"Maple sugar?"

"Made from the sap of the maple tree."

"Sap in my tea? Why, thank you!"

"You're welcome, Becky." My sarcasm is lost on him. "We're all up except for Midge and Honeybee. There's hot porridge on the range..."

"I smell it now."

"Yes – A Robin's Nest forgot to stir it. Never mind. Take your time. See you downstairs."

He's off, and I prise myself up from the pillow and reach for my mobile. Will there be a signal in Cobweb Cottage? We appear to be higher here than in the Much Jenner car park... YES! A signal at last. And I've got a text message. How exciting. Despatches from the outside world. Here it comes...

FK U. XPCT PST. AMNDA.

Now there's a nice thought. And what does she mean by XPCT PST? It's pathetic, people like her trying to text. But the rest of the message is clear. Fuming, I text back,

FK U 2 and throw myself back onto my pillow in a paroxysm of rage. Then I sit up once more and gulp down my tea (quite nice, actually. This sap stuff is rather good).

Finally I crawl out of bed but getting dressed nearly makes me want to kill myself once more – I can't face the outside bathroom, and Amanda's clothes are deeply depressing. I eventually settle on a long Indian cotton skirt, a faded black, long-sleeved t-shirt and for warmth alone, the orange poncho. If there were a mirror, I wouldn't dare look into it.

The kitchen is heaving with Mike and his children and everybody attempts to arrange their breakfasts at once. Pumpkin is scraping his porridge bowl, so I nonchalantly chuck him a quick couple of prunes. With any luck, A Robin's Nest will be around when the next nappy is filled. Mike is wagging his beard over the usual muesli, A Robin's Nest is dishing out more porridge and Honeybee is hunched over the range making toast and snarling to herself. Mike is the first to speak, spraying bits of muesli all over me.

"Hi, Becky! Help yourself to some breakfast. Heyyy! Love the poncho."

Honeybee looks round. I wouldn't have said that her expression could blacken, but it does, in the manner that black boots get blacker when you put black boot polish on them. "That's Amanda's poncho, Dad. It was her favourite."

"Really?" says Mike, munching merrily away. "I don't remember it. But it looks great on you, Becky. You should wear it more often."

"Dad, how can you be so crass? You're fucking unbelievable."

Mike stops scooping up the cereal to wave his spoon in an admonitory manner. "Now Honeybee, no swearing."

"Oh, fuck off."

88

"Come on, Honeybee," says A Robin's Nest, hoovering up his porridge. "Becky is Amanda's sister. She can wear her poncho if she likes."

"Yeah. She can take everything of Amanda's if she likes. That's what being sisters is all about, isn't it?"

"Look. I hate the poncho, but I'm wearing it to keep warm, okay? Now. I'll have some toast, Honeybee, as you're making it…"

"Eff off."

"Charming! And Mike, can you fill me in on what's happening today?"

"Yeah! Right! Now. Let's see. School starts tomorrow. There's a lot to get before then!" Mike chucks his bowl and spoon into the sink (I wonder who he thinks is going to wash them up) and gets busy with a pen and piece of paper at the kitchen table.

"There's loads to do today, Becky. You'll have to get rolling in a few minutes."

"I haven't had my toast yet! It's barely dawn!"

"Dawn? Nonsense. That was hours ago."

"Well, it's first thing in the morning, anyway. I'm barely awake."

"It's not first thing in the morning, Becky…"

"REBECCA."

"… it's nine o'clock. Boy oh boy! You've got to get used to the early hours now! See, it says here, 'From the Holt Park punctuality mandate'. Now that sounds organised! Good sign! It goes on, 'Children must be at their desks at ten minutes past eight. Punctuality is a sign of respect so we ask all parents to ensure that this rule is adhered to.'"

"I'm not their parent."

"No! Never mind! But remember Becky, it's your job to look after them? Nothing heavy, but I'm paying you fifty quid a week?"

"What? Are you telling me that I'm going to have to leave this pitiful excuse for a house while the owls are still hooting just so that they can be at their desks at eight? There's no way. They are perfectly capable of getting to school by themselves, and that's what they are going to have to do. I mean, I never get up before eight thirty. I'd get bags under my eyes. I'd die young."

"Well, Honeybee and A Robin's Nest can get to school under their own steam although it's a bit of a walk, but Pumpkin certainly can't."

"He's too young to go to school."

"Playgroup, Rebecca, playgroup. And all three of them need some supervision when it comes to making sure they've got all their gear."

"Can't the older ones take Pumpkin?"

"It's too far for him to walk."

"What about the buggy?"

"Becky, if they get ready themselves and leave taking Pumpkin while you are still snoring your socks off in bed, then I wonder what I am paying you for. Really and truly, you do need to supervise this."

"Why can't you supervise it, Mister Lovely Caring Daddy?"

"Becky." Big sigh. "You know I can't. I'm at work! This is what you are meant to be doing."

"What about Midge? She is their mother after all for God's sake."

"Bex..."

"Re-fucking-becca. Oh forget I asked. Okay. I'll get up at the crack of effing dawn every day although I tell you now it will do my health and temper no good at all."

"Fine! Great! Cool! You'll need to take them shopping. Here's the list of stuff they need. Oh, and there's class get-togethers as well today at five o'clock. They need to go so that they can meet their class teachers and new friends. Now I just need to fix that banister..."

He shoves a slender wedge of cash into my grasp and in a whirl of beard he is off through the door looking like a man who's going to mend something. He's very good at that. I've got a theory that he carries a few tools around just so he can whip them out and make a hole somewhere just as I come round the corner. God knows, in Cobweb Cottage you could chisel moon craters before anyone would notice the difference.

With a mammoth intake of breath, I go to find Honeybee and A Robin's Nest and summon them to the camper van. Once A Robin's Nest has installed Pumpkin into his seat and all is quiet, we examine the list. Quite a few of the items named can be purchased at the school shop, which is open today. Then they need lunchboxes. Oh. Rewind. Lunch *baskets*. Logos, letters and images are prohibited from lunchboxes. Baskets or bags are de rigueur. Okay. Honeybee looks appalled.

"What! I've got to trot to school looking like fucking Little Red Riding Hood with a bloody basket over my arm! No way. I won't do it."

"Don't get stressy with me Honeybee, and stop that foul-mouthed swearing."

"You swear the whole time!"

"I'm a grown-up. You'll have a fucking lunch basket and like it or I'll twist your arm till it breaks. What about you Rob? Going to make a fuss?"

"Er, no. No Rebecca. That's okay."

"So. Lunch baskets we will get at the hardware shop. Sports stuff we can get at the school shop, de da de da, blah blah blah, oh. Eurythmy shoes. And what the heck is Eurythmy when it is at home?"

"Oh Bex. Don't you know what Eurythmy is?" titters Honeybee, raising a pierced eyebrow.

"No I don't, you little smart arse. Why don't you tell me?" Dead silence.

"She doesn't know and neither do I," says A Robin's Nest, firmly. "Shall we just make a start? Whatever they are, I'm sure we can get them at the school shop, too. Come on, let's go."

The camper van thunders and farts through the village scattering old ladies left and right, and after a fair amount of wrong turning and effing and blinding we finally reach Destination School. And I have to admit, Holt Park is quite impressive. There's a scattering of utilitarian buildings, but even they cannot spoil the view of Holt Park House, a beautiful building in some disrepair, glowing with honey coloured stones and creeping vines. For a moment I gaze at it dreaming... Lady Rebecca... Riding to hounds... Thirties evening dresses... Oh yes. There's nothing like a small stately home to make one feel really quite romantic. And of course I had imagined the worst about this damn school, that the buildings were knitted or tie-dyed or something. This beautiful house really does give it some cachet.

We park right by the door, dismount, shovel Pumpkin into his buggy and set out, asking all passing hippies the way, for the school shop. It turns out to be a room steeped in extreme disorganisation, manned – or in this environment should I say, womaned - by a rather pretty, but woolly, woman named Lizzie. While Honeybee and A Robin's Nest squabble over the list and hold manky items of sportswear up against themselves we fall to chatting, and it turns out that she has a toddler of identical age to Pumpkin called Charlie who will be in his playgroup. Goody! A little friend already. Perhaps it'll be a real love match and Pumpkin will be asked over to play every afternoon. Or at least two afternoons a week. Lizzie radiates kindness. I'm sure she wouldn't want favours back.

Before we leave, I extract an invitation to coffee tomorrow morning after I've dropped Pumpkin off at playgroup. Then Honeybee and A Robin's Nest want a look around the school grounds before their class get-togethers, and in an unusual fit of generosity I agree so we spend a pleasant hour or so wandering hither and thither. Well, Pumpkin and I do, anyway. Honeybee and the Nest drop us almost immediately and slink off to God knows where. The whole set up is very pleasant, actually, although there are some surprises. Ten black piglets, for example, which scare the shit out of Pumpkin when they come barging up behind as we're crossing a perfectly innocent mud patch. It takes some time to stop the child screaming. What kind of school has pigs? I thought a few rabbits and goldfish was more the form.

Then there is a largish market gardenish sort of arrangement, full of pecking, scratching chickens. A still gasping Pumpkin and I are leaning on the fence examining these, when I hear the cracking of twigs and look up to see a man marching around the compost heap, carrying a basket.

Now, hold on a minute. The universe suddenly did something really weird. It expanded until it was one gigantic throbbing drum. And then it contracted into a tiny point charged with an extraordinary magnetic force. At least, I think that's what happened. It's difficult to describe these gigantic cosmic disasters. I shouldn't think the dinosaurs spent much time analysing the impact of the asteroid that ended their dominion over the earth, and I felt rather the same. Because, you see, it is a disaster. I absolutely and totally refuse to fall in love with a member of this insane community. If love is what I've just fallen into. I've never been in love before so I'm not too clear.

As I stand, stunned, with every sense reeling like six men in kilts at a Burns Night supper in Surrey, the man who may control my destiny approaches. I stare, quite frankly, with my jaw dropping and mentally introduce him to me as if we were internet dating.

"Hi!" he might begin. "My name's [something very cool] and I'm six feet two inches high with a mop of blonde hair, green eyes but dark eyelashes, loads of laughter lines and a six pack. I'm thirty years old, good with children, kind to animals but much more important than any of that, I sizzle in the sack..."

"Hello! Are you admiring our chickens?"

"Sorry?" I say, blinking. "What was that?"

The man grins appealingly, revealing that he has all his own teeth. Good. Because I've just noticed that he is wearing some sort of hessian smock, and while it is inevitable that we fall in love, or at the very least, exchange the bare minimum of personal fluids, I would rather not spend time with a member of a disadvantaged community. But he's opened the channels of communication so I have to pull myself together.

Now, the thing to do when you really, really, really fancy somebody, is to make interesting conversation. You can't just stand there hoping you haven't got anything stuck between your teeth. So I took the plunge.

"Erm... I was wondering how people *kill* chickens in a place like this."

"Why would we want to kill them?"

"To eat, of course."

"Oh, most of us are vegetarian."

"Oh well, you know what I mean. When they're past their sell-by date."

"Sorry?"

"Ill or something. I mean, for the chop. Literally. How do they get their chips? Does somebody bore them to death by reciting Buddhist scriptures or something? Or are they just overpowered with joss sticks and strangled with their own auras?"

The man laughs attractively. "Oh no. No, we kill them the way it's always been done. We wring their necks."

94

"How old fashioned of you. I think you're missing out on a real opportunity for karmic killing."

"Do you know what a karma is?"

"Actually, no."

"Well then. I'll have to enlighten you sometime."

My heart beating fast, I slip him a sideways look. Is that a bit fresh – or a bit naïve? Impossible to tell. His good-humoured, friendly face is deadpan as he watches the chickens peck about.

"They are nice aren't they?" he continues, leaning over the fence and frowning thoughtfully. "Funny though. Chickens are really quite close relations of dinosaurs. Genetically that is. You can see it too, can't you? Just look at their heads. And their legs."

"Oh. Yes! Heads and legs. Yukky horror scales. Just look at that, Pumpkin. Watch out! They'll hold you down and peck your eyes out before you know it."

"WAAH!"

"Oh for goodness sake Pumpkin. It was only a joke."

But poor Pumpkin, already a bit fragile this morning, just doesn't see it that way. His mouth is square, face purple, and tears are bursting out at the sides like a cartoon. I heave him into my arms and wipe off tears and clean the button nose to no avail. When I turn around with the sobbing Pumpkin in my arms, I see that our new friend has climbed over into the chicken pen and is gathering eggs and placing them tenderly in a basket.

"Look Pumpkin!," I coo. "The chickens have laid some lovely eggs for your tea. Look!"

"You could have an egg if you liked, Pumpkin. Is that your name? Maybe I can find an egg box in the shed. Mummy could boil it for your supper. Would you like that?"

Pumpkin's wails turn to sobs and dwindle out completely as we amble up the garden to the shed. The sex god rummages around, finds an egg box and Pumpkin chooses his own egg.

"There, Pumpkin! Aren't you a lucky boy! Say thank you! Thank you! Say it! Go on, Pumpkin. Say thank you, or I'll give you a Chinese burn."

"Whoa! It's okay. He doesn't have to say thank you." There's a longish pause, but neither of us make a move to go. "So, are you a new parent here?"

"Oh, I haven't got any children of my own. Can't you tell?" He looks polite but blank and doesn't even glance down at the perfectly flat tummy I'm proudly patting as the prime example of my lack of maternity. "I'm looking after Pumpkin, and there's another two who are older. They can look after themselves so I'll be at a bit of a loose end a lot of the time I expect." God. I frown at the ground in order to cancel out the outrageous hint that just popped out from nowhere, enough to make any man run a mile, but the hessian-clad one keeps talking.

"Have you just moved to the area?"

"Yes – down from London yesterday – I think yesterday. It seems an awfully long time ago. We've been really busy, what with the move and everything. I'm exhausted, actually."

"I'll let you get on then."

"No! I mean, I'm fine." Christ! Why am I having this conversation? It must be because he's got such amazing green eyes with – no, it can't be true – little golden flecks in them. Then I realise I'm staring again. So I take a step backwards and ask coolly: "So... what's with the smock?"

"What? Oh, this. Well, it's the gardening uniform. We have to wear it when we're teaching gardening. It's quite handy, actually. Got special pockets and everything."

"So you wouldn't wear it normally?"

"Well..."

"I was rather hoping you were going to say you wouldn't be seen dead in a ditch with it."

"Why?"

"Because... well, if, say for example, you were going out to dinner at a local restaurant, or to the pub, or something like that... you wouldn't be wearing it?"

"Probably not."

"That's a relief."

"Sorry?"

"Nothing. So, you're not a parent then? You're a teacher?"

"That's right."

"Really? What years do you teach?"

"Year Eight is the big one for gardening and farming."

"Oh! One of Mike's kids is in Year Eight."

"Really? Class A or B?"

"B."

"Great! That's my class. What's his name?"

"Oh... A... ah... Rob. Rob Lange."

"Rob Lange. I have to admit I don't recall the name from the list, but I'll keep an eye out for him. And I'll probably see you at parents' evenings and so on – we're quite sociable here."

"I'll look forward to it."

"So will I."

"So, do *you* have any children?"

"No, I don't, actually. Too busy looking after everybody else's."

"So you're not married then? I mean – for God's sake! Where's Pumpkin!"

"He's just here, climbing on the compost heap. Down you get!"

We stare at each other for a few seconds too long, then sounding in rather a hurry, and I'm not surprised, he sticks out a hand for me to shake and says, "I'd better go – it's been good to meet you. I'll see you around."

"Yes indeed. Bye!"

I gaze after him, casually pushing back my hair in a sexy manner as he turns to wave – that's when I realise that a whole lock of hair is stuck to my cheek with about a gallon of Pumpkin's snot and has been throughout our conversation. And Pumpkin is covered in compost. I brush him down breathing not through my nose but through my mouth, then head back to the pigs where I discover A Robin's Nest and Honeybee leaning over the fence, staring the porkers out.

"Come on, you lot! Time to go back to the House for your class get-togethers. Move it! What's wrong with you?"

"Do I have to go?" A Robin's Nest is completely paralysed with shyness and his spots look radioactive.

"Of course you do. I'm right behind you. Come on. Left right, left right, left right. They'll love you."

Honeybee's face is like a magazine illustration for How To Cope With Your Sulky Teen, but at least she's wearing the right clothes for a sixteen-year-old. Poor A Robin's Nest is a complete sight. We haven't had a chance to go shopping, and I can't help feeling sorry for him, but life is tough and he's going to have to get used to it. We march up to Holt Park House and A Robin's Nest, his head hunched between his shoulders, scuttles into the reception area. At the door is my new friend, who smiles and raises his eyebrows at me. My stomach melts within me – a very odd sensation. But looking rather cooler than I managed earlier, I smile and raise my eyebrows straight back at him. I read somewhere that raising eyebrows is a sign of attraction. Ding dong! But Honeybee whips around in the middle of the eyebrow moment.

"Don't think you need to take us in, Rebecca. And don't wait. We'll walk home afterwards."

That won't suit me. I want another chance to chat up the man who I feel may be my future. So although it goes against the grain, I say enticingly, "I've got to take Pumpkin down to Playgroup for his get-together anyway. Why don't I come back up here afterwards to meet you, and I'll give you a lift home?"

"Why can't you just leave us alone?"

You have to know when to give up. "My pleasure. Walk if you want to. And good riddance."

There are little signs scattered here and there with directions on them such as 'pottery', 'crafts', 'sculpture' and 'eurythmy'. Nothing for 'maths' or 'computer studies' I notice, but perhaps the terms are akin to swear words here. Eventually we find an arrow pointing to 'playgroup' and Pumpkin and I wander down.

We venture in without knocking as the door is open and I have to admit that although the word 'cute' makes me heave, one of the signposts should certainly have warned me that this is what this playgroup is all about. A big central table is covered with flowers and candles, with little knitted fairies, bunny rabbits and gnomes skipping about between them. A group of toddlers is hard at work kneading dough, wearing adorable little pink and blue smocks. There's a large rocking horse near the french windows which lead into a darling little garden and the toys scattered around are definitely of the wooden/woollen variety. Great white birds are flying overhead – the ceiling is very high – and there's a thick white carpet, which looks very cosy. I look around and take a deep breath. Forget Cobweb Cottage. I could move in here right now. Pumpkin spots the rocking horse, which is right on the other side of the room and runs towards it, while I look for somewhere to dump my bag. With my eyes focused on floor level, I suddenly notice that all the children are wearing slippers.

And that Pumpkin has left a very significant trail of black compost on his way to the rocking horse. Compost is also smeared liberally over the horse itself, as Pumpkin wrestles himself on top. For God's sake! They shouldn't have compost in gardens and then expect small children to go into rooms with thick white carpets and remember to take their shoes off. I say as much to a tall, thin, manic looking woman with long hair, clogs and a full-length apron who materialises at my side.

"This carpet seems most impractical. Surely bare boards or concrete or something like that is more suitable for small children," I accuse. "Look! He's made a terrible mess of it. That's going to take the cleaners ages to clear up. What is this? A school or a front room?"

"Well!" the teacher seems slightly taken aback by the logic and power of my reasoning. "We have the carpet to create a more gentle, emotionally warm environment for the children, actually. Perhaps you could go and take his shoes off while I go and get a dustpan and brush. Then we can introduce ourselves properly."

She heads off into an ante-room to get cleaning materials, and huffing and puffing I collect Pumpkin and wrench his shoes off. In the process my own shoes, or rather a pair of Amanda's sandals – rather horribly wide at the toe – spread plenty more mud around. The teacher sweeps it all up without a murmur but there are plenty of stains behind. That'll teach them to have cream carpets. It'll probably need professional cleaning.

"Now. I'm Susan," says the teacher, having washed her hands. "Who is this little chap?"

"Tell the lady your name," I instruct Pumpkin, who is struggling to drag my hand from his so that he can go and play. Of course he doesn't answer, so it's up to me to tell her the ghastly truth.

"Pumpkin! What a lovely name."

"It's a bit unusual."

"Oh, not really. We have all sorts of names here. Now. We're making bread today as a little introduction to the kind of things we do here. I'll give Pumpkin some dough and he can join in with the others. You sit here, Pumpkin, next to James and Charlotte. Here's some dough."

100

"I *see*," I said. "You *do* have some peculiar names around. James and Charlotte. Well I never. Pumpkin, you'll fit right in here."

While Susan titters uncomfortably, Pumpkin digs into the dough. I wander around for a bit, then find the loos just off the main room. The toilets are tiny – perfect for children, but a case of any port in a storm for adults. I wedge myself onto one and have a refreshing pee. There isn't a loo roll.

"Excuse me! Excuse me! Excuse me! HEY!"

"Yes?"

"There's no loo roll."

"Oh! Sorry. I didn't realise."

There's some scuffling around and after a while, the teacher brings in a roll, averting her eyes. What's the matter with her? Hasn't she seen stockings and suspenders before? This is the kind of thing that happens when you're squashed on a loo for midgets in a communal wee-ary with your knees on a level with your nose.

This trauma over, I go back into the classroom and perch on another minuscule chair, urging Pumpkin to get a move on and finish making his bread roll as I'm desperate for a fag. After what seems like a hundred years, the teacher slides the tray into the oven and explains to the children that tomorrow, they will be eating the rolls for their break. Disgusting. Why can't they have some nice chocolate milk and a packet of crisps like everybody else?

"Thank you very much," I say to Susan. "I bet Pumpkin really enjoyed that. We'll see you tomorrow at... what time was it? Five thirty ay em?"

"Ten past eight. We're not that bad," she smiles.

"Same difference. We'll see you then. Come on Pumpkin, time to go home."

As per instructions, I leave Honeybee and A Robin's Nest to make their own way back – it shouldn't take them more than about twenty minutes to walk anyway, and it'll do them both good. Halfway home, I park the camper van by the hardware shop and penetrate its gloomy interior in search of luncheon baskets. To my surprise, they are readily available 'buying them for the school, are you?' says the ancient crone who hobbles out to serve me (a serious case of forgetting to use Oil of Olay) and I purchase three. I must say, they are rather sweet. I can just see them with little red and white check covers over them, the three children setting off to school like so many little Red Riding Hoods... OH MY GOD! STOP! I'm turning into an issue of Country Living. This stops right here. Stuff the gingham, they'll have to make do with kitchen roll. I drive home, arriving at the same time as A Robin's Nest and Honeybee.

"How were your class get-togethers?" I ask, quite cheerfully for me. "I got your luncheon baskets."

Honeybee doesn't reply, but A Robin's Nest mutters something about it being okay and thank you for the basket. We form a wedge in the door and burst into the kitchen. Mike is stirring a pot of something foul on the range and he turns and beams cheerily as we stump in.

"Hi, guys! Guess what! Turnip soup for supper!"

"Scrummy, Dad," says Honeybee, wearily, and exchanges a look of suffering with me. For the first time I begin to warm to her – something in common at last. Perhaps she can have gingham on her basket after all.

Turnip soup, though, is something they'd have to give me in a drip when I was unconscious. There is no other way it would ever enter my system. "Thanks Mike, I'll pass," I say. "I think I might go out and get a takeaway later."

"A takeaway! Why would you want a takeaway? They're fine for the odd treat, but Becky, takeaway food is just loaded with salt and other additives. And they're terribly expensive. Come on. Have some turnip soup. I'm famous

102

for my turnip soup. I took some up to Midge just now, and she was raving about it."

"I'm quite sure she was raving about something – it's her natural state."

"Come on. Just try a spoonful."

Slowly but surely, I sink onto my beanbag in the sitting room with the others, and wait for my bowl of turnip soup. It looks absolutely revolting but... mmm. Not too lethal. I've never knowingly eaten a turnip before. Probably terrible for wind... In between slurps, I question A Robin's Nest closely. He's feeding Pumpkin, but seems pleased to talk.

"I met your gardening teacher today. He seems very nice. Did you like him?"

"Yeah."

"What's his name?"

"Um, Mr Mayer."

"Mayer. What's his first name?"

Honeybee fixes me with a beady eye. "Why, fancy him do you?"

I ignore her. After a lengthy pause, A Robin's Nest offers: "William? I think William. Or something like that."

"How can it be 'something like that', Rob? What is like the name William but not the name William? You must give your use of the language more thought. More focus."

"Sorry, Becky. I'll try."

"How can you give in to her like that, Robbo?" shouts Honeybee. "Don't let her boss you around like that. You talk the way you want to talk! You be yourself! Be an individual!"

"What, like you?"

"Yeah."

"You're hardly an individual! You look exactly the same as all your friends, and talk like them too."

"I do not, either."

"You so do."

"Do not."

"Do."

"Name one way I look like all my friends."

"You've got a pierced nose. And a pierced eyebrow. And a pierced tummy button. And you wear hair extensions. And all the clothes you wear come from the same shops. And you've got a tattoo of a fairy on your bottom."

"Lower back. And anyway, you've never even seen my tattoo."

"Of course I have! Every time you bend over everybody in the whole world can see your bum."

"Pervert."

"I'm not. I don't want to see your bum. Nor does anybody else. We can't help it. It's so big."

"Just fucking shut up, okay?"

"Well, you asked. And I've answered. You look just like all your friends."

"So what if I follow the fashions. I've still got my own style, haven't I?"

"Not really."

I've never heard A Robin's Nest fight his own corner like this! It's really exciting. I look over to Mike to see whether he's as thrilled as I am to see his son asserting himself, but instead of punching the air and chanting football songs he's looking very pained.

"What?" I hiss. "It's great to see A Robin's Nest stand up for himself for once."

"I hate to see them fight, Becky" he returns. "Mother Earth has conflict aplenty without having negativity on this scale in our new home. If this goes on, I'm going to have to get a shaman in."

"What's a shaman?"

"Somebody who'll be able to exorcise the negative vibes."

"Would you have to pay them?"

"Of course."

"Sod it, I'll do it myself. I could exorcise Beelzebub himself if the price was right," I yelp, horrified by the idea of Mike's precious cash flowing out into any pocket but my own.

"You're a real card, Becky. Shamans train for years, you know."

"Oh, all right. Couldn't Midge have a stab at it? Sounds right up her street,"

"She's not a shaman. She does crystal healing. Now. While I do the washing up, Becky can put Pumpkin to bed. You two can start getting your stuff ready for school. Special treat! I'll do your sandwiches so you can go to bed early. It's a big day tomorrow."

"How old do you think we are, Dad?" says Honeybee desperately. "It's not a 'big day', like we were nine years old. It's any old day. Worse than most days. This place is a dump and the school's a dump too."

"Honeybee, such beauty to learn in will create inner beauty in you."

"Sod the sandwiches. I'm going up to my room. If anybody comes in, I'll kill them. Okay?"

A Robin's Nest and Honeybee slouch off, and I wearily begin the bedtime process for Pumpkin. I can't be bothered to give him a bath, so I just wipe him down as best as I can, put a t-shirt on him and tuck him into bed while A Robin's Nest lies silently on his bed on the other side of the room, staring at the ceiling. Mike comes in to kiss him goodnight and rather than witness the revolting sight I beat a hasty retreat downstairs. My dream of a quiet moment is destroyed, as Midge – silent but deadly - has descended into the kitchen with her empty bowl and is sniffing around the prunes, Pepys tucked under her arm.

"Greetings to you, Rebecca. Everything's surprisingly calm in here," she says in glacial tones.

"You've got prune stuck between your teeth."

105

"Never mind that. How are they all settling in?"

"Fine. Delightful children."

"They are soooo soul-centred, aren't they? A testament to the positive life forces."

"Funny that you avoid them like the plague, then."

"I think that my relationship with my own children is my business, don't you?"

"Oh of course. I wouldn't want to tread on your toes, Midge."

"Thank you."

"Although it would be a laugh causing you pain, I might get blisters from the toe-rings."

"Very amusing, Rebecca. You make the fact that I only came in to give you your post worthwhile."

"Give it to me, then."

Looking as if she's just sucked on a lemon, Midge hands me a small brown padded envelope postmarked London and drifts from the room. With an exhausted sigh I wrestle with miles of sticky tape and finally unwrap a disc with DVD No 1 written on it in black pen. There's also a note from Amanda, which says: 'Hope you enjoy this. All my hatred, A'. Well, isn't that just typical of Amanda? She must know that Mike doesn't have a DVD player. And what the hell does she want me to watch a DVD for?

Putting the disc into my pocket, I wander into the sitting room and slump onto a beanbag, completely exhausted. Now the kids are in bed, my thoughts can wander and in next to no time, my dreams have transported me back to the chicken run. Mmmm. That Mister Mayer, possibly William or else 'something like that' had better watch out. If there are any girlfriends in the way I'll have to purchase a flamethrower. I hear Midge and Mike passing on the stairs. Somehow I have to touch on the experience I had today with another human being. Well, make that form of life.

"Mike," I yell, as he shuffles towards the kitchen. "Do you believe in love at first sight?"

Mike pokes his head around the door.

"Of course! That's how I fell in love with Midge. First sight. In the second year at school. We were married at eighteen. That's why I'm so young and sexy now even though Honeybee's almost all grown up. First sight. Yeah."

"You're not much of an advert for it," I say.

"Yeah we are," he says. "We may not be together anymore, but we still love each other to bits."

"All the same," I say. "I think the two of you are possibly the blackest recommendation for love at first sight I've ever met. And that counts my mum and dad who fell for each other in a fish and chip shop in 1974 and split up twenty-eight years later when he ran off with a shark."

"Maybe he was trying to avoid the expense of a thirtieth anniversary party," offers Mike, ever cautious with the cash.

"You may be right."

"What's all this about? Have you met somebody?"

"Of course not, beard for brains. Me? Now. Brew a cup of tea before I expire of dehydration. All this talking is drying my tongue quicker than a slug in a sauna."

CHAPTER FIVE

The next morning we are all up bright and early. Well, A Robin's Nest had to be, to get Pumpkin ready on time. The rest of us shoot into the kitchen at about three minutes past eight, showering paraphernalia in all directions and trying to get out of the door at the same time. Honestly. It's like a Marx Brothers film round here.

I manage to start the camper van without too many problems and we move off, A Robin's Nest and Honeybee exchanging insults in the back. Pumpkin looks a trifle apprehensive and I admit to feeling a bit sorry for him – for them all, actually. I remember my first day at a new school. It's crap. In fact, I went to quite a few schools owing to being a square peg in any round hole I came across unlike dear old Amanda, who fitted in everywhere and with anybody. Just anybody. Really. I'm a little more exclusive than that.

But enough of reminiscing! We are nearly at the gates, and a tense silence has fallen as everybody struggles with their nerves. I park in front of the main entrance and a rotund midget with dyed hair shoots out like a cork from a magnum of champagne and whacks a nasty looking florescent notice under my wipers. I step out of the van.

"What's wrong?" I say, majestically.

"Sorry! You can't park here. Teachers' cars only. We sent everybody a letter over the holidays, so..."

"We are new to this school."

"New or old, I'm afraid you can't park here."

"I am going to park here."

"Then I am going to have to take your registration number."

"I'm scared."

"And print it in our weekly newsletter."

"Oh my God! Anything but that!"

She bowls off, shooting me one of the dirtiest looks it has ever been my pleasure to receive. I turn to acknowledge applause from A Robin's Nest and Honeybee, only to see them scuttling off at high speed. A Robin's Nest looks back once, purple in the face from what I can only assume is embarrassment. Really. That colour in a complexion does nothing for the ravages of acne. You'd think having a face block coloured the same shade as a virulent spot would act as camouflage. Take it from me. It doesn't.

I haul Pumpkin out, straighten his outfit as best I can and march off to the playgroup where Susan greets us with a friendly smile. Pumpkin seems to be reassured by the familiarity of his surroundings, and dons his slippers and little blue smock without a murmur. Susan sits him down with some paper and paints and he immediately commences work. I tiptoe out, anticipating that he'll cry as soon as he knows I've gone, but mercifully there is silence. Now. I've got a couple of hours for myself. First off, coffee calls. Lizzie from the school shop invited me round and hell, I'm going in. I head back for the camper van, whipping the offensive and bossy note from under my wiper and ripping it up as I speed along. The virulent midget is still lurking around at the top of the drive and with a cheery wave, I shower her with the pieces as I exit which gives me a lovely warm feeling. You had to be there.

It takes me quite a long time to find Lizzie's house, what with one thing and another, and at least half an hour passes before I am beating my way through the wind chimes to her front door. I knock with a hand shaking for a caffeine fix. She opens the door with a weedy "Hi!" and I stream past her into the sitting room. Five hirsute women sitting on goatskins look up and say "Hi!" With a brief "Hi to you" I pass through into the kitchen where Lizzie has established herself at the helm of a kettle. "Coffee please," I say crisply. "Strong. Black." Lizzie looks aghast. I might have been suggesting drinking the blood of infants at the full moon. Then she realises that I must be joking. "Well let's see. I have the fruit teas, green tea, Rooibosch and Acorna."

"What's the most like coffee?"

"Oh, Acorna."

"Then Acorna it will have to be. Thanks."

After a wordless pause while she fixes the foul brew I grab my steaming mug and head back to the sitting room, Lizzie at my heels. Just as I sit down and force a gulp, there is the unmistakable sound of a loo flushing and another woman comes into the room. Oh dear. It's the virulent midget – actually around five feet four inches, but more virulent, if possible, than before.

I have to admit that the immediate future looks bleak. Even I feel a bit shy, if shy is the word, following the paper-chucking episode. Lizzie is still in the middle of introducing me and she finishes by saying, "and Rebecca, this is Dawn." I say, "Hello!" and give a little wave. Dawn says nothing, stares at me very hard indeed and sits as far away from me as she can manage.

There's an awkward pause, broken violently by a sharp scream from our hostess. We follow the direction of her eyes, which are, like the humble snail's, unattractively waving around on stalks and hit upon a stout blonde who is rolling her eyes to the ceiling and sighing. On her lap there is, in this order, a baby wearing only a vest, and a large, orange turd. Or make that, half a large orange turd. The other half is on the carpet.

"Tut, tut, tut," sighs the blonde. "I've done it again."

Of course, it is not she who has laid the turd, but her child. I'm just about to point this out, when she continues, looking around her in confident expectation of our approval and understanding.

"I'm having wonderful results with the no-diaper system. It's amazing how much I'm in tune with when Poppy needs to go. But whoopsie! There's always the little accident when I just don't pick up on her vibes!"

"Sorry, what system is that? Just run that by me just one more time?" I ask.

"Oh, don't you know about it? It's the no-diaper system. I mean, I've always wondered what women do in the third world, you know, and places like that, where there are no nappies. I mean, literally. Like, even the rags are used for... bandages, you know. And things like that. Well, the mothers are wonderfully in tune with their babies' natural rhythms. They are really in tune with when their baby's about to go pee pee."

"Or poo-poo."

"Yes! Or poo-poo! So they simply lift the baby up over a gutter or something, and just let her void! Which is just great."

"Why?"

"Well, it saves the world from the devastating effects of washing powder and power consumption caused by washing machines. And of course I don't need to mention landfill, although I'm sure no-one here uses disposables."

I glance round. Several mothers are looking hard at the floor.

111

"And of course, it's so much better for the babes. There are so many studies showing that disposables cause infertility."

"A good thing, surely," I venture.

"What?"

"The world's over-populated as it is. We should be encouraging third world mothers to use as many disposables as they can."

There's a communal sharp intake of breath, then Stout Blonde continues. "Well. Anyway. My babies don't have a nasty old wet dirty diaper around their gorgeous little ikkle botties, do they Poppy-Poo-Poo?"

During this exchange, Lizzie has got her butt parked firmly in a Catch 22 situation. I can see that all she wants to do is to clean up that poop and disinfect the area, possibly quarantining her sitting room from this woman and Poppy-Poo-Poo on a permanent basis. On the other hand, her wish to appear liberal and understanding of this dysentery-inducing no-diaper system is preventing her from leaping up and getting to it with a pair of rubber gloves. I take pity on her.

"Well, it sounds just fascinating. I've got some wipes in Pumpkin's nappy bag somewhere... here. Would you like some?"

"Oh! Are they washable?"

"Never mind. I'll just mop it up myself. There. And shall I do your lap? You don't want to stand up and drop the rest of it on the carpet, I'm sure. Lizzie, have you got any disinfectant?"

"Oh! Oh! Thank you Rebecca. Somewhere, probably. Come into the kitchen."

We dash into the kitchen, me holding the pile of wipes at arm's length and Lizzie finds me a plastic bag. I'm sure I hear her muttering something uncomplimentary as she digs around under the sink but when she emerges, her long, lean face –although flushed – is almost as benign as ever.

"I think that woman's system is fucked up," I say pleasantly. "Who wants a load of shit on their carpet?"

"Oh, she's all right," says Lizzie uncomfortably. "Each to their own." But she gives my shoulder a squeeze as we hurry back to the sitting room to apply the Dettol. By this time the others have started chatting again, and while I'm scrubbing the carpet with wipes and Dettol – Lizzie standing by with the plastic bag – my ears prick up, because there has been a conversation shift from the delights of defecation au naturel to personalities. The difference here is that instead of facing facts and admitting that they hate certain members of the school community with every bone in their body, they start out by insisting that they love them. As I nip to the loo to scrub my hands, a woman called Irene, unexpectedly absent, is mentioned. Lizzie comes back from throwing out wipes to agree that she certainly seems to be having problems with her son, and I regain my seat to hear Stout Blonde launch into Stage One of Session Bitch. "What an amazing woman she is. I love her, I really do. She's so special and I really admire her. And Ricky's a wonderful child. He is. But I do feel for her. And for her husband. He must really be having a difficult time. No wonder they separated. You know what? Just between us, but she's very negative. She drains me. To be honest, I find her quite difficult company. I've had to stop Orlando from going round there to play. All Ricky likes to do is to play with a toy fort, I mean, soldiers and everything! And that's just not good for Orlando. It's so aggressive. I don't know why she can't do something about it. Everybody says so. It must be all the additives in the food she gives him. Poor Irene. I mean really, no wonder Jimmy left her."

113

There's a general murmur of agreement. Stout Blonde adds complacently: "Poor thing. She's looking terribly thin."

"Don't knock it," I say. "Every divorce is a diet opportunity."

Lizzie hastily passes a bowl of dried fruit and nuts around the room and Dawn goes on as if I haven't spoken. "I know, I know. I love her too. Her back's really against the wall, and I've got nothing but respect for her. I feel terrible saying all this. Bill says that she is really having some problems. But it's her own fault. She asks for it really. It's all down to personalities. I agree with you, and I said to Bill, she's just too negative. Bill said he would be too, but you know Bill. He's such a sweetie!"

Everybody agrees with this. Smiles all round.

"I mean, what a wonderful man! I adore him! We're so lucky having him for Elizabeth. We need him for that class. It's really quite difficult this term. Oh God! Have you heard? The new boy? He has the most bizarre name. Guess."

While the others are all merrily guessing bizarre names, I develop a horrible sinking feeling. And I'm right.

"A Robin's Nest! Ha ha ha! Can you believe it? Poor boy! Who could do that to a child! His sister's just as bad, she's called Honeydew Melons or something and Elizabeth says she has pierced nipples. Can you believe it at that age? What a mutilation! Mind you, it's not surprising. Bill tells me that their home life is very unsettled. They moved into Cobweb Cottage. Well. Nobody else would, what a dump. They probably haven't got any money. Bill says the father can't keep a relationship down and there's some kind of a stepmother or helper or something who sounds like, if you'll excuse my French, a complete bitch and the mum's mad in the attic or something. Elizabeth hasn't been able to get a word out of him yet, but she says he's awful with terrible acne. Probably his diet.

114

Apparently he smells. They probably all do. They've got a really horrible dog it seems which can't help. What? What's the matter Lizzie? Oh! Whoops!"

Well, there's really nothing to say. Lizzie has been making frantic signals to Dawn for about nine hours and I am red as my lipstick, feeling like shit. I could defend myself if I wanted too, but she's right about Rob's name. It is terrible. No wonder girls like Dawn's daughter Elizabeth are laughing at him and his spots. And the rest! First I heard that Honeybee has pierced nipples. And how does this Dawn pestilence know anything at all about our home situation? From the class teacher of course. Mr Hessian Smock. Mr Nice To Chickens. William Mayer, obviously known as Bill and clearly Dawn's good buddy. Not so cute after all. Heads are going to roll over this.

Another of the women, noticing what is going on, makes a valiant attempt to change the subject and says, "I saw Mandy the other day." "Oh really? Is she still breastfeeding Sidney?" chimes in another. "He just turned four, didn't he?" gabbles Lizzie desperately. Come on! This is a face-saver. I must join in and chat as if nothing has happened to bother me. Pausing only to moisten the tonsils with a gulp of Acorna, I jump right in. If I'm positive and confident, everybody will think I don't care that Dawn said what she did.

"Four? She's crazy! The child is being completely manipulative. That's the way to raise a psychopath. I'm telling you! The child will be a mass murderer, in love with mummy, cutting off prostitutes' tits with kitchen knives before he's out of short trousers."

They all stare at me open mouthed and it is at this moment that a stout child – presumably the aforementioned Orlando and aged approximately five thunders into the room and hurls himself at Stout Blonde, yanks up her top and begins noisily refreshing himself at one of her beige and floppy founts of Venus.

115

After that, I can only make my excuses and leave, and I get the impression that with the possible exception of Lizzie, they are not sad to see me go. In fact, I think they probably disinfected the cup. The feeling's mutual, especially when it comes to Dawn. What a complete cow. But even worse, how could Professor Mayer have told her so many things about Mike's family and me? He seemed such a nice man, down by the chickens, and I was looking forward to perhaps seducing him over coffee and biscuits. But no more. He's now my enemy – official. And I'm going to have to sort this out.

As I fumble for my car keys with shaking fingers, a friendly looking woman in combat trousers and short spiky hair pulls up and gives me a big smile. She is reassuringly normal looking and looks kind.

"Hi," she says. "Are you off? I was looking forward to meeting you – my son's in playgroup with Pumpkin, so I know who you are. I'm Irene."

"Oh! You must be Ricky's mum."

"Yes." She looks puzzled, then her face clears. "You've probably heard all about me from our mutual friend. I noticed a little tension there at drop off this morning. Did you really throw a parking notice at her? Don't worry, say what you like. She hates my guts."

"I take it you are referring to the lovely Dawn?"

"Dawn. If she's in there" indicating Lizzie's house "I'll stay out. Fancy a coffee?"

"Great. Where?"

"Vera's in the village. Don't you know it? Don't worry, you will. Just follow me. Come on."

Vera's manages to distract me from my problems for a minute or two. Vera herself is incredibly ancient, and the café is a museum piece. Nothing in it has changed, perhaps even moved, since – at a guess – 1954 and that includes the rock cakes. But the coffee is good and strong.

"The ambience here is unpretentious," I say. "And the very fact that you have taken me somewhere without a crystal corner and are drinking strong coffee instead of ground barley tells me that you are relatively normal. So perhaps you can fill me in. What the hell is this place all about?"

"Don't you like it?"

"No I don't. To be perfectly honest, I think it's God's recycling bin for nutters. The village is a dump and as for the people – I've never seen so much crap served up with a sprig of parsley."

Irene laughs, then stirs her coffee thoughtfully. "Well, I know what you mean. And a few of the people here are a bit extreme. But they're very nice, in general. I mean, they really do care about issues like the environment, cruelty to animals, education, stuff like that."

"Eighties crap."

"Well, maybe Much Jenner is the land that time forgot. But it's pretty cool, really. There's a lovely community atmosphere, and quite a lot gets done in its own way."

"Like what? I'd be surprised if this lot could organise opening a door."

"Well, for example, phone masts. The subject only has to be mentioned and you have five hundred families with all the kids coming out to demonstrate. That's special. Often those sort of demos are four women and a dog."

"You give me hope. At least the morons here have retained some rudimentary sense of a reasonable standard of living. Who'd want to live without mobile phones?"

"They're demonstrating *against* them, Becky."

"Oh. Typical. I take back my kind words."

"Then, the place is a sort of centre for organic food."

"What, twice the price, triple the blemishes and none of the flavour?"

117

"You're talking about supermarket organics, Becky. If you eat local produce which has been organically farmed, you'll really taste the difference."

"Okay, so what about the school? It seems to me that it's a bunch of lunatics charging up their own arses while the kids mooch around smoking dope and learning sod all."

"You couldn't be more wrong. Seriously! It's just a different way of doing things. Believe me. It may look a bit wild and woolly because there's no uniform or anything, but it's very disciplined, actually. They have to hand in homework and be on time for school and stuff like that."

"Big whoop."

"Knock it if you like, but I can tell you that I am very cynical about stuff, and I think the school's absolutely brilliant. I wouldn't send Ricky anywhere else. The teachers are fantastic. Because it's an alternative form of education, they tend to be incredibly vocational and committed."

She sounds like a social worker, but she's well-meaning I suppose. I play with my spoon. "Would you mind telling me a little about a man named Bill Mayer?"

Irene stares.

"He's my charge's gardening teacher and I feel I should know more of his credentials," I say haughtily, and blow on my coffee.

"Right. He's lovely. A really lovely man. I can never believe that a man that attractive can be so nice."

"Oh! I suppose you could say he is fairly attractive," I say, blowing harder on my drink.

"Only fairly? If you say so. The mums faint in heaps when he passes by. One of the janitor's jobs is to rake them up and leave them by the side of the road for removal by the council. The great thing is, he doesn't even know it. He's the least vain man I know," says Irene merrily.

118

"I wasn't asking about his looks. Is he a *clever* man?" I ask, blowing so hard on my coffee that a spurt of it shoots out and hits Irene in the eye. "Sorry. Here's a napkin."

"Thanks. He is very clever, and a wonderful teacher."

"And is he... attached? I only ask because one wouldn't want him to be distracted from his duties by the ups and downs of an unsatisfactory love life, as these good looking younger teachers often are," I explain, dabbing the table.

"Right. I get you. No, he is not attached."

"Oh. That is unfortunate. A steady partner is such a help when all the gorgeous sixth form girls are bound to be lurking around making a nuisance of themselves with their young bodies and innocent charms," I say.

"But of course there are plenty of women who'd love to get attached to him," whispers Irene, looking over her shoulder first. "And first on the list is guess who."

"Penelope Cruz?"

"Dawn."

"NOOOOOO! I mean, oh really? Gosh."

"He's so nice, Rebecca, that he doesn't know how horrible she is. He thinks that just because she's divorced, she needs cheering up and so he lets her prey on him. Frankly, he needs saving."

"Have you ever thought of saving him yourself?" I ask, scenting a rival.

"Oh, he's not really my type. I only go for total losers with addiction issues and smelly feet."

"You are a wise woman. But check this out," I mutter. We shuffle our chairs nearer the table. "He told her all sorts of bollocks – well, half of it was true I admit - about the family I live with. I thought things like that were confidential! Can there be any excuse for that? Despite those good looks and personal charm, he's a closet creep."

"Are you sure he told her?"

119

"How could she know those things if he *didn't* tell her? And she *told* us that he told her. She sat there and told us! 'Bill says this. Bill says that.'"

"Oh don't worry about that. Elizabeth is a real sneak. She probably found out a few things on the grapevine, added some stuff and told her mum all about it. Dawn just wants all the other mums to know how close she is to Bill – pretending he tells her everything. I'm sure that's all it is. You mustn't let it spoil your relationship with him. You'll be having a lot to do with him with the class and it would be a pity to get off on the wrong foot."

"I'm sorry. In my opinion, any man who allows Dawn within his radar system is a washout."

"That's what I'm saying! He just doesn't get how horrible she is, because he's so nice he thinks everybody else is nice, too."

"I hate that word."

"What?"

"Nice. Boring, you mean."

"No, honestly. There's nothing boring about being nice."

"Oh yeah?"

"Look, Rebecca, I know what you mean. But really. I used to be quite tough. Now I'm as nice as I can be. It's much more restful, trust me."

"I just don't want to be 'nice'. What about, exciting? Stimulating? Exotic?"

"You can be all those things, and nice too."

"Well, I'll think about it. I've really enjoyed this, Irene. It's been a bit manic so far. I'm glad we met. Shall we have another coffee?"

"I wish we could, but it's pick up time."

"Oh God. It never ends."

We dive into our respective vehicles and I chug off to the school. I park – just where I did before, thank you very much – and go to collect Pumpkin. I peep into the classroom before he sees me and there he is, squashed into a little house made from wooden clothes-horses and muslins. He's holding a fistful of pinecones and looking very grim while the teacher hurries over. Another child has just reached the stage of holding her breath in a silent scream – you know, the bit where you think they're going to turn blue and expire on the spot. Then the scream comes out, the teacher whisks the little girl away and Pumpkin is left in possession of house and pinecones, looking triumphant.

I slide in, and between screams, ask what's happening.

"Oh, Pumpkin and Claudette had a little disagreement in Cooperative Corner," she says with a desperate smile.

"Cooperative Corner?"

"Yes. We have little sessions in there, where they focus on cooperative behaviour. Nurturing each other's ability to share and play together. You know..."

She breaks off to wrench one of her locks of hair from the screaming toddler in her arms. By now, Pumpkin has also begun to cry, as have several others. Mothers coming in to pick up their children are looking anxious.

"You know... it's lovely! They really experience each other's soul states. Of course there's the odd disagreement, but basically – quiet now, Claudette! Mummy's coming soon! – Cooperative Corner is a great success."

"So I see! Thanks for explaining," I bawl over the noise, while gathering Pumpkin's possessions, grabbing his hand and bolting for the exit. With a gasp of relief, we escape from the bedlam and head towards the car park. And suddenly, wheeling a barrow full of compost, is the stomach-churning spectacle of the man I love crossing the drive. Horrific flashbacks of my experience at Lizzie's house spur me on. Closing my eyes to his beauty, I hurry over and he puts the handles of the wheelbarrow down. A beaming smile threatens to broadside me, but with a gulp I stick to war, not love.

121

"Pumpkin, just crawl over there a minute," I say, pointing him in the direction of the sandpit. "Right, Mr Mayer. I'd like a word with you."

"Hello there! We met by the chickens, didn't we? You're A Robin's Nest's stepmother."

"Actually, I'm neither his mother nor his stepmother. I'm the au-pair."

"Oh!" Mayer looks taken aback by my tone.

"But I'm really surprised that you didn't know that, seeing as you know everything else about the family I'm living with."

"Really?"

"Yes. And not content with nosing out all our little secrets, it seems you've been spreading them around your friends as well."

"I think there must be some kind of misunderstanding. Sorry, what is your name?"

"Another thing you don't know. Amazing!"

"I promise you, I really don't know what all this is about. Shall we go and sit down somewhere and talk this over?"

"No thanks. I just wanted to say that if you want to go gossiping, do it about people who you actually know. Don't shoot Rob in the foot before he's even started at the school. Life is tough enough for him already. I am very prepared to make a formal complaint on this matter, so lay off, all right? Now, I'm not going to discuss this any further. Goodbye."

I march out, leaving Mayer still standing by his barrow, staring after me in a stunned manner. Then the whole effect is spoiled because he has to hoick Pumpkin from the sandpit and chase after me.

"Hi! Excuse me! You forgot your child!"

I thank him frostily and take Pumpkin, hugging him tightly.

"Look, there is obviously some terrible misunderstanding," he says, looking at me with anxious eyes. "You're upset now, but why don't we talk later. Feel free to call me at home, the numbers on the class list. Okey doke?"

I manage to wrench one of my bitterest smiles onto my face and march off, clasping Pumpkin firmly in my arms. But it's a bit like drowning. I'm not sure if it's true that in that regrettable situation your whole life flashes before you – I mean, how do they know? You're dead and can't tell the researchers except through a medium. But certainly right now, lots of things are flashing around. Like, I've blown it with this man. I thought I'd fallen in love at first sight, but he was mean to my kids. I mean, Mike's kids. And I only met him once for five minutes anyhow. And I want to go home. But I haven't got a home. And damn and blast Amanda.

That's only the start of it. Before I know it the novelty's worn off, I'm in an endless round of pickups and dropoffs, and the weeks seem to get worse as they pass by. I'm frantically busy running Cobweb Cottage. It's hard work for a pitiful salary and less praise. At home, I went out or picked at takeaways and ready meals. Here, I have to cook meals from scratch including scrubbing incredibly muddy root vegetables – a process I am gradually improving on, but it's wrecking havoc on my nails. At least the complete and utter lack of a social life means that I can stuff most of my pathetic salary under the mattress each week. Following my disastrous debut at Lizzie's, I am an automatic Don't Ask on the coffee morning list. Irene is always friendly, but being a single mother she's always in a rush and seems too busy to chat. My evenings are spent slumped in front of the fire for the lack of a television – rather an improvement to normal life, actually. And no matter how much I lurk around the chickens, I never manage to bump into Bill. Sometimes I see him from afar, but by the time I've casually wandered in his general direction he's trotted off with a ladder or a spade tucked under his arm. And on the few occasions I've been within striking distance, Dawn has been grabbing at his trowels and grinning up at him like an idiot.

I've never suffered from hopeless yearning before, but I'm suffering now. I'm haunted by my conviction that Bill must be a sneak of the worst order, one that gossips about harmless fourteen-year-olds to people like Dawn. At the same time, I can't stop thinking about him and indulging in the most shamefully romantic daydreams. I sometimes, but not often enough, dream about him at night. Whenever I do see him, I feel the sensation of a complete cliché – an arrow in my heart.

But, I continually argue with myself, how can a man who willingly befriends somebody like Dawn be the one for me? Whenever I go to pick up Pumpkin, Dawn's there. She's always clutching at somebody's arm, whispering away and having a giggle. Of course I realise that she's talking about me. Me and my family! Well, my sort of family. No blood ties as I am always anxious to point out. For Rob's sake I attempt to keep the peace and say nothing so that Elizabeth doesn't rip him apart in class, but there came, just after the Easter holidays, a breaking point.

I'm crouching on the floor outside playgroup, gently squeezing Pumpkin's tiny feet into his slippers, when I see her. The purple-clad one. Lurking by the door with a group of mums. Irene gives me a friendly wave, but Dawn just scowls. Then another mum comes up clutching her sprog and Dawn's onto her like a leech. The whispering starts, and sure enough, as I slip the pair of them a covert look, I catch the woman's eye. She looks embarrassed and turns away. I look at Pumpkin and he gives me a radiant smile – so lovely, so heartening, that I suddenly throw my arms around him and give him the most tremendous squeeze. Without another look at Dawn, I usher him into

124

playgroup and wait patiently until he's settled. He has a way of looking up at me and stretching out a hand whenever he thinks I'm off, but it usually only takes about five minutes.

Then I go out. Dawn is still there and when I appear, she gives me a really pursed lips, tight little smile crammed full of poison. The difference between her smile and Pumpkin's beautiful grin is astonishing. And in front of Irene and all present, she says: "Hi, Becky! How are you? Skinny as ever, I see. Tell you what, if Honeybee could give you some of her extra pounds, you'd both be just right, wouldn't you! Ha ha!" Unbelievable. I just can't let this pass. I've remained silent for weeks, but this means war. I give her one of my 'Hate You!' smiles, which consists of: Lips just open enough to bare the teeth; head dipped sideways; eyes not smiling AT ALL; nose wrinkled up in a sneer. I'm telling you, step by step, so that you can use it one day. Trust me. It's great. Then I say – enunciating every word very clearly: "Thanks for that, Dawn! You may be right. Oh, by the way, I've been thinking about that question you asked me. I believe there are three kinds of lice: hair, body and genital. As for the threadworms, I have no idea."

There's dead silence as I march off, Pumpkin clinging to my hand.

"Wait! Becky!" Irene is running after me with Ricky hard on her heels. She's laughing so hard she can barely speak, but finally manages to wipe her tears away. "Becky, that was brilliant. You're amazing! I can't believe you said that. Dawn has been so waiting for somebody to put her down. You're incredible."

"Did you hear what she said to me?"

"Who didn't? But sod that, everybody loathes her anyway. You'll have everybody on your side over this one. No worries."

125

"It was funny, wasn't it? But I'm a bit bothered about what Elizabeth'll do to Rob when she hears about it."

"Oh, Rob'll be fine. Most of the class just think Elizabeth's a bully anyway. They'll be on his side. I hear that he's settling in really well."

"He seems to be happy."

"How about Honeybee?"

"Oh, she's fine. Coping with the coursework okay. She's a grumpy little cow, but I'm quite fond of her, really. Reminds me of myself as a teenager. I wouldn't go back to that for any money."

"Nor me."

We stroll companionably through the carpark, and I catch a glimpse of Bill on the tractor bumping off down the track to the school farm. I feel the familiar lurch in my stomach and it drives me into action. There's no point in having a hopeless crush on somebody I can never talk to even though I'm at the school where he works half my life. I should get out more. I should try and meet somebody else. Forget about Bill.

"Tell you what, Irene, are there any decent pubs around here?"

"Well, there's the Dog and Bucket – it's a bit of a dive, but it's a laugh if you like hanging out with alcoholic chainsmokers and a bunch of underage drug addicts."

"My very favourite. Would you like to go out for a drink?"

"Yeah, great!"

"Really? You always seem so busy."

"I am, but I'm never too busy to have a good time."

"I wish I'd known you felt like that before."

"I should have asked you to come out with me ages ago, but you always seem in a rush."

"Okay, let's agree. Both of us are busy but we both need a bit of fun. How about it?"

"Sounds good."

"What about next Friday?"

126

"Fine. My friend's daughter Amy won't mind babysitting, I'm sure. Shall I come and get you? About eight? I know where Cobweb Cottage is."

That was easy. But it's weird. I've never much seen the point of female friends. Who wants to go out with a bunch of women, all of whom want to look the best, and who look over your shoulder trying to spot men when you're trying to talk? But now, for some strange reason, I'm desperately in need of a best friend. By Friday night when she's knocking at the door, I'm hysterical.

"Hi, Irene!," I yelp, bounding around her like Pepys with a squeaky toy. "Come in. Have a vodka and tonic – I'm just finishing off my makeup."

We thunder up to my room, drinks in hand, and I carefully apply another layer of mascara. One of the first things I did after we'd settled down was to invest in some serious makeup and it's such a relief. I'm always so busy that I haven't had a chance to wear it yet, but this evening, I'm making up for lost time. I'm wearing a pair of skintight leather – or rather, leatherette – jeans that I bought at Oxfam, and although I wouldn't have been seen dead in them in London, they look pretty good for here. Oxfam also supplied me with a low-cut, very fitted pink top and a pair of pink high heeled sandals, and I have to say, I look great. Then I turn on Irene. She is wearing, of course, combat trousers, those funny wide-toed sandals that everybody seems to wear round here, and a white t-shirt. With her short hair and no makeup, she looks like a boy. For God's sake! I don't want everybody in town to think I'm a lipstick lesbian.

"Hey, Irene! I've got a good idea. How about I put some makeup on for you?"

"Oh, no. Really. It's not my style."

"Come on! You'll never score looking like that."

"Thanks."

127

"I didn't mean it like that. I mean, you've got to look flirty. If you don't look available, nobody'll hit on you."

"I don't want them to hit on me. Honestly Rebecca, you haven't been to the Dog yet. You want people to leave you alone down there."

"Nonsense. It's always good to be chatted up wherever you go."

"I promise you, Rebecca, I'm not on the pull tonight."

"All right. You need to put on some facepaint to make me feel less like an old slapper cruising for action."

"If it'll make you feel better, you can put some makeup on me."

"And put gel in your hair?"

"And put gel in my hair if you must."

"And change your clothes?"

"No. I'm not changing."

"Okay. Now hold still."

I carefully put makeup on Irene. She's really very pretty, with lovely pale blue eyes, high cheekbones and blonde hair that when tousled with a little gel looks very trendy. When I show her the results, she seems really taken aback.

"Gosh! I look great! Thanks, Rebecca. Ow!"

I have sprayed her liberally with the nicest scent available at the local chemist. That is, the nicest *cheap* scent available at the local chemist. I aim a brief squirt down my own cleavage, pick up our drinks, down mine in one, watch her chug hers, then we're off. Pathetic isn't it? I feel quite excited. It's about a fifteen minute walk to the pub as both of us intend to drink and not drive, and it's fun. We even link arms. Part of me feels like shrieking to the skies, 'I have a best friend! Thank you, God!' but of course I don't. It would be so embarrassing.

CHAPTER SIX

"Good morning! You've got post. Shall I open it for you? You don't look very well. Have you been sick in the night?" says A Robin's Nest in a concerned voice.

"Mind your own business. Give me my post and go and make me some tea. Please. I said please! Now, push off."

Robbo buzzes away downstairs, hopefully to put the kettle on, and I take a look at my post. It's another of these crappy discs from Amanda. I chuck it in the corner with the other one and lie back on my rumpled pillow with a groan.

I've got a terrible hangover. I woke up with a mouth closely resembling the interior of a kangaroo's pouch. There's probably a baby roo tucked away in there somewhere, farting for Australia. My head is aching fit to burst and I feel that if I move, I'll be sick again. It was worth it – sort of. Irene was right. The pub is a total dump. I practically expected to find sawdust on the floor and spittoons in the public bar. The locals are a bunch of people all of whom should be on reality TV. They divided into five parts.

Fat, tarty teenage girls with tattoos and visible thongs.

Saggy, chatty middle-aged women with missing teeth and hair dyed yellow with nicotine.

Thin middle-aged men with hungry, desperate eyes and the skin of eighty-year-olds.

Fat middle-aged alcoholics who insist on dancing to every song on the juke box.

Teenage boys playing the fruit machine, staring at the telly and wondering whether they have the energy to shag the fat teenage girls.

For the first five minutes, I felt seriously depressed. The kind of bars I have been used to going to in London are crammed with young professionals in designer clothes with plenty of money to spend on champagne cocktails. Okay, they get drunk – and so do I – but somehow, it's not miserable like this is miserable. A cursory glance around the room showed that there was less than nobody I would ever be interested in if they were the last man alive. Irene happily headed for the bar, ordered drinks and settled on a barstool. I reluctantly followed suit, studiously avoiding the eye of every man in the pub. And I don't consider it a compliment that every eye of every man was trained on me. I saw what Irene meant. Here is not a place to score.

But in the end, we had a real laugh. I think. I know I've blown what was left of my weekly pittance, and the night must have been one to remember according to how I feel this morning. But in fact, I can't remember a goddamn thing. I've got a few bruises, I didn't take my makeup off when I got home, and my whole soul is cringing like a whipped hound with that horrible feeling of guilt and shame that accompanies a really bad après-bender. But I don't even remember coming home.

With any luck, A Robin's Nest will remember to bring me up a cup of tea.

As staying in bed completely still is the only way I won't be sick on the carpet, I start thinking about how much I hate it here, the men we met last night, and about how none of them are going to be a meal ticket out of here. I have got to get back to London! Okay, Amanda looks like she's in my flat to stay. Fine. I'll show her. I'm not going to hang around for a hundred years waiting for her to change her mind and let me have my life back. In an ideal world, I'd buy myself another life – one even better. That'd show her. So what I need is large amounts of cash – like winning the Lottery or something. For a few minutes I fantasize about winning the Lottery. With my first million I would buy an even better flat, one overlooking the river. With my second million, I would furnish it, get serious art on the walls and fill my cupboard with the most amazing designer clothes known to womankind. With my third million I would buy an absolutely fantastic sports car, a holiday home in Tuscany and join the poshest gym in town. My fourth million I would salt away for future expenses. My fifth million I would keep in my current account for day-to-day expenses. My sixth million would go on the biggest diamond necklace I can find. My seventh million... well, I might give that to charity. You can meet lots of celebrities if you give loads of money to charity.

Then in the middle of my rosy glow I consider that I've never bought a Lottery ticket in my life and I'm not likely to. I have studied the chances of winning seven million pounds and they are very small indeed. No, money is much more available if you can lift it straight out of a man's pocket. I know it's just so un Pee Cee, but I do love a man I can shake like a piggy bank.

The way my finances are right now, I *need* a man to take me out to dinner and pick up the tab. And more. I want presents. Big ones. And treats. I would sleep with almost anybody if he gave me the chance to hum along in a sports car with the top down and a CD of my choice at top volume instead of farting along in the VW camper

131

van with Mike's stretched Joni Mitchell tape that I've heard eight thousand, seven hundred, sixty three and a half times since last Tuesday. There are also lots of little irritations plaguing me, like, I need my legs waxed. More makeup and vanity items. And a ski-ing holiday. And many, many items of designer clothing. Basically I am open to approaches from a sugar daddy. Any old sugar daddy.

I'm sure there is a rich vein of gold secreted within the parent body at this weird school. The mums and dads here may look like a convention of unravelling sweaters, but I suspect that in many cases this is just for show. Who wants to look impoverished and out of date, you may ask? Well, it has fast become clear to me that this is a community in which if you drive a crappy, prehistoric camper van like Mike does, you are way cooler than an airbrushed blonde at the wheel of a Mercedes sports car. But I can't help feeling that many of the parents wrestling with the VW controls could afford to drive just about anything they liked, if they chose to do so. All private schools, however much they like to pretend that money doesn't exist, are at the parents' pockets with blowtorches and chisels and if the ready is not forthcoming, little Charlie and Annabel, or in this school's case, Pumpkin and Honeybee, are out on their patched arses. Loads of the men I see mooching about the place here look like tramps but logic says it ain't so.

However, when it comes to picking up a hippy with a wallet of gold, my luck has not been in. Call me a dumb blonde but I had not taken in just how unavailable the males lurking around at the school gates really are. All of them, without exception, are attached. Some to their wives. Some to their mistresses for whom they left the wives. Some to their second wives or subsequent mistresses. Some, for we are open-minded here in Much Jenner, to their boyfriends or boyfriends for whom they

132

left their girlfriends or the other way round. None of them ever seems to split in order to be alone although I bet they all said that they needed some space. Who wouldn't, I have come to realise, when sharing a house with child or children?

Naturally, I have noticed that some are what you might call, semi-attached or in extreme cases semi-detached. These are the ones who, when they learn that I am Mike's au pair rather than his partner, get a little glint in their eye and start babbling about osteopathy and Indian Head Massage. But please. Oh please. Do I really want to embark on a clandestine romance with some hairy bloke with an ex or about-to-be-ex and kids to support? God help me, I do enough wicked stepmothering at Cobweb Cottage and I don't have to sleep with Mike in exchange.

If there are no male meal tickets out of here, perhaps I ought to be looking for some sort of job other than being an au-pair. Making money is not easy, I do understand that. I mean, for a few measly coins you have to work like a dog in a dump. Plus, I am not, repeat NOT the type to stand behind a till all day. No, no. I want to be *in* that till, scraping up the right stuff with both mitts. Armed robbery, I reluctantly concede, is out. But actually earning the money in some sort of nylon uniform is a definite no-no. Perhaps I could do some sort of computer trading or something? Buy stuff over the net and sell it back for loads more than I paid for it?

Or hang on a minute. Why not write a brilliant novel, sell the screen rights for squillions and live in the lap of luxury for the rest of my life? I've always toyed with the idea, ever since a woman I worked with on the Star wrote a bestseller at the age of 23, got a six figure advance and became a global phenomenon. If she could do it, I can do it. I've always known I could. It's just a question of finding the time. Right. I'll write the true story of my adventures in diary form, a sort of hippy Bridget Jones. A yarn about moving to the sticks and hating it. As I, with all my talents, will be the author, it'll be a sure-fire success. I'm sure I'll get an agent interested on the synopsis alone. It'll be a film starring Kate Beckinsale as Amanda and somebody absolutely fucking gorgeous as me. I'll...

But if I'm to write a book I need a word processor and we haven't even got around to setting up the computer yet, for Christ's sake. It's my fault really, I just haven't been bullying Mike the way I used too. It's all started getting a bit comfortable just dossing around and earning fifty quid a week doing the school run and feeding Pumpkin.

It's tricky, of course. First of all, in order to use the computer, we need electricity so the generator will need to be running. Well, Mike does have a handle on that. We're allowed electricity on a strictly rationed basis – and if I bought the petrol for the generator myself, Mike couldn't complain. Setting up the computer itself would be a bit tricky, but fortunately A Robin's Nest appears to be semi-computer-literate, the result of hanging around at his friend's houses mucking around with their PCs.

It doesn't matter how crap I feel. In fact, the crappier I feel the better. It'll motivate me. The sooner the computer is up and running, the sooner I can make a start on funding the rest of my life. With a weary sigh I unglue my hair from the pillow and am preparing to heave myself cautiously out of bed, when the door opens and A Robin's Nest comes in, tongue protruding from the side of his mouth as he carefully carries a brimming cup of tea.

"Oh, Rob! Thank you. This may just save the life other lives couldn't reach."

I take the cup and sip gingerly. After a few seconds of slurping I experience a new dawn. There's no doubt about it, the amber nectar is doing its stuff. A Robin's Nest sits down on the end of the bed.

"Becky…"

"Yes?"

"Becky…"

"Still here."

"Becky…"

"Still hanging on your lips and getting a bit pissed off."

"Becky… do you remember that you said ages ago that you were going to get me some new clothes?"

"Oh, God! Sorry Rob. I'd completely forgotten. Why don't you go down to Oxfam and see what they've got?"

"I thought we were going to get some new clothes. You know, more, sort of, trendy."

"Were we?"

"You said you wouldn't be seen in public with me the way I look. And that was months ago."

"So I did! Oh well. I've been seen in public with you many times by now, and we've survived."

"No, but really, Becky, I would like some new clothes. I feel a real geek at school."

"Can't Midge go with you?"

"I asked her once, but she said that all that mattered was my aura. I just want some new jeans and a few t-shirts."

"What are you wearing now?"

Silently, Rob lifts his stripy cardie and shows me his t-shirt. It's Teletubbies and a bit stretched out at that. Okay, fair enough. No fourteen-year-old should have to endure this.

"All right, Rob. I'll take you shopping. We'll have to get some dosh out of your dad, and if all else fails I'll use the housekeeping. But you'll have to do something for me in exchange."

"What?"

"Set up the computer. I'm going to write a book."

"A book! Cool! No problem! I like computers. I totally forgot about keeping ours, Dad's been on about throwing it away for so long. It's all still in boxes, isn't it? I'll get onto it right now."

"That's my boy. I'll get up after I've finished my tea and join you. You'll have to show me what to do. We'll need to set up an email account and everything. Go on then! Get started. Remember to fire up the generator first."

He thunders off downstairs with the enthusiasm of the very young, but as the condition of my head and stomach means I have to crawl around like an arthritic octogenarian who has lost her zimmer frame – keeping movement to an absolute minimum - it takes me a considerable time to make myself presentable. A quick bath, or what passes for one at Cobweb Cottage, makes quite a lot of difference though, and by the time I go into the kitchen, I'm no longer actually pressing my temples with both hands. Mike is sitting at the table holding Pumpkin in his arms and looking like a martyr about to be disembowelled.

"Hello, Bex."

"Rebecca."

"How are you?"

"Crap."

"I'm exhausted."

"So am I."

"Pumpkin was up at five."

"What a coincidence! That's practically when I went to bed."

"I wonder if you can take a turn with him?"

"Sorry. Not this morning. For a start I've got a very nasty hangover to nurse, and for another start, I'm working on the computer with Rob."

"It isn't set up."

"That's right. We're setting it up. I'm going to write a best-selling book."

"Wow! Perhaps Pumpkin could hang out with you while you bang out the first chapter?"

136

"Nice try. I'm afraid it's over to you this morning."

"I need a lie-in!"

"Who doesn't? Look, I really think that on a Saturday morning, I'm entitled to some time off. I'm not some kind of Roman slave."

"Okay, fine."

"Fine."

"Fine."

"You sulk then."

"I'm not sulking."

"You are."

"I'm not."

And it's at this point, with the adults engaged in interesting and serious discussion, that A Robin's Nest bursts in to announce that the cables are attached and plugged in and whatever it is that cables do, and that we can make a start on setting up our email account. Or as Rob would prefer, playing a computer game, which he has dug up from the deepest, darkest corner of his cupboard. He shows it proudly to Mike and me. Mike looks utterly horrified and if he hadn't just taken a big bite of muesli, A Robin's Nest would have come under a barrage of questioning about why he wants to play computer games which are violent, misogynistic and a whole load of other anti-isms. I also am feeling that games are a complete waste of time.

"This is so cool? I can show you the moves?"

"Sorry to burst your bubble, but you are going to give the computer a virus, you cagoule."

"I think the insult you are searching for is anorak?"

"Oh pardon me. Anorak, then. And as we're being critical, why do you always talk in questions?"

"You just asked me a question?"

"Yes, because it was a question."

"What's the difference."

"That was a question. Normally you don't ask questions, you just talk as if you do unless it really is a question, in which case you don't ask it as if it were."

"Right... Look. Do you want to play the game."

"For heaven's sake, if it's a question, you should ask it as if it's a question."

"You told me not to ask questions."

"No, I told you not to talk like a question unless you are asking a question."

"What's the difference."

"That's a question! Say it like a question!"

"Okay?"

"No! That's not a question."

"Okay, Becky. Do you want to play the game. Game?"

"No, A Robin's Nest. I do not want to play the game, now or ever. Now piss off."

"Oh. Okay!"

I think you'll admit that my conversation with Mike, followed by this intelligent exchange with A Robin's Nest, demonstrates just how interesting and stimulating my life has become.

"Look, Rob," I say more kindly, after a gulp of coffee. "You've done a brilliant job. Let's go shopping. I'm gagging for a Diet Coke to help my hangover, and you can check out that cool surf shop on the high street in East Jenner while I drink it."

"Whoa!" interjects Mike. "I've been meaning to say to you, can you keep things like that under your bed? I don't want Honeybee developing an eating disorder."

"Things like what?"

"D.I.E.T drinks."

"It would do Honeybee good to lay off the full sugar stuff and have a good old-fashioned eating disorder. She's an absolute fat-arse."

"Becky, you simply can't say things like that around vulnerable, impressionistic teenagers."

"Oh, blah. Come on Robbo, let's hit East Jenner."

"Whoa, whoa, whoa, Becky! Where are you going?"

With a sigh, I turn back to Mike. "Ever heard of East Jenner? It's five miles up the road."

"Yes, but *why* did you say you were going?"

"Oh, I forgot. Imagine I'm smiling and showing you some cleavage. And while you're about it, why not slip me the housekeeping and a bit extra for some new clothes for Rob?"

"A Robin's Nest doesn't need any new clothes."

"Okay. I won't argue. We'll go to the health food shop instead. Just give me the housekeeping. In fact, give me the whole month's worth now. It'll make sense if I buy in bulk. I've got some great deals going down the cooperative."

"Well..."

"Don't be so tight. Unleash your wallet."

"All right. Here you are," and he slips me the readies. I send a big wink in Robbo's direction and he blushes furiously.

"Right, Mike! We'll see you later."

There's one final despairing plea: "Can you take Pumpkin?"

"Sorry, no can do. Come on Rob!"

And we're off. I'm feeling quite a bit better. The sun is shining as Rob and I head off for East Jenner, both of us singing along to Joni Mitchell at the tops of our voices. This is a very strange feeling. I can't be happy. Can I? The feeling I'm feeling feels pretty much like happiness if what I have been told of the state is correct. There are obviously some issues I need to deal with and they are:

One. I am calling Cobweb Cottage home.

Two. I'm still hopelessly in love with a humble gardening teacher. Despite the fact that he gossiped about me to Dawn, and is her best friend and possibly more.

Three. Mike's kids are... okay.

139

Four. I haven't so much as glanced at the London Star since I got that nasty shock in the car park. God knows what Amanda's doing to my column. I must pick up a copy today.

Five. I quite like Joni Mitchell.

And that's enough to be going on with, isn't it?

We grind to a halt near the shops and head for the surf shop, which just happens to be next-door-but-one to a rather good fruit and veg shop, which, I happen to recall, also sells what the nutritionists refer to as 'pulses'. I push Robbo in the direction of combat trousers, cool t-shirts and beanie hats, and pop into the store to pick up a few bits and pieces. Can't spend much, of course, the week's housekeeping is earmarked for Rob's new wardrobe. If I had a crystal ball, it'd be chockfull of vegetable and bean casserole. Very economical and nutritious I have found.

"Good morning, afternoon, whatever!" I begin to the old trout behind the till. "I'm after a superb selection of vegetables for a very pernickety family tonight so they'd better have no brown spots..."

'Like your hands', I nearly add, my head thumping with leftover alcohol, but then I have a pleasant surprise. Irene, with bulging bags at her feet, is preparing to pay, and looks up to see me with a big smile.

"Hi!" she cries.

"Hey, how are you!" I abandon the trout. "Feeling like shit?" The trout suffers a sharp intake of breath. I toss my head.

"Yeah. How about you?" says Irene brightly.

"Yeah. Like shit."

"Frankly, friend, you do look awful. Your skin's all blotchy and your eyes are all red and puffy. Go home and get Midge to sling you some homeopathic hangover cure."

"I think she'd seize the opportunity to slip me some arsenic."

"It was worth it though."

140

"When are we going to do it again?"

"As soon as I can laugh without my head banging like a rocker on acid. God though. You are hilarious. The best bit was when Bill came in. I nearly died!"

"What?"

"You know. When Bill came in?"

"I don't remember him being there."

"Don't you? God, you must have been bad. No, he came in when you were playing pool."

"I played pool?"

"Sure you played pool! Don't you remember? When you were trying to stop that bloke from winning by putting the pink and yellow balls in your bra and doing a little shimmy?"

The trout starts clicking her tongue in a most emphatic manner, and I lead Irene to a quiet spot behind the bananas and lower my voice to a frenzied whisper.

"Oh God. I do have some vague recollection. No, it's not funny Irene. It really isn't. Who was that bloke, anyway?"

"Some loser who kept pinching your bum. You won the game, by the way. Sort of. You wouldn't give the balls back until it was your turn and then you put them right by the holes and potted them with your boob."

"And Bill was there?"

"Yeah! He said hello to me."

"Did he say hello to me, too?"

"No. I said he should go on over, and he said he could see you were too busy. Then he left. Wait a minute. No. You rolled on the pool table. Then he left."

"I rolled on the pool table?"

"Yes! It was hilarious! Mind you, we nearly got chucked out."

"While Bill was there?"

"Maybe he missed that bit. No, come to think of it, he was still there because he asked me if I needed help getting you home."

"He didn't say that."

"Well, my memory is a bit confused itself, but I'm pretty sure he offered to help."

"What did you say?"

"Oh, I said that I'd manage even if I had to carry you."

"Thanks."

"You're welcome."

"God. I'm so embarrassed."

"It was a riot."

"Bill will think I'm awful! Er... Not that it matters for me, of course, but it won't do Robbo any good if one of his teachers thinks his home life's iffy."

"Oh Bill's fine. He's cool. He's probably forgotten about it already."

It' at this moment that a thin and earnest character enters the shop and slinks over to the fruit. For some reason, my eye rests on her – and is richly rewarded for she withdraws a large crystal tied to a piece of string from her pocket and holds it over the pineapples. I nudge Irene and we watch, spellbound. The whole shop – including every fruit and vegetable in it – seems to be holding its breath. Slowly the crystal begins to swing and with a satisfied smile the earnest character selects a fine looking pineapple, pays for it and withdraws.

"What the blithering heck was she up to?" I ask.

"Dowsing," says Irene.

"Dowsing for pineapples?" I say.

"That's right. Dowsing for a fine, ripe pineapple," says Irene.

"I thought you only dowsed for water," I say.

"Not so," says Irene. "You can dowse for anything, apparently. Paint colours, new houses, the lot."

"Do you have to go into the actual house, or can you do it over the details from the estate agent?"

"Oh, the details will do, I think. So long as they're in full colour."

There's a thoughtful pause.

"Well, I've found the title for the bestselling novel I'm going to start writing when my head's stopped aching," I say eventually. "'Dowsing for Pineapples.' It puts this dump in a nutshell."

We hug goodbye, and feeling crestfallen about Irene's description of our wild night out I make my purchases, rather more humbly than I'd planned, and hobble out of the shop with a large bag of vegetables and dried beans to find Rob. He's looking slowly through the racks, cringing whenever one of the very cool apparently primary school-age characters behind the counter throws a glance in his direction.

I take a deep breath. No matter what an idiot I made of myself in the pub last night, and no matter how ghastly the idea of camping out with the Holt Park parents is, I owe Rob a positive approach to this shopping trip. "Hi, Rob!" I cry merrily. "How are you doing? Any luck?"

"I dunno," he mumbles. "It's difficult to tell."

"No it's not. Look! Here's an excellent t-shirt. Here's another. Blue's your colour, let's get that one too. Now. Trousers. What sort of size are you? Right! Look. Here's the coolest pair ever. You'll look great in those. I love these too. You'll have to try this pair. Now. How about a couple of sweaters? This one with the zipper is fab. And this one looks really practical but fun too. Da, di da... you'll need a belt. And a hat. And a pair of trainers. Excuse me, can we try these in a... what are you Rob? A medium Cheers! Oh, and these too. Thanks. Now Rob, you get in that changing room and have a go with everything. I'll stand here so you can just open the curtain a little bit to show me. Go on! Get a move on!"

Rather shyly, Rob shows me various combinations. He looks great in everything. Really, I should be a personal shopper for twelve to fourteen year olds. I'd make a fortune. Even the trainers are a hit.

"Well, Becky? What do you think?" He looks incredibly happy and excited – but a little bit as if it's all a wonderful dream and he's going to wake up any minute. "What do you think? Should I keep this t-shirt? And which trousers looked the best?"

"Robbo, they all looked brilliant. It's lucky there's a sale on, because I think that the only option is for you to have everything."

"Everything! But that'll be the whole housekeeping money! What'll we eat all week!"

"Vegetable and bean casserole and you'd better learn to love it. You'll have to be on my side when everybody else complains when we have it for the fourth time running. Can I count on you?"

"Yes! Of course! Thanks, Becky!"

"Look, let's snip the labels off your favourite things and you can wear them now."

"And the trainers?"

"Of course." I borrow a pair of scissors and while I pay, Robbo gets dressed. He emerges from the changing room looking very sheepish and extremely pleased with himself.

"You look fab. Here," I address the child on the till, "could you put these in the bin for me?" I hand him Robbo's old clothes and collect my change. "Hey, Robbo! Guess what! There's enough left for a haircut. Come on."

We whizz off down the high street to a rather trendy barbers I've noticed the yoof emerging from, and Rob – under my strict instructions – has a cut the exact same as every fourteen-year-old's favourite footie star. The feeling I got as his manky locks hit the deck was fantastic. Better than drugs. Better than sex. For the first time in his life, my sort of stepson looks... well, like everybody else his age.

I've got about a quid left from Mike's housekeeping money, but it's so, so worth it. Rob is looking like a normal human being, and what's more, he's actually looking ecstatically happy. I can't stop grinning myself. I keep shooting him quick glances and saying things like, "Boy, I'm not cool enough to be walking down the road with you. I'd better keep a few paces behind," and he loves it.

I suddenly feel weak from last night's excesses, so Robbo has to carry the bag of beans and veggies back to the car. I drive home thoughtfully, and as we approach the house, I can see Mike struggling in the back garden with what looks like a bunch of drain rods. There's a huge tarpaulin or something, as well, flopping all over what passes as a flowerbed.

"Hello!" I say cheerily, as we wend our way up the path, Robbo struggling with the shopping bags, face averted from his father. "Planning a spot of sanitary investigation? I heard that the way to do it is with special little cameras, and high pressure hoses. But you've got enough rods to get the system cleared right up to Ten Downing Street there. Good luck!"

"These, my dear Becky, are not drain rods. They're the skeleton of a tepee. And here's the skin."

"Tepee? What do you want a tepee for? Planning on moving out to the back garden? And this – what do you mean, skin? It looks like a tarpaulin to me."

"It's a skin, as a matter of fact. Tepee skin. Technical term. We'll be using the tepee for... Oh! Who's this?"

"A Robin's Nest, you twat."

"God!" Mike drops his poles and gapes at his son, completely stunned. "You look completely different!"

"Becky helped me choose some new clothes," mumbles Rob shyly, clutching onto the shopping bags for dear life.

Mike turns to me. "Becky, I thought I said that A Robin's Nest didn't need any new clothes. And I believe that Midge said the same last week. What's going on? What's happened to his hair? It's short! Goodness knows what

145

Midge will say. He's not old enough to look like that. And how did you pay for it all?"

I ignore the last question, but, stepping over the poles, go in all guns blazing on everything else. "Yes, I know you said Rob didn't need new clothes. And I know Midge said the same. I can't believe you two! And as for his hair, it was revolting. All over his face like that, no wonder he got spots. Take a long hard look at your son, Mike. He looks fantastic. Go on, Rob, give your dad a twirl."

Robbo drops the shopping bags and shuffles round, grinning and blushing.

"See how great he looks? He's coming up fifteen, for goodness sake. All the other kids in his class have great clothes. You don't want him to look like a total moron for the whole of his school career, do you?"

I pick up the shopping bags, hop over the last of the poles and head into the house with Mike hard on my heels.

"He's only a child!"

"So what? You want him to look like a complete retard? You want everybody to laugh at him and bully him and not invite him to their parties?"

I make it to the kitchen and stick the kettle on. Mike is spluttering something about being an individual, free from the dictatorship of fashion, when the door swings open and a gust of patchouli informs me that Midge has entered the room.

"I can feel the negative vibes drilling through the floorboards," she says, sourly. "Can somebody please tell me what is going on?"

I point a dramatic finger at Rob. "Who's that, Midge? Can you just kindly please tell me who that is?"

"I have no idea."

"It's your son. It's A Robin's Nest. Dressed in trendy clothes for the first time in his life and looking pretty damn hot."

"Holy Buddha!" gasps Midge, histrionically clutching at her throat and staggering backwards in a spirited imitation of Lady Macbeth. "Where on earth is his beautiful, beautiful hair? Lying on the floor in some barber shop? You Delilah! And what clothes are these? Unnatural fabrics and... and... metal *zippers*? He wears buttons. Wooden buttons! Metal interferes with the body's meridian channels – it can wreak havoc with one's chi. Besides, A Robin's Nest asked my advice about his attire a few days ago and I spent some considerable time explaining – and to his perfect satisfaction, I may add – that one's aura, when exposed to those sensitive enough to read it, is more visible, in fact far more visible, than mere layers of material. Clothes are irrelevant to the truly spiritual."

"I'd like to point out that you are wearing a very carefully chosen outfit, Midge."

As indeed she is. Midge appears to have a quantity of caftans, and this one is made of silk with butterfly wings painted on the back and sides so that when she raises her arms – as she is doing now – the wings unfold. It's rather wonderful if you like that sort of thing, which I don't.

"Oh, this? Well, this dress is a manifestation of my soul. I am a butterfly, spreading my wings and fluttering in the sunshine of the spirit. This dress demonstrates that I have seethed in the liquid of my cocoon until I am ready to fly. This dress *talks* to the beholder. It tells them that in my previous life I was a caterpillar, crawling close to the ground and unable to fly."

"You were a caterpillar? I imagined you'd be Cleopatra, or something."

"Not *that* previous life, although my previous lives have been many. And I was *never* Cleopatra – she was, like, totally materialistic. I mean my previous life when I was involved in a relationship with Mike. He caterpillarized me."

147

"What?" Mike yelps, half rising from the table. She quells him with a wave of the drooping hand and a mournful gaze.

"Yes, Mike, darling. You did. When I was with you, I was earthbound, crawling, trapped by a thousand limiting factors. When we broke up, I entered a cocoon. I seethed there many moons, undergoing a complete and utter transformation. Then I emerged – yes, I did! I emerged and I was a beautiful butterfly. I still am. This dress says it all."

"Midge, how can you say that? I didn't make you into a caterpillar. I tried to do everything to make you happy. I tried to let you have all the freedom you needed to... to fly like a butterfly."

"Oh, I know you tried Mike, my love. You tried. But you're a man. It's terribly difficult for a man to do anything but crush a woman. All men dominate women. It's their conditioning."

There's something very patronising about this. "Oh come off it Midge," I put in. "You'll be saying all men are rapists, next."

"Oh, they are!"

"What, even Robbo here?"

"Of course."

"No I'm not, Mum! That's crap!"

"Don't speak to me like that."

I look around the kitchen. Mike is looking completely crushed by the idea that Midge was once a caterpillar in his arms. Robbo is puce with indignation. Midge is flapping her butterfly wings with ever-increasing agitation. We're really playing happy families here.

"Excuse me!" I shout over the uproar. "May I make a few points?" Everybody looks my way. "First of all, there is no way that Mike and Robbo are rapists. And if Midge wants to believe that she was once a caterpillar, then fine. Perhaps you and Mike can talk over the insect factors in

148

your relationship another time. This whole argument blew up because Rob is wearing some new clothes. Well, he looks bloody brilliant and there's about a million more bags full in the car. Midge, you'll admit that from everything you've said, it's obvious that clothes do tell you a lot about the person wearing them."

"Well…"

"What do you and Mike want Rob's clothes to say? 'I'm a complete plonker with parents who don't give a toss about me' or 'I'm a cool dude who's respected at home'? Come on, Mike. Which?"

"Well, the second I suppose. But…"

"No buts. I'm one hundred percent sure that I did the decent thing in kitting Robbo out and I'm sure he's going to thank me for it until his dying day, aren't you?"

"Yeah. Thanks, Becky."

"You see? Now. I'm sure we've all got a lot to be getting on with. I for one am going to have a soothing cup of tea. How about you, Midge?"

"Thank you, Rebecca, no. I can't take the negativity here. I'm going out for a walk."

"Good idea! You haven't been out since we got here and frankly… well, never mind. Let those butterfly wings soar."

Midge rather sniffily heads for the open air, accompanied by Robbo who is no doubt anxious to show off his new look to the about-to-be-stunned young people of Much Jenner. Mike slumps heavily down onto a kitchen chair.

"How did you afford all those clothes, Becky?"

"Never you mind."

"Was it the housekeeping?"

"That's for me to know and you never to find out."

Meals over the next few weeks are, it must be admitted, depressing but my spirits lift every time I look at Rob. His confidence is magically lifted by his new wardrobe. Of course he continues to walk as if he's got advanced

149

dementia, shuffling out of the door in the mornings with his head hanging to his knees and his trousers trailing behind him like some Edwardian lady's train, but as he now looks exactly like all his friends, I have no problem with his posture. I'm just glad he's happy.

Honeybee, however, gives me cause for concern. She's still putting on weight, not a sign of a happy teen, and mopes endlessly around the house instead of going out and behaving badly with her friends. I've just decided that I'll have to buy her some alcopops and get her to tell me all her problems when Irene, round for tea, drives all thought of charity out of my head.

It's a lovely summer's day and we have been discussing the rights and wrongs of childhood vaccinations, not a subject I ever dreamed would grab me, when she drops her slice of homemade cake into her homemade lemonade and cries: "Oh God! Quick change of subject. What about the Festival Games? Are you all set?"

"What are you talking about?"

"The Festival Games of course! Haven't you been reading your Wednesday What's On?"

"Wednesday What's On?"

"You know, Becka, the parent's newsletter!"

"I never bother to look at it."

"You should do. Look, I'd better break the bad news. The Festival Games start on the first Monday of June. Next week! It's the school's Big Thing this term. The kids all compete against each other – sort of, that is, there are no winners or anything negative like that – but the best bit is, we all get to camp out the night before. I promise you, it's cool."

"Camp? You mean, outside? In the mud? No loos? Like Glastonbury?"

"That's right. Look, sorry. The cake's great and everything, but I'd better head for home. I've got a lot of packing to do."

150

"If I come, can I stay in your tent?"

"That would have been great, but I'm with a load of women coming down from a school near where I used to live in the North. They're a bit intense. Not your type."

"Very well. Your doom is sealed. But I'm a monkey if I let Mike talk me into this one."

Irene hurries to the door, narrowly avoiding a collision with Mike. As the sound of her footsteps fade I shove a glass of lemonade his way.

"Mike, there are black rumours about a thing called the Festival Games. Irene said that we had to camp out. But I'm sure it must be a spurious rumour. What's the deal?"

"Oh, she's quite right," Mike replies, having downed the refreshing beverage in one. "Haven't you been reading your Wednesday What's On?"

"As a matter of fact, no. You should have told me."

"Oh, okay. Sorry. Well, you know now. It'll be groovy!"

"*Groovy*? What kind of word is that when applied to camping?"

"The children take part in non-competitive sports during the day, and the night before we all camp together and chat around the camp fire. There'll be music... talk... spiritual healing..."

"Right. You can count me out. You're their dad, you camp. I'll stay here and keep the range going."

"Oh go on, Becky, don't be so negative. It'll be a laugh."

"For you maybe. Anyway, who's going to look after Pumpkin? I've got to stay here."

"No, no, no. Pumpkin's coming too! He'll love it. Absolutely love it. Wow! It'll be a trip."

"So there *will* be drugs?"

"Oh no. Of course not."

"So the whole thing really is pointless."

"Come on Bex, I'll need you there to look after Pumpkin."

"What about Midge? Couldn't she go with you?"

151

There's a short silence as we both contemplate this possibility. Mike pleads with me with his eyes. I glare at him. He heaves a big sigh.

"Look, Bex, I didn't want to do this. But I'm telling you, if you don't come with us to take care of Pumpkin, I'll have to cut off your salary."

"You *what*?"

"I've every right. You are paid to help out. And camping out for one night counts as just that. Think about it! I need you there."

"It's torture! Unreasonable demands!"

"Some would call it a perk. People pay to have this kind of experience. There are all sorts of great things going on. Er... there'll be a home made sauna! Just like we believe the peoples of the Stone Age enjoyed. You heat the rocks, pour water over them and steam naked together in a special tent..."

"You've said enough."

"So you'll come? Cool!"

"I will not."

"Then – no salary."

"Then I'll come. On the strict condition that I *don't* have to steam naked with a bunch of losers. And I warn you, any funny business in the tent..."

"Tepee."

"What do you mean?"

"Well, we're not staying in some kind of middle class suburban tent. No. I'm building us a tepee. What do you think the skin and bones in the front garden is for?"

"Not that thing that's been lying there for weeks turning green?"

"I've been weathering it in. And tomorrow, Bex, we're going to get it built."

"We?"

"Yeah! I'm going to build it here, set it up, take it down and get it over there first thing tomorrow. I can just see

152

us – sitting round the camp fire – beating our tom toms – swaying in a rhythmic circle under the stars..."

"For God's sake, Mike, you make me want to kill myself."

"Don't be so negative, Bex. Life is a positive charge. Yeah."

CHAPTER SEVEN

It doesn't seem to be very easy, building a tepee, especially as we've had a change in the weather right on cue. On a damp Sunday morning, with the Games commencing in twenty-four hours, Mike, huffing and puffing, drags his blinking skin and bones through to the back garden. Then he sets to. I've invited Irene and Ricky round to enjoy the show. We lurk in the kitchen, prepared to bring out cups of fennel tea at regular intervals.

"He's a weird one, isn't he?" whispers Irene, opening a packet of biscuits for Ricky and Pumpkin, who are happily playing with a set of wooden blocks. "What does he want to build his own tepee for? You can get great tents at that outdoor place near Wellesley. And as we're being perfectly frank, what's with the beard? He's a bit young for it, isn't he?"

"Come on, Irene. He's just like that. Why else would we be living here?"

"Well, I can understand why he's here. But I've never really got why you're here with him."

"Don't ask."

Irene changes the subject to one close to my heart, my opus magnus, Dowsing for Pineapples. "How are you getting on?"

"Slowly. It's very difficult, writing a book. I'm aiming for a thousand words a day, but I'm getting more like two hundred. Still, it could be my meal ticket out of here. I've got to stick to it."

"How are you enjoying it here, anyway?"

"What?"

"Life here. As compared to London. Obviously you're itching for the bright lights."

"What – when I've got the Dog and Bucket just down the road?"

We both chuckle and take another biscuit.

"No, but seriously. Are you settling in?"

"Well, more than you'd think. I know what you mean about the people being good at heart. Some of them are really nice. And the school's a lot better than I thought it would be. It's lovely, in fact. But I'll tell you one thing, my life would a lot easier if it wasn't for Dawn. That woman is the nastiest piece of work I've seen outside the offices of a tabloid newspaper."

"Yes, she's a nightmare incarnate. But I think you can hold your own."

"Yeah. No worries. So... seen Bill recently?"

"No more recently than you, I suppose. Why?"

"Oh, nothing. Just... nothing. Nothing really."

"Come on. You've got a crush on him, haven't you?"

"Certainly not."

"You have."

"I have not."

"Well, I think he likes you."

There's a long pause while I attempt to control my breathing by eating another biscuit. When I've finished choking, Irene repeats: "I really do think he likes you."

"What makes you say that?"

155

"Well, at the pub that time he was showing interest."

"I too would show interest in a woman potting the balls with her breasts. That was ages ago, anyway."

"But that's not all."

"What else is there? Not that I'm interested or anything."

"Well, you know the other day when you were walking through the playground and he was there?"

I desperately wrack my brains, but come up with a blank.

"Well, anyway. When he saw you, he..."

A gruff voice comes from the garden. "Bex! Can you give me a hand out here?"

"Can't it wait? I'm busy! Irene's here!" I call out, grabbing a box of fennel tea bags and waving them at him through the door. "Cuppa?"

Mike hoves in through the door, cutting off Irene's revelation. "Lovely. But can you just come and hold this?"

Before I know it, I'm ankle deep in nettles holding what appears to be a collection of writhing snakes steady while Mike fiddles around attempting to fix them all together and Irene watches from the kitchen door, valiantly trying not to laugh. The rain drizzles gently down.

"Honestly Becky, can't you hold them still! It looked perfectly simple in the book. No, up that way! No! No, no, no, no!"

I drop the pole and walk away.

"NO! Come back!"

"Say please and I'll think about it."

"Please."

"And don't be so fucking cross."

"I won't be cross."

"Okay, then." It has occurred to me that if Mike fails to get this tepee upright, we'll be lying directly under the stars at this blessed Festival Games and so I stand patiently, watching him measuring and sawing and swearing and hitting his thumb with the hammer until an unexpectedly large tepee is standing, or should I say filling, the back garden.

"It's very big!" I say admiringly. "Plenty of room for us all in there. But isn't it meant to be symmetrical? Looks like it's got a list to the left to me."

"No, no. That's an optical illusion. Due to it's being round, you know. It's rather complicated to explain."

"Well, it's gorgeous! Come on, let's go inside. Irene! Check out the tepee!" Irene, Ricky and Pumpkin come out and we creep around the structure in search of a door. Half way round, I call a halt.

"Okay! Tell me. What happened when I was walking through the playground and he was there too?"

"Well, when he saw you, he ran his fingers through his hair."

"He didn't."

"He did."

"No way."

"God's honest truth."

"That is *so* significant."

"I know."

"Not that I fancy him."

"Of course not."

"And I still think he's an arch-traitor, telling Dawn all about our family."

"And *I* still think you're wrong about that."

"Whatever. Anyway it's irrelevant seeing as I don't fancy him."

"Of course you don't."

"That's right."

"I'll tell you one thing about Bill, though."

"What?"

"He's very moral."

"You mean, he doesn't like sex? How do you know?"

"No, no, no. I mean, he's very committed to causes and stuff like that. He really cares about things like global

157

warming and live exports. He's always organising demonstrations against this and that. Seriously, Becky. He might get on your nerves."

"Well... I'm against live exports. Who cares how it travels so long as it's tender and juicy?"

"Bill's a vegetarian."

"Oh, right. Well, I quite like fish."

"He doesn't eat fish, either."

"Oh well, for Christ's sake, I like peas, don't I? So long as they're really small and delicate. And when it comes to global warming, well, I'm all for it. Long summers at any price."

"That's just the sort of joke Bill wouldn't find funny."

"Who's joking?"

"I'm just not sure it'd work between you."

"Hey. I'm doing my best to develop a moral sense. It's uphill work. And who said I was interested in him, anyway? I keep telling you. I don't fancy him at all."

"Oh that's right, yes. Of course you don't. So the fact he ran his hands through his hair in the playground means nothing to you."

"Did he *really*?"

"Cross my heart and hope to die."

At this point, Mike breaks in with a roar of encouragement to continue our circumnavigation of his tepee and with my feelings in a flutter we crawl on through bush and bough, eventually meeting up with Mike once more. "I give up!" I say. "Where's the door! You've built it in beautifully. I can't find it at all!"

"I haven't done the door yet, actually," he responds huffily. "I was going to do it just now."

"Oh, I get it. You've forgotten the door."

"No I didn't. I'm going to do it now. Please remove yourself and your puerile imagination from the vicinity."

"Oh for God's sake. Have you donated your sense of humour to science, or something? Here's a quid! Buy yourself a good laugh! It's funny! You forgot the door!"

Irene reluctantly goes home to give Ricky his tea and after supplying Mike with a cup of tea and buttering his ego whenever I can be bothered, the tepee is finished at close of play, and we are all packing for the big camp out. Bill, the man who tidies his hair when he catches a glimpse of me, will be there. Oh, I do hope so.

Humming "I want to hold your ha-a-a-a-aaand", I pop into Honeybee's room with a pile of laundry, and am surprised by her choice of packing. For one night out by the camp fire, she seems to be taking several pairs of trousers, about twenty t-shirts, make up, a zillion cds and her mobile phone. Her sponge bag is also very hefty, and her makeup bag and a can of hairspray are also piled up on her bed. But I have learned a thing or two about teenage girls recently. Instead of insisting that all she packs is warm clothing and a sleeping bag, I simply put the pile of laundry on her bed, give her my frozen-lips-wide-open-eyes smile and exit without letting one word of wisdom escape me. She'll have to learn her own lessons in life. I'm too busy to care.

A Robin's Nest is being slightly more sensible. At least a sleeping bag and sweater are to the fore on his bed. And of course, as I am packing for Pumpkin, he has everything he needs – and I let him pack his own personal choice, a scruffy, handknitted rabbit wearing a bright green tie that he loves to cuddle at night. I'm like that. Generous.

We have long finished, and are slurping our soup, when there is a sinister rumbling noise and Mike descends into the sitting room. What a sight. My God. He's wearing a woolly hat with a pom-pom in vibrant Rastafarian colours, and sporting on his back the largest backpack I have ever seen in my life. How he can even begin to move, I can't imagine. I leap up, nearly spilling soup on

159

my leg and dash into the kitchen, returning histrionically fanning myself and acting all relieved.

"What is it, Becky?"

"Oh, the kitchen sink's still there. Just checking as we haven't washed up after supper yet."

"Very funny."

"What *have* you got in there? Big Ben? Someone'll notice it's missing."

"Oh, just a few essentials. I like to be prepared."

"Oh, you cute little boy scout."

"Come on, Becky, leave Dad alone," snarls Honeybee. "At least he's trying. Where's your luggage?"

"Here!" I say, proudly producing a fake Burberry handbag from behind the sofa. It was especially purchased in Oxfam some time ago for occasions of this very nature.

"That?" says Mike, scornfully. "What can you fit in *that*?"

"Well, I'm going to wear my clothes, obviously, and sleep in them too. Who wants to change in a tepee with ten thousand hippies squashed inside? So in here are my toothbrush and toothpaste, anti-wrinkle cream, my makeup bag, a packet of condoms, super-ridged for sensation I might add, and a packet of what is rather revoltingly known as moist toilet tissue."

"You're mad," raps Mike, with a furious 'pas devant les enfants' stare. "What happens if there's an emergency?"

"I told you. I've got the condoms right here."

"*Please* Becky. I mean, a joke's a joke."

"Okay Big Bag, what have *you* packed?"

Proudly, Mike begins to recite. "Kendall mint cake. A primus stove in case it rains and we can't get the fire started. Storm matches. Water purifying tablets. Three pairs of dry socks. My sleeping bag, liner and roll. A complete change of clothes. My one-person tent, just in case somebody freaks out and needs their privacy. A compass. A trowel. A rope. A torch which works by winding it up – clever, eh? Salt water toothpaste, travel

160

brush and a compressed towel. A pair of gaiters. 'Survive Outside' – a marvellous book, Becky. You'd do well to read it. And..."

"Tell me no more, Mike. This is like a sort of generation game for gear-addicts. I confess that I can't foresee any use whatever for ninety-nine point nine of the things you've mentioned, but to be charitable, you never know."

"That's right, Becky!" pipes up A Robin's Nest, sticking up for his dad. "It's true! You do never know! For instance, how about... you need to go to the loo in the middle of the night, but you've forgotten where it is, so you take your compass because you've already memorised a bearing, and you look at the compass with your torch – although it might be difficult winding up the torch and holding the compass at the same time – and then you tie the rope to the tepee so that you can easily find your way back, and then off you go, and you dig a hole with the trowel and go to the loo in it..."

"Gross!"

"Shut up, Honeybee. Then you find your way back with the rope, and then you purify some water and wash your teeth in it with the salt water toothpaste which is very environmental because it doesn't foam and then you decompress your towel... what else was there?"

"Not much, Robbo. You've done brilliantly," I say generously. "I think it's marvellous that Dad's managed to think of so many things, and that he's prepared to carry them out to the car, and then to the camp, and then use them for one night and then lug them all home again."

Mike is looking rather pleased with himself. I pat my little bag in a self-satisfied way. Honeybee rolls her eyes and Robbo beams round at everybody.

It takes an hour or two to pack up the car and rope the tepee on top (Mike actually has to unpack his backpack to find the rope for this, which results in an explosion of gear all over the sitting room) but finally the family is all ready for tomorrow and – exhausted – I crawl to bed. But not for long.

I happen to know that we don't actually need to be at the school before lunchtime, but being Mike, he just has to wake us at dawn with his version of the army bugle call.

"Poooo-rrrrrr-iiiiii-ggggg-eeeeee!"

Which if you need a translation, means – not porridge, a delicious oatmeal dish topped with brown sugar and lashings of organic cream – but a grey mess made from something called quinoa, which Mike says is much more digestible and comes from somewhere weird like Peru. Well, it may be digestible for llamas, but for the ordinary working girl it's frankly inedible.

After a great deal of groaning, we all assemble in the kitchen, and Mike doles out the slop. I push my bowl aside and chomp moodily on a piece of bread liberally encrusted with sunflower seeds. Yeah, yeah. I made it myself. Doesn't mean I have to like it, although my skin tone has certainly improved over the past few weeks.

"Wow!" says Mike through his beard and a large spoonful of quinoa. "This is going to be great!"

We all look at him sadly.

"Where's Midge?" I ask.

"Oh," he replies busily. "In bed. But it doesn't matter. I said goodbye last night. So! We'll be off in a minute."

"Shall we leave the washing up to Midge?"

"Um... Probably not a good idea. I'll do it," says Mike brightly, leaping to his feet. "You get the kids in the car. Don't forget Pepys!"

"Okay, Mr Keen. Come on everybody. Pile your bowls on the sink for Dad to wash, and let's get going. Don't forget your toothbrushes."

We surge out to the van and after some time, Mike joins us. Of course it won't start, and we sit shivering in the misty morning while he fiddles around under the bonnet, muttering the sort of encouraging noises VW camper van

162

owners are well-known to make to their darlings. And eventually, we are off, rattling through the village in our usual harmonious way.

I expect that we'll be very much the first to arrive, I mean, it's only ten past nine in the morning when we get there, but to my surprise, the camper vans are streaming in from all over. It's like a Volkswagen convention. Loads of tepees, or what passes for them, are being pulled down from rusty roofs, and eager children are already on the scrounge for extra firewood in the rhododendron bushes.

Mike, of course, is in his element, which makes my head ache. He's leaping around, roaring with laughter, throwing sticks for a bemused Pepys and otherwise acting like a complete idiot. Honeybee and A Robin's Nest are embarrassed enough to get back into the van – they peer out of the windows in search of friends like monkeys in a cage. Frankly, I'm too knackered to care.

Only the prospect of putting up the tepee again calms Mike down. After lugging down the poles and staring at them for ten minutes or so, he's a lot quieter. In fact, I'm hoping for a total cessation of jolly laughter, but it's not long before another camper appears to offer a helping hand, and Mike cheers up.

The weather's not too bad – only a light drizzle this morning, with a slight hint of yellow on the far horizon, so all the adults are extremely cheerful bar myself. Eventually Rob and Honeybee spy some compatriots and slink off into the gloom, so I have the whole van to myself and Pumpkin. He is happy enough pulling at his socks and eating ricecakes – I huddle on the vinyl sofa arrangement wrapped in my poncho and wishing I was in the Caribbean. After a while, Mike digs out a thermos flask and pours us both out a cup of something hot. And I mean literally, something. I can't identify it at all.

"What is this, Mike?"

"Oh, miso."

"Omiso?"

"No, miso."

"Nomiso?"

"Look, whatever it is it's really, really good for you."

"Say no more."

It's at this moment, when all the work is done and Pumpkin's long day is drawing to a close, that Midge arrives. Mike's eyebrows hit his hairline, as do mine. But his surprise is delighted, while mine is definitely under the weather.

"Darling!" he cries. "You came after all!"

"Yes. I felt I should join the soul gathering. I felt the need for a fire ritual."

"Great! Come and have a beer."

Midge shudders delicately and talks about liquorice root tea, but I notice that she latches onto a bottle like a leech in a blood bath. The three of us sit around the fire, plentifully supplied with fuel by Mike from a large pile on his left, in a fragrant miasma of woodsmoke, damp leaves and mud. Other camp fires blaze, there are gusts of laughter and the sweet pop of corks and clink of beer bottle tops. Is this what my life has become? A small point of thought enclosed by a seventies fashion item and a homemade tepee? Perhaps I could start a trend. It's rather enjoyable.

Mike passes me a bottle of beer and I guzzle on it – and several of its companions - happily for a while. Then I start getting restless. Bill might be around and although there are merry sounds elsewhere, our camp fire is a bit quiet for my taste. Honeybee and Rob are nowhere to be seen, Pumpkin is snoring busily inside the tepee and Mike and Midge are gazing into the flames together and seem indisposed for chat. I wander off, pulling my poncho well around me, and my hat half over my face in a feeble attempt to keep the fire's warmth with me. It's very dark, and the glow of fires is welcoming to one left

164

out in the cold. Looking no doubt very sinister in my semi-disguise, I lurk around the camp, absorbing the whole scene. Small clusters of people are sitting, drinking and chatting calmly – talking of the next day and how they imagine the Games will go. Their children are nowhere to be seen, but there are explosions of laughter from the bushes so I imagine that a lot of illicit pot smoking is taking place, not to mention a few games of Truth or Dare.

One fire seems more welcoming than the others for the simple reason that one member of the party is extracting a packet of jumbo rolling papers from his bag. With a start of surprise followed by a surge of hope I edge into the group, keeping well in the shadows. Only one or two of the seven people assembled notice me at first – and they, I'm sure, don't recognise me under the hat and poncho. It's rather fun, being anonymous.

"Who goes there?" says one of these revellers, laughing.

"Er... Sarah," I say, accepting a proffered tin cup of mulled wine with a willing hand.

"What class is yours in, then?"

"I'm just a friend of the school really," I say guardedly.

"Welcome."

"Thanks."

There's a thoughtful silence, then the group picks up the conversation I must have interrupted.

"So... I think he's lucky to have the children he does, really," says the girl who greeted me.

"It's not that easy," responds a beardo, looking up from what looks attractively like a leek-sized joint he's busy constructing. "There are some very difficult kids in that class. I mean, two have left and the one that came in seems to have a few problems. It upsets the delicate balance. And when it comes to biodynamic gardening, the personal relationship between teacher and kids is really important."

"Has he tried feng shui-ing the gardening shed?"

"God, yes. At least, I think so. I should imagine he's tried everything. Chloe gave him the number of a really good shaman, but I don't know if he followed it up. Here, pass this round."

"Thanks."

There's silence while people smoke without inhaling and try very hard not to cough.

"Sarah? Sarah? Sarah?"

"Oh, me?"

"Yes. Your name is Sarah, right?"

"Oh, right. Yes. Sarah."

"Well, do you want a toke?"

"Do bears shit in the woods?"

"I beg your pardon?"

"I mean, sure. Thanks."

I suck on the joint like a dying man in the desert pushes the camels aside and drains an oasis. After about an hour, I reluctantly pass it on, and practically fall over backwards. I can still hear, but their voices sound very far away. It's all I can do to avoid bursting out into demented giggles, but by some miracle, I manage to stifle them by wedging a bit of poncho in my mouth and holding my breath.

"I was in the driveway a while back, and a completely crazed mother attacked him."

"What, physically?"

"No, verbally. I don't know what she said, but he looked really upset."

"Oh yeah! I heard about that. Accused him of gossiping about her? Here, pass it on."

"Thanks. Something like that. Anyway, he told Maria that he'd been dumped in it by Dawn, but he wouldn't name any names. I'm dying to know who it was. But according to Maria, he closed up like a clam when she hinted she'd

166

like to know. I mean, he is really good like that. He knows how to keep a secret."

"He's so sweet!" bursts in another tubby female, in between puffing on the joint as if it's a tin whistle. "I mean, I really just think, he's so great! He's such a great teacher. I love him."

"Steady on, Shula."

"No, we all do! Help, I'm having a coughing fit... ah... ah... Sarah? Sarah? Sarah? Here you go. No, guys. Seriously. You just can't help being smitten by him. We are all in deep smit. The man just exudes karma all over the place."

"Who's got the joint?"

"Sarah."

"Cool."

It's at this point that I drain the dregs of my mulled wine and stagger off. It's clear to me from this conversation that if the reported facts are in any way accurate, Irene is quite right – Dawn is the anti-Christ, and Bill is completely exonerated of foul gossip and vicious slander.

Wending my way around a tent traditionally held up by guy ropes and with my balance somewhat affected, I trip over a rope, stagger forwards, tread on the front of my poncho, begin a graceful arc through the air and land bang thump in the arms of a complete stranger.

Or rather, not a complete stranger.

"Oof! Who are you?" Bill says, after catching me mid-flight and staggering backwards about four feet while severely constricting the blood supply of my upper arms with his strong and manly hands.

Now, Rebecca. Careful. After the disgraceful exhibition I made of myself in the pub all those weeks ago, it's very important that this lovely man doesn't guess that I'm not feeling quite myself. And I have a plan, for I always find that getting complex ideas across in a rather wordy way proves sobriety. Same idea as walking along a straight line in front of a policeman.

"It is my belief that you should be communicating the following question: '*How* are you?'" I annunciate clearly and slowly, attempting to free myself but giving up because I am tangled in poncho and Bill's strong arms. "You've nearly been the cause of my demise, perambulating along like that just where I was falling over."

"Well, sorry. I thought I rescued you from landing face first in the mud."

"The zephyr is evil which does not advance auspicious circumstances to no person."

"Absolutely. You've hit the nail on the head there. Great vocabulary."

"My gratitude is infinite."

"So, who is that under the beanie?" Bill asks kindly, ducking down to get a better look. I stare sternly at the ground and fold my arms – well, it takes me a few tries to fold them but I make it in the end.

"I know the voice, I'm sure," Bill persists, and gently he pushes the hat up my forehead. "Oh! It's you!"

"Yes. Problem? I mean, could it be that you disapprove of my... whatever?"

"Whatever it is, I have no problem at all with it. Are you still annoyed with me?"

"Of course."

"Why?"

"It's ages ago now, but I've never got over it. You told Dawn loads of crap about me and where I live. Elizabeth's tried to make Robbo's life a misery. All because of you." I burp sadly and goggle up at his face. I know he's got *two* green eyes, both flecked with gold, but they've morphed into one. Wish I hadn't had that last lungful of weed.

"Look, you must believe me," says Bill earnestly, continuing to clasp my arms and thus, all unawares, allowing me to remain upright. "I have never spread rumours around about any of you. I'm not that sort of person. If you want me to apologise, I will. But none of it's true. I swear that right is on my side."

I can't help being amused. Then I gradually stop giggling and just stare at him while all time seems to grind to a halt. "I love you, I love you, I love you!" I muse, open-mouthed. "It's not your radiant, youthful, glorious face," I think to myself, "it's not your athletic, relaxed body or firm, friendly hands, it's the soul pulsing out of you like the beams from a lighthouse. You say to me, 'Come in! Come in!' Or rather, not that. You say, 'Avoid the rocks! Avoid the rocks!' Because that's what lighthouses say. You are extraordinary. We could be extraordinary together. Hey, if you are a lighthouse, could I be your keeper?"

"Sorry?"

"Oh God. Ah... do you remember what I last said? It is possible that I may have been thinking aloud."

"Yes, that's possible. Or it may be that you are taking part in some kind of performance art. But I'd love to hear more. Look, now we've made a truce, why don't you come and have a drink? My tent's just over there. I've got some interesting homebrew. It's a bit muddy this year, but it's passable."

Bill takes my arm, I *think* with the unconscious gallantry of a true gentleman but I don't know him well enough to be sure, and anyway to be perfectly frank I'm a wee bit muddled. He escorts me through the increasingly muddy paths to his tent – a small, but perfectly serviceable affair that the most efficient of boy scouts would have been proud to erect and lie down in. His fire is also remarkably neat – and we are alone.

There's silence as I absorb the truly awful taste of Bill's homebrewed poison, then he begins conversation on an embarrassing, subject.

"I've never seen you in the Dog and Bucket again."

"Ah!" I swallow my homebrew in one, and foolishly allow Bill to refill my glass. "Well, now. No. Hmmm. I've only been there the once. Boy, this stuff's strong. A mild night, isn't it?"

"Very mild. You must have had quite a hangover after the night I saw you there."

"I did, as a matter of fact. Just a little one."

"I thought you would."

"Somebody spiked my drinks with alcohol, and I seriously thought of complaining to the bar staff. Irene says I rolled on the pool table."

"You did, among other things."

"So embarrassing. Why were you even there? I wouldn't have put you down as a pub man."

"Oh, I pop in occasionally for a quick half. I've got a couple of friends I have a drink with."

"I hope I amused you all."

"It certainly was funny. I've rather regretted you haven't put in a repeat performance."

We sit by the crackling fire in silence for a moment that lasts an age. Then I realise that under the influence of recreational drugs topped up with homebrew I've nodded off for a moment. What if he tries to kiss me and I'm asleep and I SNORE and suck his tongue in and choke on it? For some unfortunate reason I feel I have to make the danger of this horrible thought clear to him, but without being embarrassing. I think I can do this. I'll be very subtle. He'll never know it's personal. I crawl round to his side of the fire and, on all fours, stare at Bill with a solemn significance. He looks back, all amusement and raised eyebrows. Or at least, eyebrow. I'm still getting that two into one thing going on.

"Hello!" he says. "What's up?"

"Look," I say. "It's a well known fact that if you kiss somebody when they're snoring, they could inhale your

170

tongue and die of as... as... asfix... whatever. Choke to death. Interesting, isn't it?"

"Very."

"Just thought you'd be interested."

I crawl back to my side of the fire, pick up my plastic cup and take a big old slurp on it.

"Maybe you don't need any more of that," he says, leaning over and gently taking the glass out of my hand. He doesn't move. Neither do I. There's a long pause as we look into each other's eyes. Bill touches my cheek with his hand. It's so romantic.

But sadly - I puke on his knees.

CHAPTER EIGHT

It's always very sad to wake up with a hangover. It's very sad if you're in your very own bed and drank a pint of water before going to sleep as well as dabbing at the interior of your mouth with a toothbrush and rinsing off the makeup.

But let me tell you, it's so sad that it's downright morbid to wake up hungover, unwashed, unbrushed and dehydrated in a tepee surrounded by a bearded hippy snoring his head off, a wakeful toddler with a dirty nappy, two scowling teenagers who can't wait to never see you again, and a panting, stinking dog. Oh, and a mad, meditating Buddhist. Midge is greeting the day with her legs wound around her ears and it's a frankly unattractive sight.

There's something really horrid about camping. The smell of the canvas warmed by the morning sun, other people's feet and sleeping bags is a perfume I prefer not to inhale too early in the day. Or ever. I'd love to escape, but unfortunately if I so much as twitch a toe I'll die young, so I wisely remain motionless except for my lips. The hoarseness of my voice surprises even me and wakes Rob with a horrid shock.

"Robbo, what time is it?"

"Are you okay?"

"No. What time is it?"

"Let's see... Six."

"Oh God. Change Pumpkin if you love me."

"Well, I don't love you if you don't mind my saying so, but I do like you."

"Well then, for fuck's sake change Pumpkin."

"Okay."

"Then *I* love *you* whatever your feelings about *me*."

And with a hollow groan I close my eyes against the dawn.

Memories of last night begin to seep through my consciousness. Oh God. Did I... no. I can't have done. I must have dreamed that I was at Bill's tent and that I was sick on his leg just as it looked like he was going to make a move on me. It must be a terrible nightmare induced by drugs and mulled wine. My thoughts are disturbed by Rob, who has started chuckling quietly as he sorts out Pumpkin's nappy equipment.

"What's the joke?" I whisper crossly.

"You! Last night. It was a riot!" He shakes his head, laughing, while digging into Pumpkin's bag.

"What was a riot? In what way was I a riot?"

"Oh, you know. With Mr Mayer. He practically had to carry you back here. I mean, honestly, Becky! It's like, you're the teenager, we're the grownups. Wicked!"

"Mr... Mr... Mr... Mayer had to... *carry* me? Like, in his *arms*?"

"Yeah! He had sick all over his trousers. That's, like, so *gay*."

"Sick?" I ask tremulously. "Did he say... whose sick?"

"Aha! It's like in Spinal Tap. You can't dust for vomit!"

I fall back with a groan. Then it's all true, and it's all over. There's no way Bill will ever want to be friends – or more – after this. That's the second time he's seen me absolutely paralytic. Right. I mean it. This is it. I'm detoxing. Starting right now, I'm going on a massive health kick. I'm going to do tai chi and drink eight glasses of water a day and eat algae and drink Yogi tea and... and... all those good things. Starting right now. In the meantime, I think Mike will have to carry me home.

I miss the Games, of course. Every now and then a member of the household rushes back and attempts to rouse me but it's no good. Mike is extremely shirty about my being unable to care for Pumpkin and constantly mutters about docking my salary but even he can tell that for me, it's all over. A distant cheer, a song wafting my way on the wind, that's what the much-touted Games are for me. I manage to smile faintly when Rob bursts in to tell me he excelled against himself in the javelin throwing but that's about it. I haven't even the strength to deconstruct his triumph and ask him why he isn't allowed to excel against the other children. Even when it's home time, I'm still completely unable to move which, as I'm in the tepee, makes packing it up an impossibility. Eventually, Mike responds to my desperate appeals for help and carries me to the van in his arms. We drive home with me leaning out of the window with my tongue waving around in the breeze, trying not to vomit down the car door. And once home, I crawl into my bed for a refreshing twenty-four hour nap.

But the next day, I spring out of bed rather girlishly. This is the first day of the rest of my life – and I'm going to make the most of it. I eat my quinoa with barely a retch, and wash it down with two glasses of water as recommended by supermodels the world over. I inspect a plastic tub of vitamins in the form of green algae, the instructions of which sound like if I ingest a teaspoon of it daily, I will live for ever in a really fine state of health. It's rather nerve-racking, but after some time I manage to work up the courage to spoon some into some apple juice, hold my nose, close my eyes, and start drinking. It's at this delicate moment that Mike bounds in.

"Hi, Bex! Glad you're back in the land of the living. Absolutely bloody vital, in fact. Got a gang coming for dinner tonight. You're in charge of cooking."

"WHAT?" I then gag over the sink for a while, Mike watching in appalled fascination, and finally, with the help of deep breathing, am able to speak again. "I'm in the process of recovering from the hangover of the century, Mike! I've had to start my life all over again the healthy way! I'm in a very tender position right now, and shouldn't be overexcited. My body's in a period of adjustment."

"That's not my fault. I didn't get out of my head at the Festival Games, did I? I've invited the gardening teacher over, the one who brought you back to the tepee. He seems like a cool guy. He's bringing someone with him called Dawn. They'll be here about eight. Anything you want me to do?"

"Yes. Cook the dinner. Because I'm going out."

"What?"

"Too bad for the dinner party. But I'm going out... on a very important... date. A date. With... a friend. So I won't be here."

"Becky, you'll have to cancel it. You have to be here. The gardening bloke – what's his name again? Bill Mayer, right. He asked especially if you were going to be around."

"When?"

"This morning. Now I thought, let's not go crazy, let's do a big pot of beans and rice. With fruit salad for afters. What do you say?"

"Beans and rice? Over my dead body. This place will be fart central by the time you bring in the carob coffee. We'll have to have something delicious. I'll need to go shopping."

175

"What about cleaning up the house?"

"Are you crazy? I'm going to be cooking all day at this rate. And yes. I do need to go shopping. Things for a dinner party are different. I'll have to read recipe books and make plans. Oh, and by the way... er... you'll need to give me some more money."

"MORE MONEY?"

"Well, it's all been spent. That's what usually happens to the housekeeping."

"Like the time you spent it all on new clothes for Rob."

"I knew you'd bring that up."

"You've had this week's money. Not another penny will you get out of me."

"I can't give Bill Mayer a disgusting dinner!"

"You'll have to."

"I won't! Now listen, Mike. I'll be fine for the rest of the week. I've got plenty of beans and vegetables. Just give me thirty pounds for tonight..."

"Thirty! Are you mad?"

"I'll take care of Pumpkin next Saturday morning so you can get a lie-in. How about it?"

"The next three Saturdays."

"Two."

"Three."

"Two and the next nappy change."

"The next two nappy changes."

"Deal."

So after a flick through a dog-eared vegetarian recipe book enticingly titled Cook A Mean Bean, and feeling a bit dodgy after the algae health drink, I venture out to the shops. But this time, the mung sprouts will have to stay on the shelves. I'm buying organic chocolate and everything. It will be a gourmet experience from soup to nuts. This is my big chance to prove to Bill that I am a glamorous individual who is only sick on people's trousers on very special occasions. Everything must be perfect, and with any luck I will be able to expunge the Festival Games from his mind.

Check it out. We will begin with tiny mushroom soufflés served with purple sprouting broccoli. After a civilised pause, I will draw a large and beautiful pie decorated beautifully with leaves and other squiggly bits from the range. Far from a fruit salad, who wants that, we will nosh on a chocolate meringue roulade followed by real coffee and the best chocolates Much Jenner has on offer.

Plus. I will look absolutely fabulous lounging around before a roaring fire, with Cobweb Cottage a vision of rural enchantment. The teens will behave, Pumpkin will be safely tucked up in bed, Pepys will be shut up in the shed and Midge will stay upstairs for the duration. It's going to be great.

Of course, nobody and nothing is perfect. Although I follow the Mean Bean's methods to the letter, presumably when she was experimenting with the recipes in a fully equipped kitchen, she did not have a frantic three-year-old armed with a rolling pin helping out. And she would have been using professional pots, pans and electrical gadgets. She wouldn't have been having to turn on a rusty generator just to whip the egg whites for the soufflé... or for that matter, turning it off again when realising that there was no electric whisk anyway, and it had to be done by hand.

The Mean Bean wouldn't have a dog named Pepys jumping onto the table via a chair and dipping its pink tongue into the cheese sauce. And she would have been using a top of the range cooker. Not a Victorian bottom of all the ranges. Yes, I had it tough.

In the middle of it all, just after I knock Pepys off the table with a long swing – he makes a most satisfying thud as he falls to earth – Honeybee comes in looking more than usually sulky. I ignore her completely of course, but she hangs around, rather to my surprise, dipping her

177

finger into the Pepys'd cheese sauce and sucking it squelchily.

In the end, I tackle her straight on. I try to be kind, but I'm under pressure.

"Honeybee, if you want something, say it," I bark, knee deep in flour and greasy pans. "If not, piss off."

"Oh thanks," says she. "Thanks a lot. If I want support, I know where to come. Thank you very much." And then, if you can believe it, she bursts into tears. I whip out my heart, examine it searchingly for signs of melting, and replace it back in the deep freeze. Honeybee throws herself onto a beanbag in the sitting room and sobs loudly. I try to drown out the sound with the radio as I mince garlic, but eventually have to give in. I switch off, throw down my knife, march into the sitting room, and stand over her, arms akimbo.

"All right, Honeybee. I'm listening. What's up. Come on. Tell me all about it. Better still, tell your mum. Shall I call Midge?"

"No!"

"Okay. Tell me then."

She continues to sob. There is nothing for it. I drag up another beanbag, squash it against hers and rather gingerly put my arm around her. She's so pierced out of school hours that I'm always afraid of getting a rash. I'm allergic to nickel. Physical contact unleashes a fresh bout of sobbing, and Honeybee snuggles into my shoulder. I find it very difficult to understand exactly what she is saying, but one word leaps from the damp and snotty flood loud and clear.

BABY.

"What? Are you up the duff?"

"Oh God!"

"Who's the boyfriend? Because it's practically illegal at your age. You're only seventeen for Christ's sake."

"Nearly eighteen."

178

"That's still seventeen if my maths is correct. So. Have you taken a test?"

"No."

"Oh! So this is probably all a storm in a teacup. Have you missed a period?"

"Yes."

"When should it have been?"

"Last November."

"AAAARG!"

"I know. I know!"

"Honeybee, it's now almost the middle of June."

"I know."

"Honeybee. Are you telling me. That you are eight months pregnant."

"Yes. I suppose so."

"It can't be possible. I don't believe you."

Honeybee lifts up her fleece and I gaze, with my eyes whirling around on stalks, at a rotund lump the size of a space hopper.

"Jesus wept! Why didn't I notice?"

"I always wore baggy tops."

"And I just thought you were a fat slag."

"Thanks, Becky."

"Sorry, but... Christ! I didn't even know you had a boyfriend."

"I don't."

"Who was he?"

"Just a bloke."

"What kind of a bloke? A Nice Bloke? A Wretched Slimy Bloke?"

"Just a bloke."

"And where does this bloke reside?"

"Nowhere, really."

"Oh. 'Nowhere, really.' I see. Well, are you in contact with him? Does he know?"

179

"Well, he lives in London, and of course he doesn't know. He's the same age as me. It's all hopeless."

"He'll have to know soon, won't he?"

"Oh Becky, who cares where he lives, who he is and whether he knows or not? Look, we're not in contact. It was at a party. I don't even know his surname."

"You mean, you slept with just anybody?"

"Yes, I did. After a few too many drinks. And for your information, if you really have to know, his first name was Lee. I mean, Lee! For God's sake. There are a million Lees in Hackney I expect, and he gatecrashed the party anyway. I have no idea who he is. There. Satisfied? Nobody here knows about the baby, that's the main thing. Except you."

At this critical moment, a black cloud bursts in from the kitchen announcing the total failure of the onions to 'cook very gently until translucent'. I spring to my feet and whip in, swiping the pan off the stove with one hand, opening the kitchen door with the other and despatching Pepys off the chair whence he was poised to leap back on the table with one foot. The other foot I use for balancing purposes. That's how small the kitchen is at Cobweb Cottage.

I call Honeybee in from the sitting room and take several deep breaths – nearly choking on the black cloud, but that's by the by.

"Honeybee. I'm glad you have told me about your situation. Quite clearly we have some serious thinking to do. But right now is not a good moment. Bill Mayer is coming to dinner tonight with his great friend and my worst enemy, Dawn. And I am in the process of cooking a gourmet meal."

"You are? It looks terrible," sniffs Honeybee eyeing the burnt pan and chaotic kitchen table doubtfully.

"I need to focus on this meal. Can you please do the washing up, and help me chop vegetables and all that crap? Just for once in your life, can you be helpful?"

"Why can't Rob do some work for once?"

"You know perfectly well it's his pottery class today in the community centre. Come on. Give me a hand."

"You fancy Mr Mayer, don't you?"

"Whatever my feelings are, this evening's going to be a disaster. He's bringing the date from hell, the onions have burned, Pepys has wolfed half my cheese sauce and there's a baby on the way. It is essential that you shut up and help out. Okay. I'll say it. Please."

"All right then."

"Here's a dishcloth. Now get your arse into gear or I'll be forced to strangle you with it."

Honeybee, I have to admit, does buckle down with a will and it is surprising, given the circumstances, how much we both – I think, we both – enjoy the afternoon. Some things have to be chucked in the bin and others resurrected practically from the compost heap, but by seven o'clock something resembling a passable meal is assembled, and I am battling Mike, just arrived home after a hard day's doula-ing, for first rights to the thin trickle of water in the bathhouse. There follows a fairly major session of clothes anxiety. I think I have explained that my wardrobe belongs to Amanda, and I'm sure that you are aware that our personal styles are rather different. I go to the closet convinced, against all the evidence, that somewhere in the shawls and caftans lurks a little black dress that isn't covered with fluff. But I am wrong. In the end, I raid Honeybee's wardrobe and squeeze into a pair of jeans that shows half my arse whenever I lean forward, and what she calls a 'tummy top', which shows everything else. A pair of Amanda's old clogs and a bit of make up, my hair – alas no longer the product of a Knightsbridge salon – brushed and I look passable.

Actually, more than passable. I look like top totty in comparison to Dawn. I send A Robin's Nest, returned dewy and relaxed from his pottery, to answer the door and he staggers backwards into the sitting room, partly because the tiny hall fills up so fast with teacher, teacher's date and a welcoming Pepys, but more from the effect of Dawn's outfit.

Listen. She is wearing, and I do not exaggerate, a costume that would make eight-legged aliens with green spots and forked tongues feel instantly at home.

Starting at the shoes, a pair of stiletto heels that I know for a fact were in the shoe section in Oxfam last Friday and which I picked up in order to laugh at and noticed that there was chewing gum on the sole.

Very wide-legged purple velvet trousers with a drawstring waist.

On top, a swirling, geometrically patterned top the like of which I have not seen since my granny went mad in 1973 and bought an outfit for travelling to Australia but never went and it mouldered in her closet for twenty years.

Dark purple glittery eye shadow.

Dark purple lips.

Feathers as earrings.

Bill looks a bit shell shocked lurking in behind all this glamour, and serves him right, but he smiles at me very nicely and takes his beanbag. All this time, Dawn is having a go under the guise of being nice.

"Hello, Nest," is her opening gambit, pretending to know A Robin's Nest so well that she is entitled to shorten his name. Rob looks a bit surprised but answers politely enough. Then she turns on Honeybee. "Hi, Honey. How are you?"

This extracts a surly "fine", then there is a brief "Oh Rebecca! I didn't see you there," before she springs on

Mike and clasps him lovingly to her bosom. "Mikey! Long time no see!" Mike looked completely confused as he's only seen her in the distance once or twice, but rather pleased. What are men on?

The rest of the evening, I can really only describe through her own words.

"What a lovely house! How compact! It's really dinky, isn't it! Oh! Down boy, down! Never mind. It's just a bit of mud. Do we sit here? How comfortable. Whoops! No, I'm fine. Really. I love beanbags. So does Bill. Don't you darling? Haven't you made it cosy, Rebecca? There's nothing like a bit of clutter to make a place feel lived in. What lovely smells! I almost feel as if I'm sitting in the kitchen. A drink? Lovely! Is there ice? Never mind. Lemon? Never mind. What's that? Do I want a twizzle stick? Oh, ha ha ha! I know I'm fussy, but I'm not that fussy.

"Oh! Dinner already! How delicious! What is it? Soufflé? Isn't that made with flour? Wheat flour? Not spelt flour? Never mind. No really. Well, I *am* mildly intolerant to gluten – I could just risk it – oh. Cheese in it too? Well, I am intolerant to lactose so... I'm sure I'll be fine. I'll just push it to the side of my plate. There. No problem! Whoops! A bit of soufflé got on the broccoli. That's fine. I'll just push that to the side of the plate too. Shall I save my plate? I'm sure you don't have enough plates for all these people.

"Who's this? Oh! Hello, Midge. I've heard so much about you. Oh thank you! I hope nothing but good! Oh. Well... No, actually, they are designer. Well, I can't quite remember. Yes, you could look at the label if you really liked – Ouch. Let me loosen the neckline – oh, haven't you heard of House of Velvet? They're awfully good. Aren't you eating with us? The food's scrumptious! Oh well! It was lovely to meet you... Mike!" in a penetrating whisper "Is she All Right? Oh good.

183

"Pie? Delicious! Of course there's that same old problem with the flour, isn't there? The flour in the pastry? What a shame. I'll just eat the filling... hmmm. thank you very much, but it's an enormous portion. I couldn't possibly eat any more. I've left enough as it is.

"Pudding too? What do we have here? Chocolate roulade! Well, Becky, what an effort you have made for little old us. Bill. Have some roulade. Oh thank you, just a tiny sliver. No, really tiny. I have a reaction to chocolate... so does Bill – oh, Bill! You're eating a huge slice! You know what it does to your system! He gets terribly gassy, don't you Bill?

"Coffee? Lovely! But I won't. Herb tea? Do you have fennel? Never mind. I'll just have hot water. Delicious. What a quaint old cup. Pity about the crack or it may have been worth something. Where did you get it? Oh. I've never been *there*.

"Well, we must be going. Thank you so much for making so much effort and preparing such an elaborate meal, which we really enjoyed, the bits we could eat anyway! Ha ha! We must rush. Down boy. Down.

"Ciao!"

She exits in a gush of purple velvet and feather earrings, Bill trailing after her rather mournfully. He looks back at me as I stand, feeling really cross actually, by the door and mouthed a thank you. I shove my nose in the air and slam the door. I virtually haven't exchanged a word with him all evening. I have to take satisfaction from the undoubted fact that he was staring at me whenever he could see past Dawn's ostrich feather earrings. What an evening.

"Well!" said Mike cheerily. "That was a fantastic party, wasn't it? Shame about the food, Becky. But Dawn was really nice, wasn't she?"

Honestly. That man! Just because she said she liked his beard!

184

Rob put his arm protectively around my shoulders. "I don't know what you mean, Dad. The food was fantastic. Wasn't it, Honeybee?"

"Fantastic."

"And Dawn's a right cow. She's the saddest cow I know. Right Honeybee?"

"Too right, Robbo."

"Thanks, Becky," he continued, giving my shoulders a loving squeeze. "It was a great evening and I think Bill really enjoyed himself."

Suddenly the doorbell rings. We all stare at each other, then I race down the passageway. Bill's standing on the doorstep, looking furtive.

"Oh, hi, Becky! I forgot something."

"You did?" I lean against the doorframe seductively. Then I remember rolling on the pool table and the merry scene by his camp fire as I puked for England, and snap bolt upright.

"Yes. There's, um, something I forgot."

"What?"

"Oh, my, er, my fleece."

"It's tied around your waist."

"Oh! So it is. Hum. Well, Dawn's set off walking home."

"Really?"

"Yes. So I'll walk home too."

"Have a good one."

"In fact, would *you* like to go for a walk?"

"What, right now?"

"Why not?"

"It's practically the middle of the night."

"Well, it's only half past ten according to my watch. But the evening was so lovely, it seemed to go very fast."

"Come off it. It wasn't a lovely evening. Dawn hated every minute of it."

"I didn't."

"Yes you did."

185

"I enjoyed several minutes of it. And I'd enjoy the end of it a lot if you would come out for a walk with me."

"Where are we going to walk at this time of night?"

"You could walk me home. That would be nice."

"Well... okay." I dash in to get the good old poncho, forestall all questions from the family with a frown and upraised finger, and set off into the night with Bill. For some reason, I can't walk quite straight and keep bumping into him, which makes me feel really stupid, but after a few yards, he takes my hand and draws it through his strong and capable arm. It's a cosy limb, too, Bill's arm. I used to think that fleeces were just about the most disastrous thing that'd happened to fashion since Garfield slippers, but a sinewy man's arm encased in the softness of a fleece is surprisingly erotic.

"Sorry I puked," I blurt out.

"That's okay. I still..."

"What?"

"Never mind."

"No, go on."

"Okay. I still find you - irresistible. I can't help it. Even though I'm a teacher... It's not so bad, actually. You're not a parent. I don't think au-pairs count."

"You find me..."

"Irresistible. Even when you're covered in vomit."

"Really?"

"Yup. That's why I called Mike and asked to come over for dinner tonight. I knew I had to make my move before somebody else took a fancy to your poncho."

Everything suddenly seems significant – the tiny hairdressers, a puddle glimmering in the street light, the far off sound of traffic. I very slightly draw in my arm, so that we're walking closer together. And I must admit, I'm finding it increasingly difficult to breathe.

"Why did you ask Dawn to come along?" I gasp.

"Of course I didn't."

186

"Well, correct me if I'm wrong, but there was a mountain of purple velvet at the table that certainly answered to the name of Dawn."

"Look Becky. She came in through the front door without knocking just as I was finishing off the phone call, and invited herself along."

"Why didn't you tell her to eff off?"

"I'm not like that. I find confrontations very difficult. She's rather a powerful personality."

I've just got to ask him flat out. "I know it's none of my business, but is Dawn, or has Dawn ever been, your girlfriend?"

"No. I have to admit that I sometimes think she'd like to be, though."

"You 'sometimes think'? Look, everybody knows that she's chasing you like a ferret chases a rabbit down a hole."

"Well, this is one rabbit she won't be able to sink her teeth into."

"Are you sure? A powerful personality could be just what a fluffy little bunny like you needs to keep him in order," I say, aware that I'm sounding like a C-rated straight-to-video film script, but caring nothing for it.

"There's another powerful personality around here that this little bunny likes better," says Bill, joining in the general schmaltz.

"And who might that be?" I enquire coyly.

"Come inside and I'll tell you."

We have reached Bill's front garden. His is a sweet little cottage with a green door and windows covered with various stained glass thingies that catch the light in a rather attractive way. We're surrounded by lavender, rosemary and wild geraniums and the moon is full overhead – a light breeze stirs the sweet smells from the plants.

187

After a tiny hesitation he turns to face me with downturned eyes and gently takes my hands. Then he looks up and I nearly faint. He's close enough to smell, and what he smells of is lemon verbena and woodsmoke. He's so tall... and his eyes are so melting... those little flecks in them drive me crazy... and he smiles at me... and my lips part and...

Just at this critical moment, there's a piercing shriek as something enormous thunders down the path and hurls itself at the pair of us. Bill is thrown back against the door and I am knocked straight into a lavender hedge with somebody attempting to throttle me. Once more my whole life flashes before my eyes – or it would do if my eyes weren't popping out of my head – and I struggle to heave the killer off my body with no success until Bill leaps forward to my aid. In the process he falls, and all three of us are rolling around in the tiny garden. I leap onto the person's back, grab a handful of hair and shove downwards as hard as I can into a clump of something green and spiky. There are muffled screams, and with an almighty effort, the attacker throws me off his back and snatches up a heavy flower pot. I am sprawling in the path and death by garden earthenware is clearly about to be delivered, when the moon – God bless it - comes out from behind a cloud, and we are all able to see each other's shocked faces. There's a frozen silence, jam-packed with horror and amazement.

Well, it's just the three of us. Me, Bill... and Dawn.

"Dawn! What the hell is going on!" Bill enquires, quite nicely, considering the circumstances. Meanwhile, I'm rubbing my throat and gasping for breath.

Dawn puts down the pot and briskly brushes the debris from her velvet top. "Rebecca! Well, really. What are you doing here, of all people?"

"I could ask you the same thing," I choke, enraged beyond bearing by her barefaced cheek.

She looks the picture of innocence. "Me? Oh, I thought Bill was being mugged. I saw him struggling on his doorstep, and dashed to the rescue. Bill, darling, I think I'm injured. I might have broken my wrist. And I'm covered in cuts and bruises."

"You're not the only one," I rage. "For fuck's sake, Dawn, you nearly fucking killed me! You're a psycho!"

"Well obviously, Rebecca, if I'd known it was you, I wouldn't have attacked. I thought I was saving Bill's life and I think he should be jolly grateful."

"Oh, I am, Dawn. Thank you very much," he says.

"Bill! What are you doing? Thanking Dawn for nearly murdering me?"

"Well, it does seem to have been an honest mistake."

"Honest mistake, my arse. Ask her what the hell she's doing, creeping around your house in the middle of the night looking for muggers."

"Yes, that's a point. Dawn, what *are* you doing here? We thought you'd gone home long ago."

Dawn stands up and continues brushing herself down. After a pregnant pause she mutters: "I left something when I was here earlier."

Bill, now also on his feet, looks concerned. "What?" He finds his key, throws open the door and stands by ready to retrieve whatever it is Dawn's pretending to have lost. I'm quite sure she'd love to say 'my knickers' just so I'll think she's having a mad, passionate affair with him and it's quite possible that if Bill were not right there she'd give it a try, but in the end she says sourly: "My fleece."

I can hardly keep a straight face, but for the second time that night I point out that the garment in question is firmly tied around her waist.

"Oh! Silly me. I didn't see it there. Well, goodbye Rebecca. I'm sure you're longing to get back home after all this excitement. Any chance of a cup of fennel tea, Bill? Perhaps with a spot of honey? I'm feeling very weak

189

after my ordeal. One does after an adrenaline rush, doesn't one? I'm sure mother tigers in the jungle have just the same sensation after they've rescued one of their adorable little cubs from a boa constrictor. Sorry, Rebecca. No offence. Come on, Bill. You look shattered. Let's have a nice hot drink and a natter."

"Oh! Well, er, okay. Becky, you come in too. Do!"

"Actually, I won't. Fennel tea's not my thing, even with honey."

"I've got coffee."

"No, really. You'll be fine now you've got Dawn to protect you from all those muggers out there terrorising the good folk of Much Jenner. It's a pity she didn't walk you home in the first place – she's got the weight behind her when it comes to all-in wrestling. In fact, Dawn, I'm not sure you shouldn't take it up as a career. Oh – one last thing. He wasn't struggling."

CHAPTER NINE

I indulge in a lie-in the following day – much deserved in my opinion – and am mildly surprised on waking to discover that this has been permitted. Usually, Pumpkin 'escapes' up to my room (a handy euphemism for Mike shoving him up the stairs to 'accidentally' wake me up). My first thought is of Bill. Then Dawn springs into my mind, and the way Bill kow-tows to her at every opportunity, and I gnash my teeth and screw myself up into a little ball. Then I remember that Honeybee is pregnant and find myself springing out of bed like a gopher emerging out onto the prairie on a sunny day. There is much to do.

The air is chilly, so I don an amazing garment of Amanda's. I don't know what you'd call it, but this is an item of clothing, which, I think, thin celebrities would avoid like butter. But it's wonderfully warm if you're living in a dump like Cobweb Cottage. It is an all-in-one fleece zipper suit with no waistline, gathered at the wrists and ankles. It makes me look like Tinky Winky after a heavy night.

I wend my way down into the kitchen and, because it is a sunny day, head straight out into the garden to think about what a wuss Bill is and – let's face it – have a fag.

191

No sooner do I light the match than Honeybee is in my midst with that familiar scowl back on her face.

"Put that out!"

"What?"

"That cigarette!"

"I haven't lit it yet."

"Well, don't."

"Why not?"

"You can't smoke around me and the baby."

"Look Honeybee, you were in the house until a nanosecond ago, and I came out here to smoke in peace. For God's sake. You're a teenager. You're the one meant to be smoking, not me. Here, treat yourself."

"Becky, just quit smoking," she commands, pushing away the packet with an outraged hand. "Yeah!" comes another voice from the bushes, and Rob materialises. "Give up smoking! It's so uncool to smoke. And you'll die of lung cancer."

I defiantly light my cigarette to howls of protest.

"Mr Mayer hates smoking," says Rob in his innocent way. "He says it makes girls mouths taste like ashtrays when he kisses them."

"What a BIG FAT LIE!"

"Well, okay, he didn't say that, but he definitely said he hates smoking and then Daniel Zuckermann from my class said the stuff about the kissing, I heard him."

"Oh well, if Daniel Zuckermann says so, it must be so. And I mustn't minimise my chances of getting off with Daniel Zuckermann." I stub out the cigarette with a casual, "perhaps it is time I quit. Especially with the baby coming, eh Honeybee?"

There is a theatrical gasp from Rob, then the cracking of twigs as he flees into the house.

"Whoops! Have you told him yet?" I ask Honeybee.

"Of course I haven't. Fourteen-year-old boys are zombies. He'd probably ask where the gooseberry bush is and can he come too to pick the baby up."

"Oh well. Time enough to educate him in the facts of life. I might buy a manual of some kind. He'll survive for now."

We hitch ourselves up onto the wall at the end of the garden and Honeybee, sounding bored, endeavours to ascertain whether I had a nice time.

"When?"

"Last night. When you went out for a walk with Mr Mayer."

"Oh, that. Well, it was okay."

"What happened?"

"We were just about to snog like fourteen-year-olds on Spanish Fly when Dawn sprang out from nowhere, nearly strangled me, threatened me with a flowerpot then went in for a cup of fennel tea leaving me out in the cold crying my eyes out."

"Oh come on, Becky, what really happened?"

"He wanted to discuss Rob's progress at school so we walked back to his house while we had a chat and then I came home."

"That sounds boring."

"It was."

"Better luck next time."

"Thanks."

"Do you think I should have an epidural?"

"I'm sorry?"

"Come on, Bex! The baby. I'd like to have an epidural."

"It's a bit early for those kind of decisions, isn't it?"

"Not really. It's due in eight weeks, remember."

"Oh dear. I suppose you're right. But we haven't even told Mike, yet. He's bound to have opinions, birth being his life's work and all that."

"That's just it, Becky," Honeybee says earnestly. "I don't want Dad taking over the whole thing. He'll drive me crazy. He'll want to give me antenatal classes himself and everything. Actually, Becky, I was wondering if you'd like to be my birth partner?"

"You've had a birth partner. That's why you're up the duff."

"Don't be daft. A birth partner is somebody who's there when you're actually giving birth, not the person who impregnates you."

"Me? Be there at the birth? You must be joking."

"No, really."

"Why me?"

"You're so capable. You'd know just what to do. And I really feel you'd be supportive."

"Well, that's almost the nicest thing anyone's ever said to me. I'll think about it. But won't your Mum be upset? Shouldn't you ask her?"

"Oh, I'm going to ask her, too. I'd like two birthing partners, one for yin and one for yang. Mum'll be really good at finding the right crystals and things like that. She's good at massage, too."

I contemplate the idea of myself and Midge, hand in hand over Honeybee's bump, poised to massage and aromatherapise and all the other things one does when a baby's about to come out and to be honest, I barely see it happening. But on the other hand... I've got quite fond of the girl recently. She's grown on me.

"I'll think about it. Come on, it's freezing."

Mike is hovering around the back door, evidently waiting for us to come in. For some reason, he is very much on his best behaviour – indeed, almost loving. As soon as I appear, he dumps Pumpkin into Honeybee's arms and hustles the pair of them out of the room. Then puts his arm around me despite my efforts to shake him off. Before I know it, I'm projected onto a beanbag. The way

194

he spills mint tea all over my trousers then tries to mop it up with a dirty dishcloth is really quite touching. Any idiot can see that Mike is building up to something and there's nothing to do but to sit quietly waiting for whatever it is to happen. When I am plentifully equipped with fresh mint tea and a rice cake ("to keep my strength up"), he draws his own beanbag closer and breathes these surprising words: "Alone at last." I lean away, and look at him sideways over my teacup.

"We so seldom get these cosy moments," he continues, edging still closer. I turn a shoulder to him and cross my legs.

"I hope you know that I'll always love you Becky, and support you in everything you do, and every decision you make. You're very much a part of this family now, Becky, and very involved in all our rites of passage."

"Well, thanks."

"So obviously, while I am shocked about the baby..."

"How do you know! We were going to break it to you later!"

"Rob told me just now. It's sad that I had to find out from him, but..."

"Well, perhaps it's better. She would have found it hard to tell you herself. There are issues at stake here."

There is a pause, then Mike draws a deep breath. "I can understand that you are trying to take the objective view on this, Becky. I understand that the 'I' and the 'she' are symbiotic... separate, yet part of the same body..."

"That sounds interesting."

"I have so much support in my heart."

"That's great."

"And all the love in the world."

"Good man."

"I'm willing to try again. That's if there's a loving heart ready to welcome me."

"I'm sure she'll do her best to be loving right back. Every good girl loves her daddy, after all."

Mike looks very surprised. There is another pause. Then he asks rather cautiously, "I've never asked about your father, Becky, and you've never mentioned him. Is he a good bloke? Did you have a good relationship?"

"He's all right. Or was, when he was around. Very different from you, of course."

"Different from me! And dead! An absent father, then. In fact, do you ever find yourself looking for a sort of father figure?"

"Actually, he's not dead, he's in Australia and mind your own business anyway."

"Right. Got it. Anyway, like I was saying. Yeah. Hey! How about going on holiday?"

"You what?"

"I thought we could take a mini-break together."

"Ski-ing?" I say hopefully, mentally calculating whether despite my love for the divine Bill I could bring myself to sleep with this man just once more in return for a week on the slopes.

"Well, I was thinking more of renting a country cottage in the middle of nowhere."

"Excuse me for pointing out something so obvious, but look around you, you twat," I snap, rejecting all ideas of sexual favours. "We already live in one."

"Yes, but somewhere really romantic. The latest thing for people in our position is knitting breaks."

"Now you really are taking the piss."

"Not so, Becky. It's a wonderful experience. Each person takes wool and a pattern, very carefully chosen of course, the colours and textures have to have emotional warmth and seasonal resonance, and we knit by a roaring fire and when we feel a bit exhausted, we just have a cup of cocoa and wait until our energy's up again."

"And then we knit on together?"

"That's right! Whaddya think?"

"I think you should shove your knitting needles up your nostrils and attempt to jump start your brain which appears to have evacuated the premises."

"Becky! You're so harsh! Tell you what. Shall we light a few scented candles? Recapture the mood?"

"What mood?"

"The mood. You know. The mood we were in."

"I'm certainly in a mood and it's getting worse."

"But Becky, this isn't very romantic."

"Romantic? Why should it be?"

"Well, it would have to be a bit romantic, wouldn't it, if we were going to get back together?"

"Get back together? We never were 'together'. One night doesn't make 'together', then or now. What on earth are you talking about? Another shag? I'd rather eat worms. Unless it was in Switzerland, in which case I'd close my eyes and think of ski-ing instructors."

"But what about the baby? The baby we'll knit for on our mini-break? Doesn't every child deserve two parents?"

"There'll be no mini-break, Mike, and I'd also like to point out that every delivered child thus far in human history has had two parents if you write off successful cloning as an urban myth. But let's analyse what you mean by 'the baby'. What baby?"

"Becky love, you don't have to pretend anymore. Rob says you're pregnant. You were talking about it in the garden with Honeybee, confiding in her. He came rushing in to tell me in his joy. I know it must be mine. Mine! I'm going to be a father again. And I'm going to support you, Becky, every step of the way. Even if we *don't* get back together. I'll even be your doula for free."

"Most generous. Or it would be. Mike, I am not – and possibly never will be – a mother. There is a baby, certainly, but please get off my beanbag and prepare for a shock. It's Honeybee's. She's eight months pregnant.

Sorry I can't manage to break it more gently than that but I had a rough evening last night and I need coffee, not something that should be served on new potatoes."

It is at this point that Pumpkin informs me that he has a stinky nappy and leaving Mike in a quivering heap on his beanbag, I lever myself up with a heavy heart and escort him to the outhouse for a general cleaning session, after which I settle him at the kitchen table with a few nuts and bang the kettle on the stove. As I dig around for bowls and spoons, collect together the various foodstuffs necessary for a healthy breakfast and tread my slipper socks into horrid things, I can't stop myself from thinking about Bill and Dawn. On the plus side, I almost kissed Bill, and he almost kissed me, and never in my life has a non-kiss seemed so sweet. On the negative side, I was busted on my potential boyfriend's very threshold by a one-woman hit squad determined to wage war on my romance. Also on the negative side, Bill didn't chuck her out on her ear with a few well-chosen expletives. But the way he looked into my eyes... yessirree, I'm crazy about him. I am, I am, I am...

I so am, in fact, that for virtually the first time in my life, I feel the need for a breath of fresh air. I want solitude. I want to walk through the fields dreaming of a future in which Bill moves up to London and gets a job, possibly as a model - men in their thirties are in demand at the moment I heard recently. And I'll get him some fabulous clothes and an expensive watch and really, I'll change him out of all recognition. I must be alone. Decisively I throw the wooden spoon into the porridge and yell for Mike to take over on feeding Pumpkin. The shocked father simply issues hollow groans from the sitting room so I give up on him and call Robbo who, as always, is more biddable, although he does plead with me to take Pepys too. In a weak moment, I agree, race upstairs, chuck on some jeans and a sweater, pop on Honeybee's walking boots, grab the dog lead, attach Pepys, and exit slamming the door behind me. As I march off, the attic window opens and Midge's head appears.

"Do you have to shake the whole house to bits?" she enquires peevishly. "You've upset my ear candles."

I ignore this remark, wouldn't you? And sally forth.

It's rather pleasant having a dog to go on a walk with. Without a dog, I would feel weird. I would think that people would be looking at me and thinking, 'why is that woman on a walk? She has no dog'. And that would be depressing. But with a hound at one's heel, one can walk anywhere with perfect confidence. I discovered early on in our acquaintance that Pepys is a veritable catalyst for social communication. As always, it takes me aeons to traverse the high street, with pensioners and children popping up in droves to pet him. Pepys, naturally, is not shy and has no reservations. "If thou wilt scratch my ear," he pants to all comers, tongue pinkly trailing, "I will love thee for ever and will eternally be thy friend. And if thou hast a biscuit, I will abandon the wanton woman by my side and flee to thy abode."

On this particular sunny day, a rather attractive man stops to ask his breed. Of course, this is a chat-up line. Now I know why so many female film stars have doggies tucked under their arms. Not only is it always a topic of conversation when the going gets tough, it gives Leonardo Di Caprio an excuse to cross the room and make conversation.

Obviously my heart is spoken for, but for the sake of good manners – and he is quite a fox – I answer haughtily: "A Sliding Wisehound."

"Really!"

"Yes. That's right. A Sliding Wisehound. Very rare breed."

"Yes, it must be. I've never heard of it. Is it registered with the Kennel Club?"

"Indubitably."

"That's funny."

"Why?"

"I'm a member of the Kennel Club – I breed Rottweilers and miniature poodles – and I've never heard even remotely of a Sliding Wisehound. I would have assumed that he's a mongrel, actually, but I just wanted to make conversation."

"He is certainly no mongrel if you *don't* mind," I say flirtatiously. "And why did you want to make conversation?"

"Because you're the prettiest girl I've seen today in Much Jenner."

"That's saying almost nothing at all."

"Are you walking across the meadow?" he says, as we turn into the recreation ground and bear right to avoid the 12-year-old footballers.

"What's it to you?" I ask, bending to slip Pepy's lead off.

"Oh I just wondered if you were walking that way, because if so, I could walk with you?"

Just as I'm hesitating – for a bloke in the hand is worth a Bill in Dawn's bush, although not otherwise – when the boys' football suddenly shoots past my head, making me duck. Just as I'm about to blast them with my rage, I realise that Pepys is bolting after the football straight – please God no – onto the road. There's an appalling screech of brakes, a sickening thud as a red car hits a white van, and silence. Pepys is nowhere to be seen. That'll teach me.

Without thinking, I race up to the road in frantic search of the dog. All my senses seem heightened – I am instantly aware that nobody is hurt, that the drivers of both vehicles have got out unharmed, that the ball has been retrieved by a passer by, and that the little group of people on their knees are not praying but are gathered around Pepys. I reach the group, and stare. He's still breathing, in tiny shallow pants, and his eyes are closed.

200

"Oh God," I breathe. "Look, it's my dog. What... what..."

"I'll wrap him up in my coat," says the man who was chatting me up half a century ago. We'll have to move him off the road. Where's the nearest vet?"

"I don't know," I say. Somehow I can't think of anything to do. I'm literally frozen to the spot. One of the onlookers says that there is a vet very nearby, just down the road in fact, well within walking distance, and the man, clasping Pepys, sets out. I trot at his heels anxiously, and a small crowd follows, murmuring amongst themselves.

It turns out that the vet, bless him or rather her, it's a lady, is on the premises and when she understands the nature of our visit, boots a springer spaniel out of her surgery so fast he's a blur.

"Who's dog is it?" she asks, looking around at the sea of faces.

"Mine!" I blurt, forcing myself to the front. "He's called Pepys and I think you should just put him down straightaway."

"Well, let's see what's wrong with him first, shall we?" she says kindly, and carefully takes Pepys from the Kennel Club bloke, who looks at me and says, "Sorry. I was taking up too much of your attention."

"What? Oh, whatever. It doesn't matter," I say distractedly. "Look, I'd better go in with him. Goodbye." And I follow the vet into her surgery. She gently runs her hands over Pepy's body while he whimpers. "What I'm looking for are long bone fractures, the femur, humerus, radius, ulna, a pelvic fracture or dislocated hip, spinal or chest injuries, a ruptured diaphragm, maybe," she explains brightly.

"Oh God," I say.

Then she whips out a syringe and starts filling it from an ampule.

"Goodbye, Pepys," I sob.

"No, no," she says. "There's no question of putting him to sleep. This is simply a painkiller."

A huge sob suddenly bursts out from a depth I never knew I had. "Oh, fuck! Sorry! good!" I choke. "Poor old Pepys! Thank God you're okay!"

"The bad news is, he's probably got a lot of damage in that back right leg. I'll do full x-rays to make sure, but I'm fairly sure the leg's the only serious problem. Are you insured?"

"I haven't got a clue. I wouldn't have thought so. Why? Will it cost a lot?"

"Well, I'll have to work it all out, but somewhere in the region of a thousand pounds I'm afraid."

My tears magically evaporate, leaving trails of mascara in their wake. "You're kidding! This is a dog's leg here, you know, not David Beckham's right kneecap."

"Sorry. It's what things cost. You're much better off getting insurance. We have some leaflets out in the waiting room. With any luck there'll never be a next time, but you never know, it could save you a lot of money in the future. Well! I'd better get this little chap x-rayed. And you'd better get off home and have a nice cup of tea. Don't worry about leaving him here alone," she reassures me. "He's not in any pain. He'll be fine."

"Oh. Okay. I'll go then. Bye Pepys." I stroke Pepys's head, and stagger out of the surgery. I don't know what I expected to see in the waiting room, nothing more than a collection of leaflets about insurance I suppose, but I'm stunned by a sea of anxious faces.

"Is he going to be all right, then?" asks one young woman, her pleasant features contorted with sympathy.

"How's the little fella doing?" blurts out a middle-aged man. The Kennel Club bloke is leaning against the wall at the left, bracing himself for the worst, I can see. This is amazing. I feel like some lowly sapper telling the war cabinet that the commander in chief has survived a bomb.

"He's going to be fine," I announce, with a fresh flood of tears. "If we can pay for it!"

"What?" shouts everybody. "Haven't you got insurance?"

"I'll have to check," I say. "But I shouldn't think so for a minute. And it's going to cost a thousand pounds. I don't know how we'll manage. It's my fault, I should have taken better care of him. But I've only got a couple of hundred quid saved. I mean, that's nothing! And his real owners aren't exactly flush. I live with them, you see," I explain, sinking onto a red leatherette chair. "I'm the au-pair. But I'm really, really fond of that dog. He's called Pepys."

"Now, now, now," soothes a lady pensioner, patting my shoulder. "Don't you get upset. There's plenty around who'll help out I'll be bound."

"That's right," says the young woman. "Let's have a whip round!" Before I can protest, coins and notes are being thrust into my hands. I can't believe it. How can complete strangers be prepared to donate their hard earned cash to somebody else's uninsured dog?

I'm sitting there, stunned, when the door opens again, and the most familiar, beloved eyes in the world meet mine.

"Oh, Bill!" I cry, and fling myself into his arms. "How do you know what happened? I can't believe you're here. You came to support me! You are a wonderful, beautiful human being."

"What's up?" he says wonderingly, supporting me with one arm and a basket with the other. "I've bought my bantam cock in. He's got a floppy comb."

"Oh!" I say, extracting myself from his embrace. Bill dumps the basket and firmly gathers me in once more. "Well, it's Pepys. He's had a horrible accident and all sorts of hideous, expensive things have to be done to him and if it wasn't for these kind, amazing people here..." I

203

fling my arm out in an all-encompassing gesture "I wouldn't be able to begin to pay for it. Because the accident was all my fault."

"How did it happen?" asks Bill, his voice strained with concern. I catch the eye of the Kennel Club man and turn quickly away.

"Well, I let him off the lead and I was a bit distracted by some kind of bug or gnat or something, and he chased a football, and that was it really."

Kennel Club Man sidles out of the door I am mightily relieved to see. How could I ever have dreamed of letting any other man chat me up? Bill is the only man for me, and when I even glanced elsewhere, Fate taught me a lesson. I look up into his warm eyes and it seems to me that the love shining out of them is the whole world. It's like, I wish I could press pause. Or better still, rewind and play in slow motion. Except that nothing could be better than this. Nothing.

"Come on, I'll take you home," he says gently.

"What about the chicken?"

"He'll live. Let's go."

I thank all my new friends and walk outside with Bill, where, on the pavement, I am somewhat aghast to see a bicycle with a large basket reclining. Bill pops the chicken's basket into the bigger basket – making chicken in a basket as I am swift to point out – and urges me to sit on the cross bar.

"You must be bloody joking," I say.

"Of course not. It'll be fine, if you're up to it after the shock. Come on!"

And so, to my astonishment, I find myself shooting back to Cobweb Cottage at what seems ridiculously high speed on a bike that has seen better days with the most wonderful man in the world pedalling for England. I scream all the way, I have to admit, which certainly dispels some of the romance.

204

When we get home, I check that Honeybee's still upstairs which, thank the lord, she is. I wouldn't want her to give birth on the spot when she hears the dread news. So Bill, although unaware of why he has to whisper – at least, men can't whisper but he tries - breaks the news in a wheezy rumble while I collapse on a beanbag and muffle my sobs with a clean dish cloth. Mike and Robbo, the only family members downstairs, are so shocked to see me emotional, and so relieved to hear Bill's first statement, which is that Pepys is going to be okay, that the actual accident takes rather a back seat. As I thought, Pepys is not, and never has been insured, but I shove the whip-round into Mike's hands, explaining how kind everybody present had been.

"Well, it's only what you expect round here," he says, pocketing the dosh. "It's a great bunch of people. Wow. But anyway, Bex, these things happen. I'd never expect you to pay. Much, anyway."

"You wouldn't? But it was my fault!"

"Whatever. You didn't mean it. Anybody can get distracted."

"Ah... yes. Well, I've no intention of ever being distracted again, in sickness or in health," I say emphatically. Then I smile at Bill, who grins back, waves and slips out. I could kiss the very door handle he touches.

But the mood doesn't last. The moment Bill's footsteps are heard fading down the pathway, there's a change of atmosphere.

"Well, Rebecca," says Mike grimly. "Obviously I'm still reeling from the shock of hearing about poor old Pepys, and I must get down to the vet's myself in a minute to see what's happening. Yeah. Wow. But first we all need to have a bit of a chat about the news you broke to me so tactfully before you took your walk of doom."

"I thought you agreed it could happen to anybody!"

"I did. In front of Bill. But I'll think twice about you taking Pepys off the lead again. I bet you were chatting somebody up."

"The idea!"

"Okay, okay. Now. Honeybee. We've got to decide what to do about this little problem."

"I'm glad you see it as a little one."

"I was speaking metaphorically."

"I bet you don't know what the fuck that means."

"How can you go on like this, when Pepys is in hospital and Honeybee's about to pop?" yells A Robin's Nest. We both stare at him, open mouthed. At least, I do. You can't really tell with Mike, because of his beard.

"Is this a family conference?" Rob adds, thumping himself down and aggressively scratching a spot. "Because if so, I should be in it. So should Mum. And Honeybee. It's her body we're talking about. She told me everything just now. Sorry for getting it wrong earlier, Dad."

"Oh, he was only too pleased," I say dryly.

"What did you say, Dad? Did you offer to marry her?"

"When the pair of you have quite finished having a joke at my expense, we'll start discussing this issue," says Mike in a temper.

"Now. First things first," I say. "Honeybee is pregnant, and we all know what that means."

"Yes! I'm going to be an uncle!" pipes up Rob.

"Quiet, Robbo. It's much more serious than that."

"You're not kidding, Bex," groans Mike. "I'm going to be a grandfather. I'm too young. I mean, seriously too young. I can't hack the responsibility."

"Oh for goodness sake. You lot are only thinking about yourselves. I'm going to be a step-aupair-gran but you don't hear me complaining. No, I am only thinking of one thing. And that's Honeybee. How is she going to cope with school during the pregnancy? Where is she going to have this baby? And how do we go about having it adopted?"

There is a horrified silence. Mike and Rob both stare at me as if I have suggested sex with Rottweilers. Then there is a roar of protest.

"Adopted? My nephew? My granddaughter? Are you heartless? What kind of woman are you? What do you think Honeybee is? A cow? You are so uncool. You cruel person. No way!" they rage.

I raise an admonitory hand. "Hold it right there. I'm only suggesting the unthinkable simply because it makes sense for Honeybee. She's only seventeen. She is a bright girl with a real future ahead for her if she doesn't tie herself down with a baby and all that that entails. She'll find looking after a child hard work at any stage of her life, let alone now. She's only had about five periods in her life for God's sake. Honestly. It makes sense. And what about all the desperate couples out there who are dying to have a baby?"

"And how about me?" comes a voice from the doorway. It's Honeybee, screwing in her nose-ring at the door. Both Mike and Robbo leap to their feet and wrestle her to a chair. She gives the nose a final twist.

"I know it's mad to be pregnant, I know I shouldn't be keeping this baby. But I've just made up my mind – I'm going to bring it up myself."

There's a short silence, then we all start slurping our decaffeinated beverages and muttering "good for you".

"And now," says Honeybee in a cheerful voice, "if nobody's got anything better to do, I'm going to pop my tongue stud in and do some antenatal exercises while you lot get busy and clean up this house. It's just not fit to bring a baby home to."

"But Honeybee," I venture. "There is just one thing. Bringing up a baby by yourself isn't going to be easy.

207

Seriously. Mike works, I won't be around for ever and frankly, you're still at school. How will you cope?"

"Well," says Honeybee happily, "this morning, I had a family conference with Mum by ourselves. Mum knows she has had her problems in the past. But Pumpkin is only three. My baby can be his brother or sister – and Mum's prepared to step in and take care of them both."

"Forgive me for saying so, Honeybee, but Midge doesn't look after Pumpkin now. Is she offering to look after your baby as well? Because if she is, examine this offer carefully. It may not be copper-bottomed."

"Like I said, Becky, Mum has had problems. But knowing that I am expecting a baby has given her strength. She says she is preparing to take control of her life again. I know it sounds unlikely. But she is going to come down and look after Pumpkin again, *and* my baby, while I finish school."

"Honeybee! You mustn't take this literally. Midge couldn't look after a hamster, let alone Pumpkin and a newborn baby. Robbo! Back me up on this."

A Robin's Nest looked at me sadly. "Amanda was really nice. And you're... quite nice..."

"Steady on."

"But Amanda used to go on about us needing a stable influence in our lives. Well, we don't want a stable influence. We just want our mum."

"And do you think you're going to get your mum back, just because Honeybee's having a baby? Look. She'll care for you all for about five minutes then sling her hook back to la la land. She's nuts!"

"Thank you for that, Rebecca."

We all turn around to see Midge posed in the doorway clad (it doesn't seem possible but I saw it with my own eyes) in a tie-dyed caftan. One be-ringed hand is draped on the doorframe, the other is pressed histrionically to her heart. She is simultaneously managing to exude mother-love, and fix me with a very hard stare.

"When Honeybee came up to me this morning, I felt it. I felt it..." - with a pressing of the hand on heart - "I felt it *here*. My child, my beautiful daughter, to become a mother. And coming to me. Her mother. How could I let her down? Could I remain in a meditative state when the time has come for action? Of course I could not. Some may say, and by that I mean Rebecca, that I cannot stay the course. Some may even say that I will throw in the towel, as it is so picturesquely phrased, after a mere few weeks. But I can tell you, that I will not! I will be a mother for Honeybee's little angel. And for my own little angel. Pumpkin, come to mummy."

Pumpkin, rather sardonically continues to chew nuts and so Midge has to leave her vantage point by the door and swoops down on him with kisses and bangly hugs. Honeybee is watching all this with tears in her eyes, and even Robbo is smiling weakly. Mike looks like he has died and gone to heaven.

"Midge," I begin. She bends her gaze upon me, clasping Pumpkin a little more closely as if I am about to kidnap him and dash off to South America.

"Midge. I'm really glad that you have come down to support Honeybee. No, really! I am. Honeybee needs all the support she can get. But I think we've all got to be realistic here. Honeybee should finish school..."

"And finish school you shall, my darling, with mummy in charge of the wee ones."

"Like I said, Midge, Honeybee should finish school and the only way she can do that, as you appear to be pointing out, is if somebody is looking after her baby. And there's Pumpkin to look after as well. I've been in charge of Pumpkin for a while now, and it's not easy. It's exhausting! And there's everything else as well. Running the house, making sure Honeybee and Robbo are kitted

209

up for school, driving everybody everywhere, looking out for Pepys, making sure that Mike doesn't destroy the house in a random fit of DIY..."

"Hey! My DIY is fantastic! This house wouldn't be the way it is today without it, I'm telling you."

"You're doing a great job. I'm just trying to point out that running this family is a lot of hard work. Midge, you can't just swan in and encourage Honeybee to keep this baby. Somebody will have to look after it and it is very unlikely that you'll be able to cope."

"I resent that statement," says Midge in low and thrilling tones. "You are taking too much upon yourself, Rebecca. Really, who are you? Simply an au pair. And one who has slept with her employer I believe, thus ousting the children's stepmother."

"Now, hang on, Midge. The children's stepmother?"

"Amanda was the children's putative stepmother, as you know very well, Rebecca. And you destroyed the relationship between her and my husband."

"Oh, so Mike's your husband now, is he?"

"When was he not?"

"When you were planning for your children to have a stepmother when they had a mother of their own, thanks, that's when."

"I am not only a mother. I am a free and creative spirit, who has needed to wander."

"Up to the attic?"

"I wander in spirit, Rebecca, something you would not understand."

"Also, I am not *just* an au-pair."

"You are paid fifty pounds a week to look after this family. That makes you into a menial little au-pair, as far as I am concerned."

"It's true that Mike and I have a private financial agreement..."

"You are an AU-PAIR!" screeches Midge, suddenly losing her cool. "And you're sacked!"

"You can't sack me! You're not my employer. Mike?"

Mike is whey-faced and refuses to speak. The teens are hunched over their mugs and Pumpkin looks bewildered from one face to another. This is dreadful. I am simply not going to be sacked by Midge at my own table. Not that it's my own. Perhaps this has got a little convoluted.

I mean to say, "Midge. Let's calm down. The main thing is, Honeybee is having this baby. And we need to decide what is to be done. I suggest that you have a stab at looking after Pumpkin for a few days while I continue running the house. That'll get you back into the swing of things, and we can all let this news of Honeybee's sink in a bit before taking any big decisions. How about it?"

But I do say: "FINE! FUCK OFF THE LOT OF YOU! AND BY THE WAY MIDGE, PEPYS IS ON HIS DEATHBED! AND SERVES YOU RIGHT!"

Then, with Midge in hysterics, I storm off upstairs to pack my bin bags.

211

CHAPTER TEN

It's fine. It's great. I can't wait to be out of this dump. I maniacally pile all my – I mean Amanda's – clothes onto the bed. Can't be bothered to fold them. Just cram them into the bin bag. Here's the orange poncho. I'll leave that behind. No I can't. It holds too many memories. What's happening? I throw the poncho out of the window.

I don't know where I'm going, that's the first thing. And I don't know what I'm going to do. I should get some kind of a job. I should stay with a friend. Which reminds me, I have been in this position before – and I didn't have a friend to stay with. That's why I'm here. Mike was the only person I knew who would take me in. Things have changed since then. I could stay with several people. Annette, for example. If I could cope with a raw, vegan diet. More likely Irene. She's a laugh. Then there are Anna and Paula and Suzanna and Kathryn and Felicity and Emma and Anne-Marie and Fiona - to my surprise, I really can think of several people who would gladly unleash their futon rolls for little old me.

And of course, there's Bill... But better not think about that. It might be tempting fate. And no matter how often I ride on his bicycle, now the magic moment has passed, I can't help remembering that he never has told Dawn to go and sink her fangs into another man's neck.

I pick up my bin bags. A final glance around the room establishes that I have taken rather less than I came with, but all that I want or can manage. I descend the stairs and throw open the sitting room door. They are all sitting around like ghosts at the banquet with Midge as the evil queen, whitefaced and tightlipped, at the head of the table (actually, on the biggest beanbag).

"Goodbye," I say dramatically. "I will see you around."

"Not if I see you first," rasps Midge. "You dog-killer."

"Well, at least I'm not a dog, Midge. And now I'm off. Don't ask me where I'm going because I don't want to see any of you ever again."

And I stride out into Much Jenner, scooping up the poncho from the front garden as I go. You never know, it may well come in useful. Waste not, want not. I am getting a bit more into recycling than I want to be, but never mind. A quick visit to the telephone box establishes that Irene is happy to have me as her guest, and I am on my way to a better – a calmer – a less healthy lifestyle.

Irene is determined to cheer me up. The moment I walk through the door she thrusts a bloody mary into my hands and plies me with cigarettes. Ushering me to the sofa (goodbye beanbags!) her face is a picture of concern. Naturally, I can't help milking the moment for all the drama it's worth, and I clasp my drink in a shaky hand and look as pale and traumatised as possible while I tell her about the last twenty-four hours.

"So what happened? What's up? You sounded so upset on the phone. Are you okay?"

"Things of moment have occurred, Irene. Let me take a moment." I slurp my bloody mary and wordlessly she refills my glass. "Go on, have a fag. It'll calm you down."

"Actually, I've given up smoking."

"God! It must be bad. Since when?"

213

"Last night."

"Oh for God's sake. Have one."

"No, really. I'm purging."

Irene, who is supposed to smoke only at parties anyway, stuffs the cigs back into her bag and sits on the floor in front of me, gazing earnestly up at my drawn features. I finish the bloody mary. She leans over for the jug and refills my glass.

"So, go on! Tell me everything!"

"It's a long story."

"It can't be too long for me."

"Well, last night, the first thing is that Pepys got run over today. God, it seems like a million years ago. He's going to be okay but..."

"I know all about it," she interrupts.

"How?"

"The grapevine. They've already got a fund started at the Dog and Bucket, and Vera's going to put a jar up at her place. And I think that there's going to be some sort of event at the school as well. Suzanna's son is a brilliant drummer and I think he's going to do a marathon drum in the gym with everybody sponsoring him..."

"Stop! You are joking?"

"Of course not! When it comes to a crisis like this, everybody wants to help."

"But it's not their dog!"

"So what?"

"Well... I'm at a loss for words."

"Okay, let's change the subject. What else has been happening?"

"Well, so much has happened since then, but Bill and Dawn came over for dinner last night. Now, that really *does* seem like something that happened in the age of the dinosaurs. Dawn put the comparison into my mind. Never in my life have I known such a raptor. Other," I add thoughtfully, "than myself."

214

"Dawn?"

"Bill brought her. By accident, *he says*."

"Right... go on."

"So it was a disaster. Dawn hated everything and was rude as I don't know what. The food was disgusting and Pepys – oh, poor Pepys - kept farting because he'd eaten a dead mole earlier in the day, poor little love. Anyway, after they left, Bill came back."

"Why?"

"He said he'd forgotten his fleece. But it was tied around his waist."

"So..."

"So he asked me to go for a walk and I did and we went back to his house and ended up almost snogging on the doorstep."

"Rebecca, you have always stated most categorically more than a million times that you *don't* fancy the sexiest man at Holt Park. So did you force yourself just to piss Dawn off?"

"Ha, ha, very funny. Okay. Gloves off. I do fancy him, as you very well know. And not only that, I think I'm madly in love with him. I mean, the other day, I actually read a leaflet about food colourants. And he turned up at the vet's with his chicken, and gave me a lift back to Cobweb Cottage on his bicycle. I mean, I actually rode on the man's cross bar. It was very erotic. Except in potholes."

"Then truly, my friend, this must be the real thing. But back to last night. What happened on the doorstep? Why was it only *almost* snogging?"

"It was all going very well, when suddenly I was hurled to the ground."

"Bill hurled you to the ground? He wanted to do it in the flower bed?"

"No, you idiot. *He* didn't throw me to the ground. Somebody else did. And when the fur had stopped flying it turned out to be Dawn. She thought I was mugging Bill, not almost snogging him. Or so she says."

This goes down big with Irene. The tears are pouring down her cheeks she's laughing so hard. "I can just see it! God! I can just see you! God!"

"Anyway, Bill got her off me and asked her what she was up to and she said she'd forgotten her fleece."

"She didn't."

"She did. And it was tied round her waist."

"So she was there to get into Bill's trousers?"

"Certainly. Anyway, he wouldn't tell her to go."

"He didn't?"

"No. And she went in and put the kettle on. And he asked me to come in too for a nice hot drink and I told him to shove it and went home."

"Quite right too. What a wimp."

"Yeah. Oh, and I've missed a bit. Honeybee's told me she's eight months pregnant."

"Now you *are* joking with me."

"No. No joke. Then while we were talking it over, Midge came downstairs and tried to make out that she'd look after Honeybee's baby and start taking responsibility in her household again."

"Well, that's nice."

"Yes, if you can believe her. So I said it was all crap, and she sacked me."

"She sacked you? I don't believe it. Midge needs all the help she can get."

"I'm just telling you the facts. She sacked, and I packed, and now I'm here. Can I stay for a while?"

"You can stay as long as you like, Becky."

"Thanks. And I'm going to have to find a job."

"Nice one."

"It's going to be a nightmare. I've got hardly any money. It's a bit complicated."

"Don't worry about that. My house is your house, and we'll soon find you a job. Everything's going to be okay."

After Irene's given me a nice big hug and I've had another few bloody marys, I feel mysteriously sleepy and have to have a little lie down. Then I unpack and we have something to eat and watch a video. Then the telephone rings. Irene answers, then hands it silently over to me.

"Hello?"

"Hello? Is that Becky?"

"This is Rebecca."

"This is William."

"Who?"

"Bill."

"Oh! Hello."

"Hello."

"How did you know I was here?"

"I called the house to ask after Pepys, and Rob told me you'd walked out after a bit of an argument with Midge. I'm glad you've got Irene to go to, but you could have come to me – I hope you know that. Anyway, are you all right?"

"Oh, just dandy. How are you?"

"A bit down actually."

"Why?"

"Well, it was lovely seeing you at the vet's."

"Yes, it was. Thank you for the ride home."

"You're welcome. And I feel like we made up after last night's disaster."

"Maybe we have."

"Then, when can I see you?"

"Are you asking me out on a *date*?"

"Well, yes. Yes I am."

"And who will be on this *date*?"

"You and me, of course. And Pepys if he's better."

217

"I'm not joking. Will Dawn be coming along to share the popcorn and rattle the ice around in a supersized cardboard cup?"

"Ah."

"Because you know what, Bill, most people consider that two people on a date is plenty. Unless they foster a split personality, they consider that three is a crowd."

"I know. I'm sorry."

"So, are you going to tell Dawn where to go? Preferably where the sun, stars and moon don't shine?"

"Well, it's a bit tricky, actually. She is a parent of a child I teach..."

"So you said. Does that mean you have to spend your entire life with her?"

"Look Becky, I'm different from you. I just don't have it in myself to be unkind. She's lonely since her husband left her. She looks on me as a friend."

"Wait a minute. Rewind. Did you say that you're different from me *because you are kind*? Thereby implying that I am *not* kind?"

"Oh come on. I didn't mean it like that."

"Well, what did you mean?"

"Okay. I'll be frank. You are different from me."

"Explain."

"Er... you drink. You smoke."

"Not any more."

"Really? Great! Okay, you don't smoke. But you drink. And you care about the material things in life. And you choose your friends because they're fun, not because they need friendship. And you have a pretty hedonistic way of looking at life."

"What do you mean by that?"

"Well, that life's for you to have a good time in. That life's just there so you can get what you want out of it. I'm not like that. I love the way you throw yourself into the world, but I'm more introspective. I don't care much

218

about money or fast cars or any of the things you've told me mean a lot to you. So I suppose that you wouldn't understand when I tell you that I have to be friendly with Dawn, because she needs a friend. But it shouldn't make any difference to me and you."

"Excuse me, it does make a big difference to me anyway, and I find what you have just said to be very insulting." My voice is trembling and I feel so angry and upset that I'm about to burst into tears. "If you want to know what I think, I think that it's you who's different from me. Frankly, you're pathetic. It's quite obvious to everyone who knows you that Dawn is after you hammer and tongs. But you just don't see it. You don't see that she's mean and manipulative and unscrupulous and that she's prepared to stop at nothing to get into your house and have you look after her for the rest of her life.

"And as for your being so unmaterialistic and all that crap – I've got no time for that at all. You go around looking like a living saint pretending that money doesn't mean anything and that all you need to have a good time is seven joss sticks and a self help book, but you're deluding yourself. What will you do when you're eighty years old with no money and a pair of walking sticks? You'll be wishing you'd been more clever with your money then, all right. And what's wrong with enjoying the good things in life? I'm not ashamed of liking designer clothes and fast cars and good food and champagne and well-dressed men."

"But Becky, I know it's a cliché, but without love, all the things you've mentioned are totally meaningless."

"Love? Hah! Don't talk to me about love. I've had enough of 'love' to last me a lifetime. My family's a fucking joke – my mother's disowned me, my dad might as well be on another planet for all the hope I have of ever seeing him again, my sister... well, enough about my sister. I haven't got time or energy to fill you in on the details. And as for friends and boyfriends, well, I've learned that nobody sticks around long enough to love me even if I could summon up the energy to love them."

"What you say makes me feel very sad."

"Don't be. You've no right to feel sad about anything to do with me."

"Why don't you give me a chance? Can't we meet up and talk?"

"After what happened last night? Forget it. I'm not looking for a life filled with the Dawns of this world. I'm not ready to share anybody. And to be perfectly frank, you can't give me what I want out of life and you never will be able to. Let me just make it quite clear once and for all that I am not here out of choice, and that I will be leaving as soon as possible in order to live in London among people who actually have a real life. And of course, I won't ever see you again."

Despite myself, a big sob bursts out from nowhere at this juncture, and his voice increases in urgency. "Becky, this is crazy. You're going to write the whole thing off because I don't wear a suit and work in the city? It's madness. If I can accept you for what you are..."

"Oh yeah? Despite yourself? Well, I'm sick to death of the whole thing. I do hope that you and Dawn enjoy the rest of your lives together. Goodbye!"

"Becky, don't go..."

But I slam the phone down, smile defiantly at Irene and burst into tears.

"Becky! Come here. Big hug. Listen Becky, you're going mad over this. You know you're crazy about Bill. Call him back."

"Oh don't you start. Honestly Irene, all I want to do now is to get the hell out of this place and go back to London where I belong."

"Well, why don't you?"

"Because I haven't got any money, that's why."

220

"How much do you need?"

"Loads. Enough to buy myself a penthouse flat and a whole new wardrobe of clothes." I wipe my eyes and blow my nose. Irene heads into the kitchen and puts the kettle on, calling over her shoulder, "A penthouse flat? You're joking."

"No I'm not."

"So how are you going to get the cash? Become a high class prostitute and tout yourself down the Co-Op?"

"Don't make me laugh. Seriously, I want to write this book, but I'm losing heart. Perhaps I'll just do a straight screenplay. Or more likely, I'll have to meet a rich man somehow. Join a dating agency. I can't move back to London like this. I've got to get my glamour back. I'm not being vain, it's a question of principle. It's all to do with my sister... oh, it's fucked up."

"I didn't know you had a sister."

"Oh, I do. She's my identical twin, actually."

"No way! You're kidding! That's so cool."

"Not really. She hates my guts. It's a bit complicated as a matter of fact."

"Nothing's too complicated for someone of my intelligence. Tell me all."

"Well, have you ever wondered why I'm here in the first place?"

"Not really. But now you come to mention it... why are you here in the first place?"

"I did the deed with Mike."

"Obviously a catastrophic mistake. But that doesn't explain why you're here. I've never got the feeling that you're madly in love with him or anything. Having said that, just recently he's been looking a bit like the cat that's got the cream."

"What do you mean?"

"I mean, like a man who's had a shag. Are you a closet item?"

221

"Far from it. As far as I know, he's a sex-free zone."

"Are you sure?"

"As I personally can be. But the fact is, we did do the nasty – once only I hasten to add – at a time when he was, inconveniently, my sister's boyfriend."

"Oh, Becky."

"Oh Becky is right. But that's what happened. But I've suffered for it. Her idea of revenge was to get into my flat when I wasn't there, and take it over along with my handbag and all its contents, my job and my entire wardrobe of beautiful, beautiful designer clothes. And sixty-three pairs of shoes. Breaks your heart, doesn't it?"

"That's amazing. Sixty-three pairs of shoes! Why couldn't you just chuck her out?"

"Easier said than done. Because we look exactly alike, everybody thought she was me including the doormen at the flat, my work and everywhere. And because I'd never told any of my friends or colleagues that I've got a twin, everybody swallowed her story hook line and sinker."

"But couldn't you just go into work and explain?"

"She took over the newspaper column I used to write and told the world she has an evil lookalike stalker pretending to be her. It made the nationals. So everybody was after me."

"Oh God! You mean that thing in the Star! I actually read about that! Clever. So what about your mum and dad?"

"Mum's on her side. She blamed me totally for what happened with Mike. And Dad's in Australia and he's completely useless anyway. So there I was, with no money and nowhere to live and no job and no life, and nowhere to go but Mike's. So I did. And he moved down to Much Jenner within the week to begin a new life among strangers. And here I am."

"My God. What a story."

"I know."

"So what are you going to do now?"

"Well, my idea of the best revenge I could have on Amanda for what she's done to me is to move back up to London with an even flashier apartment and much newer clothes, and start again only better. That'll show her what I'm made of."

"Good one. And how close are you to getting the million?"

"Not close. I've saved up about three hundred quid."

"Well, it's a start."

"I know," I reply modestly. Then I let out a blood curdling scream and Irene nearly jumps through the ceiling.

"What is it? What is it?"

"I left it at Mike's house! All my money!"

"Where?"

"Sealed in a plastic bag in the water tank."

"Why?"

"I don't trust Midge an inch. Money means nothing to her – she just likes spending it. And because she thinks that all possessions should be shared, I knew she'd have no worries about nicking it from my handbag. So I hid it really carefully. I'm going to have to go back there and fish it out. Oh FUCK!"

"WHAT?"

"I've got to get on the computer too."

"Why?"

"My book! Dowsing for Pineapples! I've got up to five thousand words. It's been a fucking nightmare. You've no idea how difficult it is, writing a book. I'd rather drink bleach than start all over again. Really. I'd kill myself. There's no way I can just leave it on their computer. I'll have to go and get it somehow. I could email it to you here, couldn't I?"

"Yes of course. So, are you going over there now?"

"Of course not. It's the middle of the night. But tomorrow! God! I hope nobody'll go on the computer. What if they start nosing through my files? What if they

223

do something dreadful like delete all those five thousand words? I wouldn't put anything past Midge – especially if she reads it."

"Becky, Midge doesn't even know how to turn a man on, let alone a computer."

"True. I had forgotten."

"No more time for talk now. We'd better go to bed. It's been a very exciting evening what with one thing and another."

"Too right. Come on. Early start tomorrow."

But of course, once safely tucked up in Irene's spare room with my bin bags piled around me, I can't so much as close my eyes. I can't help running through the conversation with Bill again and again. He thinks I'm 'materialistic'. 'Hedonistic'. Riddled with bad habits. He didn't use the precise words, but he obviously thinks I'm greedy, shallow and self-centred. Am I? Am I all these things?

I turn over, punch the pillow and try to think about immediate plans rather than my broken heart. My cash and my five thousand words are at Mikes, and I need to get them back. I suppose I could just knock on the door and explain, but I'm feeling strangely reluctant to see anybody. My pride has definitely been injured. I haven't heard a word from anybody at the house, and until I do, I shan't be making contact. Why should I care whether or not the kids miss me? Or whether Pumpkin is eating his prunes? Or how Pepys is doing?

Okay. I'm calm. Calm. Zen. I'll give them a couple of days to get back into some sort of routine. Pepys should be back from the vet's by the end of the week, so I can give him a cuddle goodbye when I go in to pick up my stuff. A good day would be next Tuesday. Pepys will be back by, say, Friday, so he'll have had the weekend to recover, and on Tuesdays Midge has yoga in the village hall at nine fifteen and I'll bet any money she goes straight there after dropping off Pumpkin, on the scrounge for herb tea.

Mike will be at work, the kids will all be at school, Midge will be tied into a knot on the floor of the village hall and as the door's never locked, I'll simply walk in, switch on the generator, turn on the computer, email the book to Irene's address, hoick my money out of the water tank and leave. It's a cinch.

Having made up my mind, and having told Irene that I won't take Bill's phone-calls, all I have to do is wait until Tuesday and it seems a long time coming. But when the great day arrives, I am ready for action. The family should leave Cobweb Cottage at about eight, so I wait until nine to be absolutely safe. Then I creep down the lane and push open the door with caution. I listen and there appears to be nobody around, but just in case I call out.

"Anybody here? Hello?"

Nothing. I'm sorted. I tiptoe through to the sitting room where I discover Pepys, lying curled up on a beanbag with a blanket, looking sorry for himself.

"Oh, Pepys!" I cry. "My darling likkle doggie-oggie-poggie!" Which isn't something I'd care to repeat in public. And I cuddle him for a good five minutes, trying to breathe in only through my mouth. No matter how much I have learned to love this dog, there's no doubt about it – he smells like an open sewer.

Then I pick up a few letters and a couple of Amanda's envelopes full of her daft DVDs, stuff them into my handbag, dump it on the sofa, put the kettle on and go out to switch on the generator. The familiar chug-a-chug warms the cockles of my heart – until it cuts out. With a muffled curse I attempt once more. Once more there's a feeble effort followed by death. Great. It's run out of petrol. I only have to leave the house for five minutes and any form of organisation is over. I'll have to go to the garage. The cans are in the familiar place in the shed and

225

I set out on the fifteen-minute walk to the mini-Tescos plus petrol station that makes all our lives so much easier. All the way, I feel absolutely fed up. Honestly! Mike really should think more about running the household than he does. Midge is pathetic. She can't be expected to know about things like the generator. They are all absolute crap at any organisational skills and can't remember jackshit. Memory is like a muscle. It must be flexed. If you simply have a routine of thought and consideration, you won't forget anything. Failing that, a good calendar, diary or notice board will do the trick.

I'm half way there before I realise I've left my handbag on the sofa.

Pursing my lips and clenching my fists around the cans I trek back to the cottage, then to the garage where I do finally manage to make contact with gasoline, then back to the cottage once more to fill up the generator and switch it on. I turn on the computer and while it boots up, go into the kitchen to put the kettle on.

The kitchen is full of steam – I suddenly remember that I put the kettle on at least half an hour ago, and it boiled dry some time ago. The kettle doesn't look like it used to and I have to remove it to the sink with oven gloves. So I fill a pan with water and stick it on to boil. Boy, do I need a cup of tea by now. While I wait for the water, I hug Pepys once more. It's a funny thing, but I really am missing this dog. With him in my arms, licking my face frantically, I wander around Cobweb Cottage, having a little nostalgic moment. I can't look at the beanbags without imagining Dawn flumped on one like a giant purple velvet piece of crochet work. That's nasty. But I can't look at the porch without seeing Bill standing there saying he'd forgotten his fleece. That's nice. I can't see Pumpkin's high chair without remembering how angelic he looks lying asleep at night, flushed and damp, with his limbs sprawled out like a rag doll's. And I can't look at

226

the outhouse without picturing Honeybee and Rob jostling for position in front of the tiny mirror, one to do her make up, the other to examine his acne. It's funny, I'd never thought I'd love a teenager except of course in the Mrs Robinson sense. Which idea, in the light of the experience of actually living with a teenaged boy, I have very much discarded.

Pepys is too loving and wriggly and licky to have around when one is trying to do something serious so I gently pop him out into the back garden along with his blanket and shut the door. A breath of fresh air will do him good. Then I fix myself a lovely cup of tea, and I'm just about to sit down at the computer when there is the fell sound of feet striding up to the front door. The idea of being caught here and having to chat with anybody, especially Midge, gives me hives. With my heart jangling around in the region of my tonsils, I dive behind the sitting room curtains. They are floorlength and of a thick green velvet, so it is unlikely that anybody will find me unless they feel like watering the rather depressed cactus that lurks, alone and friendless, on the windowsill.

Through the muffling folds of curtain, I hear a man's voice inquiring – I think – as to whether anybody is at home. Damn. A visitor. I could have faced it out and chased him off. But it's too late now. He's in the sitting room, I can hear rustles and bumps, and I really can't leap out from behind a curtain to greet him. No, I'll stay put. As long as nobody's here, he'll go away again. I'm sure that what he's doing now is looking for a pen and piece of paper to write a note. I can hear him coughing and rustling around. Heck. Piss off! I try a little thought transference on the lines of 'There is a pen and a piece of recycled paper in the kitchen. There is a pen and a piece of recycled paper in the kitchen. There is a pen and a piece of recycled paper in the kitchen.' But it doesn't work. In fact, he seems to be settling in. I wish I'd

227

brought the cup of tea behind the curtain with me. It's very hot and dusty in here. Just as I have this thought, which arrives simultaneously with the realisation that my tongue is as dry as a tampon in the Gobi Desert, I hear him pick up my cup of tea and – I assume – feel the temperature of the cup, for he says reasonably clearly, "Blimey, that's hot. Someone *must* be here." And he renews his calling up the stairs, of course to no avail. However, he seems to be a philosophical soul, for on realising that the cottage is as empty as he had first assumed, he returns to the sitting room and with a great deal of slurping and gratuitous smacking of lips, drinks my tea down to the last drop.

"Pity to waste it," he says, then with a grunt, sinks into a beanbag. It's not long, however, before I am frozen with horror once more. There is noise on the path. I hear the merry sounds of teenagers. It's A Robin's Nest and Honeybee! What the heck are they doing home at this hour? The stranger in the sitting room is similarly taken aback. He levers himself out of the beanbag and shuffles to the window, narrowly avoiding bumping me through the curtain – indeed, he even takes a piece of material in his hand to sneak a look out - and I can clearly hear his heavy breathing. Then he mutters, "Blimey! This isn't her. Don't know who these are. Must be the wrong house." At this moment, I hear Rob say, "Come on Honeybee. Don't be a pain. We'll only be here five minutes. I'll just get it quickly. Wait while I go upstairs."

The stranger obviously decides that rather than having to face an awkward introduction to strangers in the 'wrong house', he will lie low for the few minutes that Rob needs to collect whatever it is he needs to collect. Judging from the sounds, I imagine that he has dived beneath the table against the wall, which has a kind of gingham curtain tacked around it to conceal Pepy's dog basket and collection of toys. For a few moments there is a tense pause, with only the sound of Rob clumping around upstairs to break the silence. Then the tap of footsteps tells both the stranger and me that Honeybee has entered the sitting room. "Come on Rob!" she yells. "You're taking ages! I can't be bothered to wait!" There are muffled cries from upstairs, and Honeybee gets out her mobile and begins texting. I can tell by the sounds. Do teenagers ever do anything but text each other? It seems unlikely. And what they text each other about is equally mysterious. Meanwhile, I'm getting hotter and hotter and more and more pissed off.

Footsteps thunder down the stairs and Rob rushes into the room. "Here you go, Honey," he begins. "I've got the bag..." But Honeybee has shushed him sharply. There is a tense, listening silence. Then the unmistakable sound of the gate clicking travels into the room. I can picture Honeybee and Robbo gazing at each other with wild surmise, then Honeybee hisses – "Quick Rob! Duck behind the beanbags. Someone's coming." There is a rustle of beans, and the front door creaks open once more. Our suspense doesn't last for long.

"Mike, my darling. Your aura is positively pulsating!" purrs a woman who can only be Midge.

"How's *your* aura, sweetie?" replies Mike, for it is he. "Is it excited?"

"Vibrating. Oscillating. Come here," she cries.

And without further ado, there is a smacking of lips – and it's nothing to do with my tea this time. There's no doubt about it. Mike and Midge are having a snog. A snog! In this house! This can only mean one thing. They're having an affair. How deceitful! I can't believe it. I can't understand how they can have been so secretive. And it's all getting a little personal. Even I, with my ears clogged up with dusty curtain, can hear puffs and pants and the most revolting sentiments.

Midge says: "Oh Mikey, Mikey, this is so... oh!"

229

Mike replies: "Oh Midge-kins, darling, can I just... ah!

Midge yelps: "Oh Mikey, my lover, cover me in kisses all over!"

Mike squeaks: "Oh Midgey-Midge, I can't last another minute without you!"

And there's a thud as the two of them hit the pile of beanbags behind which their teenage children are hiding. A fractured silence is followed by Midge screaming hysterically at the top of her voice and Mike leaping back and – I imagine – crashing over the coffee table.

"It's all right, mum. It's only us," cries Rob.

"Yeah, it's us. And what the hell is going on?" Honeybee adds. "What are you two doing here?"

"I might ask the same of you!" replies Midge, in her haughtiest manner.

"Mum, can you stuff your boob back into your caftan?" says Honeybee scornfully. "It's not a sight worth seeing at your age."

"I beg your pardon!"

"That's okay. Anyway, what the fuck are you and Dad up to? You've broken up, remember?"

Mike joins in. "Your mother and I... well, there's a lot of love there, you know. It's kinda difficult to explain. It all started back at the Festival Games. Yeah. We just sat by the fire..."

"That's right," interrupts Midge coyly. "Gazing into the flames..."

"And I felt an overwhelming urge to nuzzle into her underarm..."

"He actually kissed my underarm..."

"And I said, 'Why don't we reignite an old flame..."

"And I said, 'I can't put out the fire inside..."

"SHUT UP!" I yell uncontrollably, but as Honeybee and Rob shout the same thing at the same time at twice the volume, I get away with it.

"Messing around like this is fucking with our heads," adds Honeybee, with, if I am not mistaken, a sob in her voice. "We've had Mum, then Amanda, then Becky, and now Mum again – I can't cope. It's disgusting."

"Look Honeybee, Amanda was a transitional girlfriend," he replies.

"So? And anyway, what about Becky?"

"Becky was a big mistake. The biggest mistake I've ever made."

Hah! I almost give myself away in a gigantic surge of rage that nearly precipitates me out of the curtain and onto the carpet. The curtain must have twitched considerably, but nobody says anything so I assume they're all so engrossed in the unfolding human drama – or soap opera, if you will – that it's ignored. But on a personal note, I do put my hand on the cactus while attempting to steady myself and that induces five minutes of such pain that I miss quite a bit of the ensuing dialogue. When I come back on stream, Honeybee is explaining that adults behaving like this is no example for their children and Midge is hotly contesting the point.

"My darling Honeybee. What consenting adults do between themselves is private and must always be so. And you say we should resist our animal urges, but I ask you, why should we? And indeed, how can we? How can we resist the cosmic forces which drive man and woman, or should I say, spirit being and spirit being, together? I ask you all that, and I ask you now."

There's a dramatic pause. Then Rob says, "What about animals?"

"What?"

"What about animals? You talked about man and woman and spirit beings and all that, well, what about animals? Is it love which drives *them* together?"

231

"I wasn't talking about love. I was talking about cosmic forces. And they drive everything together. We all make mistakes – look at Honeybee, for example."

"Why me, Mum?"

"Well, you've made a mistake. You're up the duff."

"Mum! That's not something I expect you to say."

"A vulgar expression only, which I picked up from Becky. So sorry it slipped out. What I meant was, the cosmic forces have resulted in a new spirit being in your womb and it's causing quite a bit of trouble for everybody who loves you. And while we're on the subject, Honeybee, why are you and A Robin's Nest here at all? Why are you not at school?"

"Why are *you* here? You're meant to be at yoga, and Dad's meant to be at work," she counters.

"I skipped yoga for once, and your father is in between deliveries," says Midge. "I asked you why you and your brother are not at school and I expect an answer."

There's a long pause, then Honeybee replies defiantly. "We came to collect our things."

"What things?"

"Our things. Our bags. If you must know, we packed last night. We're leaving."

"And where, may I ask, did you think you were going?"

"To Becky's."

"To Becky's?" Midge almost screams.

"Yes, to Becky's. We want her."

"But you can't possibly go to Becky's! She hasn't even got a home of her own. She's staying with that horrible counter-Buddhist Irene. What do you *mean*, you were going to Becky's?"

"Well, if you want the truth, Mum, we're fed up here. It's only been a matter of days, and the house is already a dump. You'll never bother with the shopping. There'll never be any ironing done or anything like that. It'll be boring! You'll just spend all day up in your room like

232

always, and nobody will look after us. We'll just have to watch after Pumpkin all day long and sit around in a mess."

"How outrageous. I didn't bring you up to be an arch-anti-feminist, Honeybee. I've got better things to do than to cook and clean and iron and look after a family all day."

"Oh yeah? What exactly do you do, up there? Write books like Becky?"

"Becky does *what*?"

"She's clever. She's writing a brilliant book, which will sell for millions, just like Harry Potter and Bridget Jones and the Da Vinci Code."

"And what's it called, this brilliant book?"

"'Dowsing for Pineapples.'"

"I *always* dowse for pineapples! She must have based it on me. I'll sue."

"Whatever. At least she's doing something worthwhile with her time. You're alone most of the day – are you doing something worthwhile? I shouldn't think so. We reckon you just sit up there all day long practically asleep."

"I meditate. There is a place for action, and a time for meditation. To each his own method of contributing to the world. Some contribute materially, I contribute spiritually."

"Well, it doesn't get us very far, does it? Becky was fun. She made the house fun and she made it nice. Now we're going to go and stay with her and if you don't like it, Mum, you can lump it. She's going to be my birth partner, too. You can get stuffed."

"Honeybee!"

"No, I mean it, Mum. We're fed up. Right, Rob?"

"Er, yes. I'm afraid so. Sorry, Mum."

There's a sniffling noise, and I realise that Midge has broken down in tears and the soft 'hoosh' of a beanbag

233

informs me that she has sunk down onto one. Mike is murmuring comfort. At last she speaks through her sobs.

"This has been a dreadful shock. Dreadful! My nerves are in tatters. Such a battering, such a fluttering, I'm in a desperate state. Mike darling, can you race upstairs and get me my rose quartz? I find it very soothing to hold at moments like this."

Mike thunders upstairs and there are clinking noises from the attic. Midge continues. "My darlings. Why didn't you say something before? I thought you liked living in a relaxed atmosphere. I imagined that you enjoyed running your own lives."

"Well, we do Mum, sort of," explains Rob. "But it's just a bit too much, really. We just need a bit of attention I suppose. Only a bit, though."

"Only a bit! Oh, it's too sad. I thought being liberal parents in an open relationship would be the best way I could ever bring up my children."

"But Mum," says Honeybee, "You're not in an open relationship. You've split up. So I don't understand anything."

"We have split up, of course. But we love each other. In an open sort of a way, we are together once more..."

"But it can't be open. It has to be closed. That means that you have to stop going upstairs the whole time, and you and Dad have to be properly together! If you can't do that, there's no point in anything."

"I do love Mike, and he certainly adores me, of course. We could attempt to rebond our auras in a permanent fixative, I suppose."

"Stop talking crap, Mum. I can't understand a word you're saying."

"I mean, we could give it a go."

"It has to be more than that, Mum. It has to be proper. I think you guys should get married."

"Married! An obsolete, archaic institution designed to repress women and destroy healthy sexual and spiritual intercourse with the entirety of the human race!"

"You're talking out of your arse, Mum. Marriage is where it's at. Love for ever. Sworn fidelity to the end of your days. An equal relationship forged by God and the law into an indissoluble bond. What could be more cool than that?"

"What do you say, Midge?" cries Mike from the direction of the doorway. "I think Honeybee's right. And I do love you. I always did! Shall we give it a go? What do you say?"

"I don't know what to say. You haven't asked me very properly yet."

"Well, I'm asking you properly now." There's a thud and a soft exclamation of pain, which I assume means Mike has dropped onto one arthritic knee.

"My darling Midge, in the blessed presence of our two children..." (And me and somebody else unknown, if only he knew it) "Will you become my lawful wedded wife? To have and to hold? From this time until the next time? In sickness and wealth and poorness? And so on? What do you think?"

"Oh Mike! Oh... Oh.... Oh, go on then."

"Wow!"

"Yay, Mum! Yay, Dad! Hurrah!" There are general hugging and kissing and jumping around sounds, then Rob shouts out, "Pepys is in the garden! Let's let him in! He's got to celebrate too!" In another minute Pepys limps in, and after covering everybody with muddy paws and licking it all off again thoroughly with his large pink tongue, he decides that it's time for a lovely little rest in his basket and crawls under the table.

Let the games begin.

There's an astonished silence of the canine kind, then a frenzy of yelping and a sharp cry of pain. Go, Pepys! I had no idea he was any kind of a guard dog, especially as he's

235

in recovery from a serious operation. The excitement is making me hyperventilate behind the curtain, and I would give any money to see the ensuing scene, as the stranger crawls forth to the gasps and general astonishment of all. Honeybee lets out a sharp scream, and somebody – probably Mike – evidently hurls himself on top of him. A fight scene ensues, there is a series of puffs and gasps, then a few strangled words: "Stop! Help! Listen!"

"Listen to what, arsehole?" puffs Mike.

"To me! I'm no stranger!" comes the muffled response.

"No stranger, eh? Who's ever seen this man before? A Robin's Nest? Honeybee? Midge?"

"No I haven't darling," yodels Midge shrilly, "and he looks most suspicious to me. Why, his shirt alone tells a sorry tale. What normal person would wear a florescent green tank-top covered with pink palm trees?"

"I might say, who would wear a mauve caftan covered with turquoise shells?" responds the intruder with some spirit.

"Get... out... of my house... and... away from my... family," Mike grunts as – at a guess – he bangs the intruder's head on the floor. Honeybee is still screaming, and Midge seems to be comforting her. Rob is possibly assisting Mike, if rather more high pitched grunts and 'gotcha's' are any indication. Pepys sounds like an infomercial about dogs worrying sheep so I assume he's got a chunk of trouser leg.

"No, wait!" the man whimpers. "You've got it all wrong! I'm no burglar. Let go. Get the dog off my leg! Okay. Sit on me, but take your hands from around my throat. Let me explain. I know somebody who lives here. I'm a friend! More than that, even!"

There's an alarming roar from Mike as he sees the light. "You! You! I'll kill you! I know exactly who you are. And now I'm going to string you up alive. I'm going to rip your intestines into pieces and tie them into knots. I'm going to stick bamboo up your fingernails and tear out your nasal hairs one by one and flay you with a cheese grater and boil you up like a fondue sauce. So get ready for extreme violence!"

"Why?" shrieks the intruder, his voice falsetto with alarm. "What did I ever do to you?"

"You impregnated my young daughter, that's what you did to me. And now you're going to pay the price."

"Impregnated your daughter? What are you talking about?"

"Don't pretend you haven't seen this girl before. Honeybee, come here. Admit that you slept with this man eight months ago."

"What?" yells Honeybee. "No way! You must be joking, Dad! Look at his shirt! Give me some credit! At least my bloke had a pierced lip!"

Mike turns back to Suspect One, sounding a little rattled. "So, are you telling me that you *don't* know my daughter?"

"Now – but I know my own daughter. She lives here. I'm Bob Crisis - Becky's father."

It's at this point that the heat and dust behind my cosy curtain finally defeat me and I fall into a dead faint, hurtling into the room face first rolled up in velvet fabric like a shroud. My last memory is the sound of the curtain ripping as it tears from its moorings. And then everything is black.

CHAPTER ELEVEN

"Becky! Becky!"
I come to with somebody squeezing my cheeks together like old ladies do to babies. I'm being shaken, and before I know where I am, a jug of water has been thrown over my head. That, I'll wager, is Robbo getting over-interested in my little problem. But I open my eyes to avoid further outrage, and there they all are, crowding round me in a circle with anxious eyes fixed on my face.
Well, I have to say it. The drama!
"Where... where... am I?"
"You're here at Cobweb Cottage, Bex," says Mike in his most soothing, doula, "Big Push Now" voice. "You've had a little faint but you're feeling much better now."
"Am I?"
"Would you like to sit up?"
"I suppose so."
They all cluster round grabbing bits of me and heave-hoing with a little too much enthusiasm for my liking. Is it for this I have been vegetarian for weeks? I should be light as a feather. They are definitely making too much of a meal of it. Finally I'm settled on a couple of beanbags

and it's only then that I remember. Sorry, blocked it out for a minute. Daddy's home.

"Dad? Where are you?"

"Here I am, Toots. How are you doing?"

"Stop talking with that completely disgusting accent."

"Sorry, Toots! Comes natural to me after all this time."

"Well, stop it. And don't call me Toots."

"Right, Toots."

"What are you doing here?"

There's a long pause and I can see, despite my weakness, that Dad's attempting to register emotion. I take advantage of the pause to drink him in. He is clad, as I'd gathered from behind the curtain, in a green shirt covered in pink palm trees, a pair of surf shorts pimpled with grinning piranhas and flip flops.

"Stop thinking about why you're here, Dad. If you're going to be here longer than five minutes we've got to get going."

"Where?"

"To the shops."

"Why?"

"To buy you some respectable clothes. You can't go around here looking like that! It's disgraceful!"

"Lor... Lorraine bought me this outfit."

"She must have been stoned out of her box."

Dad looks a bit pleased by this. At his age, perhaps he thinks it's cool to have girlfriends who smoke dope on Friday nights. But Robbo eagerly chimes in.

"Oh yeah, Mr Crisis! You should definitely let Becky take you shopping. She's got brilliant taste in clothes. She got me loads of really cool gear last time we went out."

It's at this point that Mike makes very obvious signs to his family that me and my dad should be left alone together and with many an elaborate whisper, nod of comprehension and walking on tiptoe, they all shuffle out. I turn to my father and give him a very hard stare.

239

His hair – brushed from one side to the other to take years off him, he *hopes* – wilts visibly.

"So Dad? What the fuck *are* you doing here?"

"Lorraine and me... we're finished. I knew it was never right, Becky. I had to end it and come back home where my heart was."

"You mean she dumped you?"

"No! No! Nothing like that."

"Yes she did."

"She did not."

"She did. Stop lying to me."

"Okay, she dumped me. For her kite surfing instructor."

"Serves you right."

"Sorry. I'm just so sorry for all the heart break I've caused!"

"Oh, that's okay. I'll make sure you suffer for it. Wait a minute! Does Mum know you're back?"

"I don't know. I went round to your flat straight from the airport, and Amanda was there. She's looking fantastic!"

"Yeah, yeah. So what happened?"

"Well, she explained that she was staying at your place for a while. I knew there'd been trouble because your mother phoned me telling me not to send you any money."

"Oh, right. Thanks for standing your ground."

"I didn't *have* any money! Lorraine wanted a new deck and what with her clothes bills and the sports car and the kite surfing lessons and everything, I was broke."

"Didn't your job pay well?"

"There's a blip in the market at the moment. People don't want humour in their car stickers any more, they want eco-commentary. And Lorraine's brother just isn't moving with the times. If I told him once..."

"Enough car sticker market news. What happened at Amanda's?"

"Well, I thought I could stay with her while she broke the news to your mother that I wanted to come home."

"You mean, you want to get back together with Mum?"

"Of course! The whole thing's been a terrible mistake. I just want her to forgive me and for us to start all over again. I'll be a better person this time, I promise."

"Save your promises for her. So, why aren't you staying with Amanda?"

"Well, it was a bit awkward, really. She was very busy. A lot on. Some bloke with floppy hair hanging around. Film crew arriving in the morning. That sort of thing. So she gave me your address down here and I spent the last of me cash on a train ticket and – well, here I am!" He attempts a salute. I roll my eyes.

"So what do you want *me* to do?"

"Negotiate with your mother?"

"She wouldn't even let me speak a word. She'd hang the phone up on me."

"Why?"

"Because I nicked Amanda's boyfriend, and she can't forgive me."

"Amanda's boyfriend? What? Is he here?"

"Yes. He's the one sporting the facial fungus."

"Boy, Toots, I wouldn't have thought he was your type."

"No more he is. It's a long story. I wouldn't have thought Lorraine was your type, either."

"No more she is. That's a long story, too."

"So what are we going to do?"

"Can I stay here with you?"

"No. Actually, I'm here under false pretences. I got the sack ages ago. Oh don't look so surprised. I was working as their au-pair. Forget it. Another long story. Anyway, I'm not meant to be here – I just sneaked in to get some stuff. I'm staying at a friend's house and it might be a bit much to have you stay there too. I'll have to have a think about it. Oh come on Dad. Take that look off your face. I'll look after you."

"Oh Toots! Forgive me!"

241

"Eeeeee... go on then. Let he who is without sin cast the first stone."

"Toots! Say it! Say, 'I forgive you, Dad!'"

"Oh, all right. I forgive you, Dad, sort of, for now and only because you're so pathetic."

There's a burst of clapping and we look round from an embrace to see the assorted hippies jumping around clapping and cheering in the doorway – a sight that forces an unwilling smile from my lips.

"Come on, everybody!" Midge is getting a little carried away. "Let's light some candles, form a circle, and dance a rhythmic celebration of spiritual intercourse and cosmic togetherness!"

"What kind of intercourse?" My dad's looking a bit alarmed.

"Don't worry, Dad. She's a nutter. You'd better just go along with it."

While Midge is busy lighting candles and muttering incantations to herself, Mike clasps my dad firmly in his arms.

"G'day, Bob! G'day!" he says.

"Er, G'day to you, too!" my dad replies, brightly.

"It's a wonderful g'day, isn't it? Tell you what. Midge and me, we just got engaged!"

"That's good news."

"Yes, isn't it! Wow! There's some kind of karma going on today, that's for sure!"

"For sure," my dad agrees.

"Everybody! Form a circle!" Midge is busy organising us all. We join hands, some of us more reluctantly than others, and begin to move round, circling the coffee table on which is balanced about forty three scented candles and a joss stick. Faster and faster the circle moves, and Midge is getting terribly excited, chanting away like anything. Some of us – I regret to include myself in this number – are giggling, when suddenly there is a dreadful

242

cry. The circle breaks up immediately, and Honeybee bends double, clutching at her bump.

"Honey! What's wrong! What's wrong! Is it the baby?" I cry.

"Oh! Oh! Yes, I think so! I've been having little pains on and off all day, I thought it was wind! It's too early!"

"Only a month, don't panic!"

"I'm not fucking panicking... aaaargh!"

"Quick, Mike. You're the midwife."

"Doula."

"She's in labour! Help!"

"I'll run upstairs and get my Bach Flower Remedies," cries Midge and exits with caftan awhirl. Rob rushes into the kitchen and I can hear him filling the kettle. I put my arms around Honeybee.

"Call an ambulance!" she gasps. "I don't want to have my baby naturally! I've made it quite clear I want loads of drugs and a caesarean if possible! I want it all as artificial as possible! It's all in my birthplan!"

"Honeybee, you're only doing this to annoy me and you know it," says Mike, soothingly. "You stay right here and have your precious baby like Mother Nature intended. Daddy will deliver it the natural way."

"No! No! Anything but that! Ben, call an ambulance! I'm dying! I need an epidural!"

"You can't be that bad. You've only just started."

"Don't you fucking tell me how bad I am! Get on the phone!"

"Look, sit down. I'll make you a cup of tea with two sugars. Rob's got the kettle on. I'll call the hospital in five minutes, okay? But we've all got to calm down."

Midge rushes in with her case of remedies, uncorks a few and starts showering them over Honeybee who puts her hands up to protect herself with a cry of rage.

"I'll have none of it, Mum! I want pethidine!"

"Now, now, Hon-bun. You don't know what you're saying. You're delirious."

"Oh, God!"

"What!"

"I've wet myself!"

"Fuck! The water's have broken!"

"BECKY WILL YOU CALL FOR A FUCKING AMBULANCE!"

"YES I WILL BUT STOP SWEARING AT ME!"

"I WANT TO PUSH!"

"THEN PUSH FOR ALL I FUCKING CARE!"

Then I'm not quite sure what happens, whether it's the Bach Flowers or Mike's bedside manner or perhaps Rob hit her on the head with a cosh without my noticing, but all of a sudden Honeybee completely calms down and changes from a screaming nightmare to a silent, concentrating creature. Mike seems to know that this is a good moment to sort out a few things.

"Right, everyone. Rob, it'll be your job to go and get all the towels and sheets you can – clean ones. Becky, can you make sure that there's plenty of boiling water to hand? Midge, my darling love, why don't you go and have a little rest? You look pooped."

"Oh, well, if you think so!"

"I know so. Go on. Go on, darling."

"Oh, well, call me when anything happens! I'm not forgetting that I'm Honey's co-birth-partner. I'll just come in for the last bit, perhaps. It's all a bit messy, isn't it? Do you think the 'waters' will stain the beanbags? She was sitting on mine, you know."

"I don't know, Midge-kins but I'll tell you what, we'll swap. In the meantime, would you like to look after Bob? He's looking a little lost."

"Of course! Bol, would you like to come up and have a little rest as well?"

"Erm..."

"It's all right, Dad," I break in, en route back from the kitchen having put the kettle on. "She's not going to tear the shirt from your back. Tear it up, maybe and I wouldn't blame her, but your body isn't in danger. She just wants you to read some Buddhist tract to her at a guess. Is that right, Midge?"

"Yes. I love to listen to the great thoughts of Buddha as I slip off into dreamland. You are safe with me. Indeed, you may find enlightenment – and a friend."

"Er, right. I'll come up with you then. If you're sure."

"Oh, quite sure, Bol. We'll be well out of the way upstairs. I've got some really wonderful philosophical readings to introduce you too..."

"It's Bob, actually."

"Oh, Bob! So sorry. Bee Oh Bee, Bob, you mean? Such a funny little name. The stairs are this way. After you."

"Thank you... Oh! Help!"

My dad is knocked sideways by an enormous pile of sheets and towels that Robbo, ever keen, has hurled down the stairs but after we've excavated him, brushed him down and set him off in the right direction, he and Midge seem perfectly happy.

Their voices fade atticwards. I look at Mike and he looks at me and we both look at Rob and he looks at us and then we all look at Honeybee. She's lying in the foetal position over two beanbags and appears to be fairly comfortable.

"Right," I say decisively. "It's time to get something done."

"Good one," replies Rob. "What shall I do now?"

"Is that water boiling?" asks Mike.

"Yes," cries Rob after having a quick check.

"Then let's have a nice cup of tea!" I say triumphantly. And we do.

It's a funny thing, giving birth. It seems to take a terribly long time. I'm sure it's all very interesting for the person who is actually attempting to expel a miniature human

245

being from their body, but frankly, for the bystanders the early stages are a complete bore. And the fuss that is made! As I understand it, for Mike gives me a crash course in the three stages of labour over our tea, all that happens is that the cervix opens over a number of hours until it is big enough for the baby to get through. The baby is usually pretty small. Then the uterus contracts to push the baby out over a ludicrously short distance. For goodness sake. It's a walk in the park compared to constipation or a really bad hangover. For example. Constipated people really do have something to deal with. You know how long your colon is? Something like twice around the entire planet and tying a bow too – that's how long. Now imagine that that whole length is packed with half-set cement, and imagine attempting to evacuate it. Ouch! And a really bad hangover. I've had a few of those. Fancy being stuck in a bed, unable to move without throwing up, unable to move your head without agonising pain, tormented throughout by rational and irrational feelings of guilt, embarrassment and shame. Now that's nasty.

Having a baby – phooey. The good body does it all for you. Mike explains that this dilation of the cervix and the uterine contractions (I think I've got that right) happen involuntarily. Well, you know what that means. It happens without you making any effort whatsoever! So whenever Honeybee is making a big fuss about nothing, I kneel by her head and explain this to her very loudly and slowly. Sadly, she won't listen to reason and in the end even Mike, who hates a confrontation, asks me to leave her alone. In a bit of a huff, I retire to a far beanbag and open a good book. Well, a book, anyhow. Not that I had time for much reading since moving to Much Jenner, but at least in London I had access to things readable. Mike's book collection is much dominated by things like Homeopathy for Diabetics and The New Age Herbalist.

Now, I pick up Siblings Without Rivalry and learn that all of us have been doing it wrong since birth. After a while, I fall gently asleep.

A terrible sound wakes me. For a moment I can hardly remember where I am, then the sound of feet pounding down the stairs and Rob's cry of "Are you okay?" reminds me. It's the New Age Home Birthing Centre and I am a birthing partner, about to assist a teenage mother to bear her first child. I leap to my feet. Midge and my dad have emerged, and everybody is standing around Honeybee in various states of anxiety. Mike has managed to sort her out with towels and blankets covering the beanbags and just as well, for as we watch with bated breath, out shoots something that should never be seen in public. Remember what I said about constipation? Well, having a baby would appear to be the universal clear all. Midge sinks into a far corner with a corner of her caftan over her mouth and nose. Rob heads swiftly for the kitchen. Mike looks completely unfazed and starts fiddling around with wipes. My father, I note, is looking frankly curious and has settled down with a front row seat.

"Dad!" I hiss. "Honeybee might not want a complete stranger, watching her give birth."

"It's all right, Bex!" I hear her gasp. "It's okay! Dad, I want to push!"

"Just breathe, darling," Mike says calmly. "Just keep breathing."

"She'd better if she wants to live," I say darkly. "Can't you give her more constructive instructions than that?"

"Becky, just give me a moment, okay?" replies he. "Come into the kitchen. Back in a minute, Hon-bun."

We go into the kitchen. "Becky," he begins in the most patronising of tones, "You must remember that this is my job. Let me get on with it in my own way."

"But anything could go wrong! I think we should get a midwife."

"I am a midwife."

"But you said you were a doula!"

"Trust me, Becky. I can deliver a baby. Do you think I'm going to let my own daughter come to any harm?"

"I wouldn't put anything past you. Oh all right, I'm only joking. Pray carry on. You're doing a fantastic job I'm sure. Where would you like me to be? Honeybee did ask me to be her birthing partner, after all."

"Why don't you sit by her head, hold her hand during contractions, and generally encourage her along?"

"Can't I deliver the baby?"

"I thought you said you wanted her to survive the process."

"It can't be difficult! You told me all about it, and I've been looking at the pictures. I simply turn the baby's head as it emerges from the birth canal, check the cord, then..."

"Seriously, Becky, you'd better leave this bit to me." There's another deep groan from Honeybee. "I've got to get back. Now, can I trust you to behave?"

"Oh, all right then. Let's go."

So there I am, sitting by Honeybee's head, holding her hand and screaming along with her in the bad bits, when something really weird happens. Honeybee grips my hand convulsively and says: "Dad, I'm hallucinating. Is it normal?"

"Now, Hon-bun. What do you mean by hallucinating?"

"Well, I've just seen Becky walk past the window. But she's here, isn't she?"

"I'd better take your blood pressure. Just calm down. Everything's normal."

Then, I walk into the room! Not me, the Becky who's sitting on the floor by a stinky beanbag chanting breathing exercises, but the old me. The glamorous, tarty, gorgeous, designer-suit-clad me. And I stand in front of me and say,

"Hi, Becky! You look in your element here. How too, too sweet."

We all freeze with shock, and it takes some time before I can respond to Amanda – for it is she.

"Oh. Right. Hi."

"Is that all you have to say to me?"

"At the moment, it is, actually. You may not have noticed, but Honeybee's having a baby here and I'm a bit preoccupied," I reply haughtily. "I'm her birthing partner, as it goes."

"Oh! Darling Honeybee. I didn't notice you lying on the floor there. How are you?"

"Not great at the moment actually, but thank you for asking. AAAARRRRGGGHHH!"

"Just breathe," intones Mike soothingly.

"Hello, Mike," purrs Amanda.

"Oh, hi Amanda. How are you? All right?"

"Oh, I'm just fine. Well, you don't all look very pleased to see me, I must say. But never mind. I've got a little surprise for *you*, Becka. Come on in, boys!"

I look over towards the door, and see that a man with a camera is lurking. Not just a camera, actually, a sort of video contraption. In fact it looks suspiciously like...

"Surprise!" says Amanda, triumphantly. "You're on television!"

Now, I've seen stuff like this before. Jeremy Beadle. Candid Camera. Somebody gets made to look a complete fool and I can see that in this scenario, it's going to be me. The eye of the camera is scanning the room, and comes to an abrupt halt at Honeybee's beanbag. Taking advantage of the moment, I grab Amanda's upper arm and drag her into the kitchen.

"What the fucking hell is going on?" I hiss.

"Let go of me. Let go! Right." Amanda ostentatiously dusts down her arm. "Well, we're going to be on

249

television. That's what's going on. As a well-known media celebrity in my own right..."

"In my right, you mean!"

"No, in my right. I'm fifty times the success you ever could have been. So, as a well-known media celebrity in my own right, I offered a producer I know the chance to film identical twins taking over each other's lives. You've been secretly filmed for weeks..."

"WHAT? You must be joking!" I'm spluttering with rage. I could lay her out right now on the kitchen floor. "That's... that's... outrageous! I could sue you. I will sue you. What do you mean, filming me? Where? When? How?"

"Oh, we've got some nice little moments. I especially love it when you're snogging a bloke on the doorstep and you get mugged. Or something. Anyway, it's one of the highlights. Oh yes! And you getting off your face in the local and rolling on the pool table. That's a classic. Great television, great television."

"Now, wait a minute. Just wait a minute, here. Other people are involved. You can't just put them on telly without their permission."

"No problem. We just blank out their faces. Surely you've seen the kind of thing. You're the only person we're interested in – you up to your antics. Really. It's hilarious!"

"I'm suing. I'm definitely going to sue you for damages, breaking privacy laws, the works. You can't get away with this. The law will protect me."

"Well, you could try! But we've got a special budget for that kind of thing. We really don't care. Becka, I promise you. The show's going to be great. Calm down! What's your problem? You're going to be on TV! Everybody wants to be on TV. So just take a few deep breaths. This is going to be great. Let's *use* that adrenaline and anger.

"Now, the other thing is the DVDs. Of course, I sent them before I came up with the idea, but waste not, want not.

250

We can really use them. Your reaction while you're watching will be fantastic. Of course, we won't get that one hundred per cent shock of the new, but you can fake it up. Where are they?"

"What DVDs? What the hell are you talking about?"

"The ones I sent you, of course. Through the post? Popped through the ikkle letterbox? Come *on*, Becka. Wake *up*!"

"God, somewhere, I don't know. I never watched them."

"GREAT! Even though that's *fucking* disrespectful. It took me hours to film them. But still, that's fantastic. We'll get a really fresh reaction."

"I don't want to watch them. Thanks all the same."

"But I made them just for you! To tell you all about my wonderful new life and how I'm about to become a Hollywood star and how I wear all your clothes and spend all your money and shag Simon eight times a night and have the most outrageous orgasms all over the place!"

"Just as well I didn't bother. They sound incredibly boring."

"Now, come on Becka! This is going to make fabulous television! I love it that Honeybee's giving birth while you watch. Perfect timing. You couldn't have arranged it better."

"I haven't arranged anything!"

"No." She looks me up and down scornfully. "You don't look as if you can arrange a flying fuck. Now." Amanda smoothes down her skirt and makes kissy shapes with her lips. "Come on! We're ready for our moment in the sun!"

I follow Amanda out looking extremely surly, but I'm taken aback by her next action, which is to burst into tears and clasp me fondly in her arms.

"Oh! Oh! I can't bear it!" she sobs, while everybody looks on in surprise and in my case, horror. "Becka! It's just... just... Becka! We all make mistakes. I know I've made mine. But can't we patch things up?" She draws back and roasts me with the fakest appealing look I've ever seen. "Sis. Big hug? Come on, you tart. Fucking hug me! It's okay Steve, we'll edit."

I'm just about to shove her backwards over the beanbags when Honeybee lets forth a heartrending groan. I hurry over and clutch at a damp little hand, peering into her eyes. Honeybee looks up at me with a small, frightened smile.

"It really, really hurts, Becky."

"I know sweetheart. I know. Just breathe, like Dad says. In... Out. In... Out. In... Ou..."

"BECKA! CAN YOU CONCENTRATE FOR ONE MOMENT PLEASE!" Amanda is getting irritated. "If you won't do the reconciliation scene, we might as well get on with the DVDs."

"I've told you, I'd rather shove beans up my bum than watch them."

"Oh, you and your little jokes. Where's your DVD player?"

"We don't have one."

"What!" Amanda spits with rage. "It's all right, stop filming, Steve. We've got ourselves a little problem here. Of course you've got a DVD player! It's part of the computer. A Robin's Nest!" Poor old Robbo jumps sky-high as my sister wheels round on the attack.

"Why didn't you tell Rebecca that she's got a DVD player on the computer?"

"Well," stammers A Robin's Nest, "I couldn't have done. Because it actually hasn't."

"Of course it has!"

"Well, no. It hasn't."

I interrupt. "Amanda, it's all just too bad, but you can't take it out on Robbo. Now, would you kindly mind leaving the room, you *and* your cameraman. We've got a baby coming here."

"No! There's no way I'm leaving without you seeing those DVDs. Don't worry Steve," she shouts across to the cameraman. "Keep your eye on the ball – with any luck we'll be able to film the birth and me cuddling the baby. I'd better get Simon to go and buy a DVD player right now."

"Simon's here?"

"Yes, he's waiting in the car outside. I didn't want him under my feet in here, but he comes in useful sometimes. Like right now. I'll send him off to the shops pronto."

I smile sardonically. "No you won't, Amanda. Haven't you realised? It's half past nine at night and the shops closed hours ago."

"But there is a shop? An electronics shop on the high street?"

"Well, yes. But it closed at five thirty."

Amanda stares at me for a moment with steam jetting from her nostrils then turns on her heel and leaves the room. I hear her barking instructions at Simon outside, then after a bleat or two from him the car takes off at an alarming pace. I continue breathing with Honeybee. It's obviously taking ages having this baby, but somehow I'm not getting tired or bored. There must be some hormonal or chemical symbiotic thing going on.

Suddenly, there's a screech of tyres, and after a moment, Amanda strides back into the room clutching to her perfectly upholstered bosom something that looks suspiciously like a DVD player. Simon, wearing some remarkably foolish floral Helmut Lang trousers, follows meekly behind. I give him and his floppy fringe a searing glance. The Editor of the London Star isn't nearly as sexy as I remember. Bill could knock him round the block and hang him up by his braces.

I turn to my sister. "What's that, Amanda?"

"A DVD player, of course."

"Where the hell did you get it?"

"I bricked the window of the electronics shop. Simon," she turns and withers him with a glare, "refused to help so I had to do it myself. Oh, don't worry. I left enough cash to pay for it and to have the window repaired. And a little note saying sorry but it had to be done."

"You're barking mad!"

"So what if I am? We've got a television show to film here. I'm not having it fucked up. The shop manager will understand. Now, where are the DVDs?"

"In my bag. It's on the table."

"Where's the computer?"

"Under that blanket. But you'd better get onto Robbo if you want anything like that. He's in the kitchen."

Amanda storms off and I hear her issuing terse instructions. Rob dashes outside to switch on the generator, back inside to set up the DVD player and turn the computer on. In a surprisingly short time, it's operational.

"Cheer up, Honey," I whisper into her ear. "This should cheer you up. Amanda making a complete and utter arse of herself."

"I don't think I want to give birth watching something like that," groans Honeybee. But I notice that she keeps one eye on the screen between contractions. Amanda inserts DVD 1 then stands with arms folded, legs akimbo and with a most unpleasant smile on her face. This is most impressive. Little Miss Love You Too turns into Mizz Evil Slut-Bitch in a few short months. It's a laugh, really. Makes it all seem worth it.

Rob presses PLAY.

CHAPTER TWELVE

In fact, I would secretly have loved to have watched Amanda's DVDs. I really would. Not that I told her that, of course. I wouldn't want to give her the satisfaction. But I was too busy holding Honeybee's hand, rhythmically panting and spraying both our faces with the bottle thingy I keep for the ironing. Amanda, however, watched her own work with a great deal of interest – as did everybody else in the room. Even Mike forgot to keep an eye on what was going on below until Honeybee let out a mighty scream that shook Cobweb Cottage to the rafters and straight back again. Pepys – who had crept out to have a look at Amanda swanning around in my designer clothes - yelped and fled back under the table.

"It's coming! It's coming! I can feel it! Oh! Oh! Christ! Fuck!"

"Don't swear, Honeybee," I say austerely. "It's not good for the baby."

"Fuck you!"

"Just breathe, Hon-bun," intones Mike, fiddling around down there. "It's crowning!" I crane over to have a look at a greasy, damp object protruding from between Honeybee's thighs. It looks terribly big. Oh God. I don't know whether to burst out crying or throw up.

"Quick, Bex!" Honeybee is shouting.

"Quick what? Whaddya want? Water? Some Rescue Remedy?"

"The mirror, of course!"

"Cocaine would not be a good idea right now. On second thoughts, maybe it would."

"What are you talking about, Bex? For God's sake! Pass me the mirror!"

There is, as it happens, a mirror close to hand – almost as if it has been left there on purpose and I pass it. Honeybee tries to hold it near the crowning head, then passes it impatiently back to me.

"Hold it so I can see the head. Quick!"

Suddenly I get it, and I whiz between her thighs and hold the mirror in position. She watches the head, I watch her. The sweat's streaming down her face, the shit has hit the beanbag, it's a nightmare. They should put twelve-year-olds in a labour room. That'd put them off doing the nasty.

"Rebecca! You've got to watch this bit. It's one of the best moments!" That's Amanda, still going on about her blessed DVDs.

"Mands, can't you see I'm holding a mirror for a woman in labour here?"

"I spent *hours* making these fucking things."

"Look, it'll rain fifty pence pieces before you'll catch me watching them."

"Becky, hold her leg up!" says Mike. I hold a gory right leg in the air and shut my eyes. "Rob, support her back!" Rob leaps to Honeybee's back and rather gingerly puts his hands in place. There's a tense moment, with Mike talking Honeybee through an almighty push and suddenly Steve the cameraman, who has moved closer in for the big moment, cries excitedly: "Look out! Here it comes!"

I open my eyes without thinking, there is an amazing slithery moment, and all of a sudden a purple baby –

purple all over – emerges in a gush of blood and other unnameable fluids. The cord, about which I have recently read so much, is surprisingly thick and odd looking. I drop the leg with a shriek.

"I want it to pulsate!" moans Honeybee.

"Don't be obtuse," I snap. "Not to mention obscene."

"It's all right, Becky," says Mike in his best bedside manner. "It's all perfectly normal. Would you like to snip the cord when it's finished pulsating?"

"I would hate it!"

"Oh, go on Bex," says Honeybee who is laughing hysterically, almost drowning out the sounds of Rob cheering, the telephone ringing and Amanda's DVD soundtrack. "Cut the cord! Isn't she beautiful? Isn't she gorgeous?"

Well, of course she isn't, she's hideous, but it's not my place to say so. Mike thrusts a pair of scissors into my hand and I shut my eyes and cut the cord with his fingers around mine. Then it's all over. The baby is whisked by Mike from Honeybee's nether regions to her chest and lies there in a little naked pink bundle. Mike softly covers them both with a folded up sheet. Honeybee still has tears running down her face and Mike is mopping his eyes. I suddenly burst into racking sobs.

Amanda puts her hand over the telephone receiver. "I'm just on the phone," she hisses. "Some bloke about some protest or other. Shall I just tell him to fuck off?"

"No, don't do that. Just get the time and place down and I'll sort it out later. Oh God! Honey! What's the matter?"

"Dad! Dad!" Honeybee has started panting and screaming again. Mike, suddenly very alert, dumps the baby in my arms, leaps to her side and begins to palpate – to use a medical term, as I am now competent to do – her abdomen.

"Okay, Hon-bun. Don't worry. There's another one in there."

257

"What? It's twins? What are you saying! How come you didn't know! AAAARRRGGGHHH!!!"

And it doesn't seem many minutes – turns out it was nine on the nail - before the whole process is repeated once more. I juggle Baby One, Mike fiddles around, the crowning happens all at dizzying speed, Baby Two slithers out.

"Thank God," shouts Mike triumphantly. "She's all right! Three cheers! Wow!"

"Twin girls? I don't believe it!" says Honeybee, looking ecstatic with happiness. Even Amanda has turned the sound down on the DVD player although Simon is still rigidly watching, for it is not every newspaper editor who wants to see a teenager give birth to twins – honest. Both babies are safely cleaned and wrapped up in sheets. Honeybee nurses the younger one, and I gaze into the older's eyes, or where they would be if she would open them.

"They're beautiful," I breathe. "They're gorgeous."

"It must make you feel a bit funny."

"Why?"

"Well, twin girls. Which were you? The older or the younger?"

"The older, of course."

Amanda has crept up behind me, and all of a sudden her hand descends onto the baby's tiny foot and she's stroking it.

"Can I have a cuddle, Becka?"

"Sure." I pass the baby over and Amanda and I sit side by side, gazing at the baby's tiny, crumpled face while the silent DVD plays behind us and Steve creeps round on my left side. For one moment I contemplate making up with my evil twin – but one look at her smiling face changes my mind. It's all for the camera.

"How a human being can change so much in a few short months I will never know," I say conversationally, as if to the baby.

"Are you talking about me?" replies Amanda.

"Of course."

"I always had it in me to be a winner. But because I foolishly cared more about pleasing others than myself, I never exploited my potential. Anyway, you're a fine one to talk. You're unrecognisable."

"Rubbish. I haven't changed one bit. I've simply allowed the warmth of my inner child melt the ice shield I erected to protect myself from pain."

"Don't bore me with the New Age bollocks. You've gone soft – it's as simple as that."

"If that means I'm a decent human being, so be it," I reply decisively.

"If I've changed into somebody who's going somewhere and has the confidence to live life to the full, then so be *it*!" she asserts.

"Okay then. Let's call a truce."

"Agreed. Steve! Get your arse over here. Come on Becka, let's hug."

"Thank you, no."

"This is a beautiful moment," says Rob, solemnly. "I think we should celebrate, don't you? Shall we get out some of Dad's elderflower fizz, 2002?"

"No!" I cry. "Anything but that! I'll go down the offy and get a bottle of champagne. Amanda, you could stay here with... what are you going to call them, Honeybee?"

"Well, I did think that if I had a girl I'd call her Victoria. So the older one can be Victoria. And another girl's name I really love is Sarah. So the younger one can be..."

"Over my dead body!" Midge suddenly appears in the door way with my father bobbing helplessly behind her. "Sarah? Victoria? What kind of middle class, middle-aged, middle of the road names are these? My

259

granddaughters must be individuals! They must express their personalities in their own ways! The name is the portal to conversation, to intimate knowledge, to love. Why can't you call them beautiful names, like..." she hovers over each tiny, sleeping baby. "Like, Sky and Mairwen? Like Ayesha and Opal? Like Rhiannon and Sabra?"

"What a lot of funny names you know, Mum. Do they all mean something?"

"Of course. Amanda! What are you doing here?"

"I'm making a television show."

"Really? Am I looking my best?"

"Mum!" Honeybee grabs Midge's attention back to what is truly important. "I was telling you about the names. Victoria and Sarah mean something too. Victoria means 'victory', so she'll be a winner. And Sarah means, 'princess' in Hebrew. And that's just what she is. So I'm sorry Mum, but that's it."

"You'll regret it, darling."

"I promise you, I won't. Now come and have a look."

Midge goes over and takes Sarah from Amanda's arms. The sight appears to quieten her, and she settles down quite calmly for a cuddle. Something occurs to me.

"Honeybee, how do you know about what names mean? Do you have a book?"

"Yes, it's in my room."

"Do you know what *my* name means?"

"I did look it up, actually. It means a 'noose'."

"That's optimistic."

"Well, more like string. Round wrapping paper. Sort of."

"The ties that bind, like that? Blood is thicker than water?"

"Well, I suppose you could take it like that. Why not?"

"And what does 'Amanda' mean?"

"I looked that up too. It means 'fit to be loved'."

"Oh, right. That's ironic."

Before I can blink, Amanda has seized her opportunity and thrown her arms around me in a last ditch attempt to get the embrace on film. Over her shoulder, I catch a glimpse of the DVD still silently playing. "You cow! You're dripping champagne down my John Galliano dress! My favourite party dress ever! How could you! What are you doing now? My God. I don't believe it. You've spilled it on the rug, now. Do you know how much that rug cost? Or how old it is? Or what part of the world it comes from?"

"Did you get that, Steve? Great." Amanda switches off the computer with a firm finger. "Actually, Becka, no, I don't know anything about your rug. But I'll have it cleaned. Now, didn't you say we should have some champagne? I could send Simon out for it if you like."

"That's okay, I feel like some fresh air."

"I'll drive you myself."

"I'd rather walk."

"Then I'll walk with you. We've got stuff to discuss. No Simon, you stay there and have a cup of tea or something. I don't need you for now. Steve, keep rolling."

Sulkily I agree and we totter off into the night, Steve shuffling along behind at a discreet distance. It isn't too long before I forget him completely, especially as on the way we have a little discussion about the future.

"So, what do you want to do now?" asks Amanda, linking her arm in mine. I equally firmly remove it.

"I don't know. What do you want to do is more like it. I take it you're going to let me have my life back?"

"Well... I suppose so."

"You suppose so? What's that meant to mean?"

"It's a bit tricky, isn't it?"

"Why?"

"Well, my career has really taken off."

"Ideal. I'll take over when *you've* taken off."

"But you're not me."

261

"No, but they think that you're me and that's the next best thing."

"Not really. Face it, Becka, the job is what I've made it. You couldn't have done all the things I've done."

"I question that. But even if I couldn't, I can carry on with them, can't I? I'll just take over from you. They'll think I'm you, and we'll all go on from there."

"You couldn't fool them for a minute."

"What do you mean?"

"Take a look at yourself! You simply are not an urban fox anymore. You're a bit of a mess, quite frankly. And you haven't got a clue what I've been up to. It would take days to fill you in. And all the people I know! It would be a nightmare introducing you to them all without them realising it – not just in this country, but in America and Europe too. And what about Simon? He's linked in with my job. He's my glamorous boyfriend in Sex and No Supermarkets."

"What?"

"Haven't you even heard of my new show? It's a huge hit! It's going over to the US and everything. And there's something else, as well. After this reality show comes out, everybody'll know all about you. There's no way you can pass yourself off as me, so perhaps we could compromise."

"How?"

"Well, you could come and live in my flat..."

"My flat."

"Whatever. We could live together at the flat while you get readjusted to city life, get a haircut and a really good facial, stuff like that. I'll bet you haven't even been waxed for months. We'll get you some new clothes..."

"I'll wear my own, thanks. They're all there."

"That will not be possible. I'm sorry to say, Becka, but to be frank, you've put on weight."

"What? *What?* WHAT?"

262

"You have. Face it. But hey! It suits you! Don't get resentful. You're a new person now! It's just the way it is. I'm a new person too. You think I could come down here and live with people like Mike and Midge?"

"I was planning on it."

"Oh, please! Just so not me any more. No, I think the best thing is for you to come back up to town and live with me. We'll try and carve you out some kind of a little life up there. Perhaps you can be my PA. It'll be fun coming up with a twin sister nobody knew anything about. Of course, you'll have to be known as 'Amanda' from henceforth. Here we are! The off licence! Now. What kind of champagne shall we have?"

"I like that stuff – it's only six quid."

"Get real, Rebecca. We'll have the very best Much Jenner has to offer. I'm paying, of course."

"It's senseless extravagance when there are people starving in the third world."

At this point, there are hasty steps and a tap on my shoulder. I turn round and face an enormous fake fur grape with shiny vine leaves trailing down the sides and a head shaped like a cork with eyeholes in it.

For a moment the shock is too great. So much has happened today. My father. Honeybee's baby. Honeybee's other baby. Amanda. Simon. The DVDs. For a moment I think the strain has all been too much and I have lost my marbles. The world seems to go all hazy for a moment and I have that strange, dreamlike sensation you get when you've had too much vodka and not enough crisps.

"Hi!" says the grape cheerily. "Are you here for the protest?"

"Er..."

"I knew you wouldn't let us down."

The voice sounds familiar, although muffled under the cork and the grape itself seems to be aware of a communication problem, as it raises its arms and begins

263

to tussle with the cork over its head. At last the cork pops off and Bill's amiable face, rather hot and with tousled hair atop, is revealed. I stare in frank amazement, then hastily sneak a peep at Amanda. Saved! She's still looking intently at bottles of champagne, with a distinctly uneasy off-licence owner explaining degrees of brut-ness and fizzability beside her while shooting glances at Bill. He has the restive look of an off-licence owner who prefers his grapes in the bottle rather than bouncing around the shop. Bill attempts to put his arm around me, but the extraordinarily bulbous shape of his costume – which has been padded with no thought to any future world shortage of cotton wool – prevents him, and he has to be content with taking my hand and leading me outside.

Four more grapes, three green and another red, are jumping up and down on the pavement, waving flags and tambourines.

"The costumes are fantastic, Bill! Who made them? I love the vine leaves and the corks are amazing."

Bill beams. "Dawn and Paula were up all night sewing them together, and Pete and I made the corks out of cardboard."

"They're great."

"Your costume is in the car."

"I *beg* your pardon?"

"I didn't realise we were meeting you here. I thought you'd be coming to my house to get changed. I was looking forward to seeing you. I've felt terrible since that phone call."

"I'm sorry too, but Bill, what do you mean, my costume's in the car?"

"Well, it's in the car, of course! A red one. I'll run and get it now. Shame you aren't wearing the green tights, but never mind. You can slip the costume on over your clothes. It doesn't matter if you get a bit hot. All that padding will keep you nice and warm overnight."

264

"Overnight?"

"It's an all night vigil, remember?"

"Of course I remember! But I'm just a bit tired, that's all. When did we talk about this?"

"Becky, are you all right? We talked about it an hour ago! I phoned you just before we set off, first at Irene's but you weren't there, so I thought I'd try Mike's. One of the grapes let us down, so I phoned to see if you would take her place. You took down the time and venue, and here you are. Aren't you happy to be here? Becky?"

"Delighted," I fume. I now realise, of course, that Amanda took the phone call from Bill and didn't tell him that she wasn't me. She's been known as 'Rebecca' for so long now that she would answer naturally to the name, and why should she bother telling some bloke on the phone the reason she sounds exactly like me and answers the phone in the house where I used to live?

Bill takes both my hands in his. "Becky," he breathes. "Let's forget the past. Let's start again. Let's get you into your costume."

I look wildly round for Amanda, but she's at the till. Bill makes a dash for his car, and returns with his arms full of grape. Within a few seconds, I am immersed in fake fur and shiny vine leaves. As soon as my head emerges from the top, a cork is popped on. Bill's right. It's incredibly hot. Still, at least Amanda can't see me in here, but I can see out through the eyeholes. It suddenly occurs to me that I have no idea what we are protesting about. I pick up one of the flags and read the motto as accurately as I can through the cork – it seems to say, "We're Feelin' Vine!" which doesn't tell me a lot.

"The costumes get the message across, don't they?" I venture.

"Absolutely," beams Bill. "I think we'll get some real attention with the all-night vigil."

"Oh yes. You mentioned that. Is that literally, an all night thing? You mean, until breakfast and sunrise and all that?"

"Of course!"

"Right." I say wisely. "I think an all-nighter is better in so many ways. Um, sorry, who did you say we were supporting?"

"WIVES."

"What?"

"The Workers In Viticulture of Europe. We're protesting in sympathy with their outrageous exposure to agri-chemicals and horrendous working conditions. Come on, Becky. Here's a tambourine."

I begin to beat it half-heartedly, but by the time Amanda emerges from the off-licence hotly pursued by the owner, who is very anxious to pull down his metal grill, I am dancing around with the other grapes frankly chanting my stalks off.

"One two three POUR!

A glass of wine is so much MORE!

Five six seven GRAPE!

From chemicals we must ESCAPE!"

The grapes are all bouncing off each other, a crowd is gathering and I hold Bill's hand tightly. Our eyes meet through identical eyeholes. We remove our corks with a pop, gaze into each other's eyes and still chanting, move closer together – craning our necks rather, I have to admit, in order to meet over the costumes.

"One two three POUR!

A glass of wine is so much MORE!

Five six seven..."

"Rebecca!" Amanda snatches the tambourine from my hand, and pulls me sharply away from Bill, who bumps into a green grape and bounces away to the other side of the pavement. "What on earth are you doing?"

"Protesting."

"Come away at once. The police will be here in a minute. Come on!"

"I don't want to."

"Becky! Who's this?" asks Bill, bouncing back off a purple grape and arriving directly in front of us.

"Oh! Bill!" I cry over the uproar. "This is Amanda. Amanda's my sister. This is Bill."

"Hello, Amanda. Gosh! You two look very alike."

"Yes, well, we're twins actually. Identical twins."

"That's great! Where have you come down from, Amanda?"

"London."

"That's quite a way to come to support our protest. We're very grateful."

"I'm not here for any poxy protest! I've come in here to buy a simple bottle of champagne and you people are cluttering up my path. I'll drop my carrier bag in a minute, and then you'll owe me sixty three pounds and ninety nine pence. Come on, Becky. You've got to cut people like this out of your life for ever. I did – and look at me now."

My shoulders slump, and suddenly I feel terribly tired.

"Come on! We'll just go back and wet the babies' heads, then we'll head back to London."

"Are you going to London, Becky?" asks Bill, looking confused as well he might.

"Um…"

"Of course she is," cuts in Amanda. "She's coming back with me. My boyfriend's waiting to drive us up and we'd better get a move on."

It's at this moment that Dawn trundles up. She grabs Bill's hand and gives us both a hard stare. It practically blisters my skin, even from inside her cork. I hear her muffled voice inquiring as to whether "Bill-kins" has finished his "chat as there is serious protesting to get on with." Bill looks at me helplessly. I feel sliced apart with rage. It's the same old story, again and again and again.

"Yes," I say lightly, turning to Amanda. "Let's go."

"Look, I don't know what's going on here," breaks in Bill. "But am I getting this right? Are you planning on leaving, Becky?"

"You always knew I was planning on leaving. And now I've made up with Amanda, there doesn't seem to be any reason not to leave at once, really."

"What about me?"

"I'm sorry. What can I say?"

"You can say that you're staying here."

"There's nothing here for me."

"There's me! I'm here for you!"

"Oh, you've got Dawn." We both look at Dawn and I'm quite sure that inside her cork, she's smirking as hard as a giant grape can smirk.

"I don't want Dawn," Bill whispers tactfully, trying to move away from her vicelike grasp.

"Really?" I don't bother lowering my voice. She's welcome to hear it. "Well, she wants you, and it seems to me that you aren't doing enough to stop her. Anyway, this is all irrelevant. I've got to go. I'm sorry." I turn away, feeling my eyes fill with tears and have taken quite a few steps before Bill calls out.

"Becky!"

"Yes?"

"You can keep the costume."

"Oh. Thanks. Well, it'll always remind me of you."

"Thanks!"

We both try to laugh, but I feel more like collapsing on the ground in tears. At least the grape costume would break my fall. Amanda tugs on my arm.

"Come on, Becka. Let's split."

She hurries me down the street – several times I nearly stop, but Amanda tugs on my arm each time. We get back to the house, where my attire causes some merriment, I may say, although I never felt less like laughing, and after a change of clothes and a rather gloomy glass of expensive champagne each (none for Simon, Amanda decrees, as he's driving), we are ready for the Big Off. Amanda stands impatiently by the door tapping her high-heeled foot and glancing at her watch from time to time, while I make a grand procession around the room hugging and kissing everybody as if my life depended on it. Even Midge gets a reasonably affectionate farewell, and as for Mike! Well. I never thought I'd kiss a beard with such enthusiasm again.

Saying goodbye to Robbo is the worst. Honeybee is clearly upset but is very absorbed in her babies – Rob is desperate. He hugs me for what seems like ever and when we finally break apart he's in tears. No sooner do I see his pink wet eyes than it sets me off and honestly, you won't believe it but it's true, I was never closer to just bawling my head off in public. To cover it up, I mutter something about saying goodbye to Pumpkin and hurry upstairs. First I gather together the few possessions I feel worth exporting from Hippyville to London, then leaving my bag at the top of the stairs, I tiptoe into Pumpkin's room. He's lying in his bed, all warm and pink and gorgeous so heavily asleep, so innocent and so divine that I can't imagine the state of mud and food and mischief he gets into during the day. I hang over him, whispering sweet nothings and dropping tears on his pyjamas until I feel like jumping over a cliff, then leave the room and bump straight into Pepys who has limped up the stairs after me, clearly aware that there is something wrong.

"Oh, Pepys! Pepys!"

I scoop him up into my arms and descend the stairs, my bag bumping on my shoulder, my head aching with the effort not to cry. What's wrong with me? Why is leaving a dog – and a mongrel at that – breaking my heart?

269

With one final hug, I deliver Pepys into Robbo's arms and stand for one more minute in the doorway taking a last look at my family. Well, I can call them my family can't I? Why not? Mike has his arm around Midge, and both of them are trying hard not to look too happy, and Mike, at least, I know will genuinely miss me. Rob's wiping his eyes furiously and Honeybee is looking wretchedly at me over a baby's fluffy little head. Pepys is whining. I take a deep sigh...

"For fuck's sake, Becky. Get a move on!" snaps Amanda.

"Wow, Amanda, you certainly have changed," says Mike, startled.

"I've never seen such a bunch of losers. Let's go."

She wrestles the bag from my shoulder, pushes me before her through the door and before I can say Jumping Jack Johnson, we are speeding through the night to London. Amanda and Simon are in the front, listening to Classics FM in between her taking calls on her mobile. I'm squashed into the back with Dad and some of his bags. Occasionally we look at each other and grimace.

CHAPTER THIRTEEN

"So, Becky. These are your tasks for today."

Amanda speaking – and I haven't even got up yet. After a short and troubled night, I awake in the spare room of my own flat to find my evil twin sister standing over me with her digital organiser and a pad.

"I've got lunch with the people from Channel 4 – but that comes after the interview with Marie-Claire at ten so I'll have to leave here in fifteen. What I need you to do is this. The most important thing is to race to the travel agents – the address is here – and pay for all the tickets to New York. She's holding them until twelve, but not a minute longer so it's absolutely vital. It's tickets for the whole team, including you. So don't miss the deadline. Bring my passport – no, forget that, I can't trust you, I'll take it myself. Just make sure you don't forget yours like the disorganised divot you are. Then go to the dry cleaners – this address - and pick up seven suits. Call Jackie at Meridian to tell her I can't make the 17th. Call High5 PR to tell them that I will be coming to the show at Tate Modern but that I don't know who'll be coming with me – it'll be a celebrity though. Then I'll need you to pick me up from the Channel 4 lunch in the car and take me to Sloane Street where I need my hair done before the party tonight. All the phone numbers and information is here. I'll leave you to it, then."

"Hold on, Amanda. What the hell's going on? I haven't had a cup of tea yet and I don't even know what you're talking about."

"You're my PA, right? Otherwise known as Dedicated Slave. And I need you to jump to it."

"Fuck off."

"Look at you! A big fat slob, lying around in bed when you ought to be out doing deals. I haven't got time for this. If you want to earn some cash, get up and at it. I'm a busy woman these days."

"Where's Simon? I thought *he* was your number one dogsbody."

"Oh, he left at half four for the airport. He's going to New York ahead of me to prepare for the shows. You'll have to book your own ticket, of course, but I'll pick up the tab. And the studio will make sure you get a good hotel room."

"And Dad? Where's he hanging out?"

"Well, I couldn't have him lounging around on the sofa all day. I sent him out for breakfast. You'll find him round the corner if you hurry. And you'd *better* hurry. You've got a lot to do before you earn your salary."

"Yes... about that, Amanda..."

"I'm offering you a very generous amount, you'll find. Quite enough to get you back on your feet."

"But I'm planning on getting a job elsewhere. I can't just trail along in your slipstream."

"That comes as rather a surprise," she says somewhat sarcastically. "You're so unemployable. I really do think you'd be better off working for me for a bit. I mean, I'm going to have to charge you rent, you know."

"It's my flat!"

"You can't afford it."

"Well, whatever, I'm going to try and make it on my own. I don't need you to bail me out."

"Well, it all sounds like a load of half-baked nonsense to me. I've got real work to do – I don't need to hang around listening to wild fantasies. I'll see you later."

And in a swirl of designer scarf and expensive scent, she grabs her passport out of the drawer of the bedside table and she's gone.

The first thing I do is – literally – to wipe my bottom with her list of instructions. I'm very sorry to say that my bad old self resurrected for that one moment of time. After flushing it away, I feel much better. Then after a shower and a root around in Amanda's wardrobe for jeans and t-shirt and making do with a Jean-Paul Gaultier top and Prada hipsters I set off in search of my father. He is, as described by Amanda, 'round the corner' at a table for two, looking gloomily at a plate liberally smeared with ketchup, egg yolk and cooking fat.

"Morning, Dad. You'll kill yourself with crap like that," I greet him seriously. "What are you, the food police? They don't sell tofu and brown rice in greasy spoons."

I pointedly order some toast, brown, no butter. "What's your plan?"

"Well, Toots, I thought I'd go and see your mum and see which way the wind blows there."

"God speed your steps."

"Eh?"

"Good luck, cobber. Do you only speak Australian now?"

"No, no. I just... never mind. So what do you think? Will she have me back?"

"Like a piranha snatches at a finger trailing in the river water."

"You really think so?"

"I do."

"You really, really do?"

273

"I do. I've told you I do. She's crazy about you. I mean, you'll probably be sleeping on the sofa for a few nights, but it'll be okay. I promise."

"Thanks, Toots. I think I'd better get off straight away."

"What, right now?"

"There's no time like the present."

"True."

"Bye!"

And he's off just like that, leaving me to pay his tab, I might add. And that leaves me all alone, sipping weak tea and crumbling dry toast in a greasy spoon south of the river. I've had better days. Suddenly, there's a screech of tyres and a snazzy sports car snarls to a halt outside the café. As a human tornado hurtles through the door and towards me I give a guilty start. Has Amanda realised what I did with her list of instructions?

"Glad to see you finally got out of bed. I forgot to give you money so I've had to come back. I haven't got a minute to spare," she announces briskly, snapping open her handbag. "Where's Dad?"

"Oh, he's gone off to make it up with Mum."

"What a loser."

"They've been married for thirty years."

"I hope she kicks him out on his arse. Men. Only one thing they're good for."

"Sex?"

"No, production of seed. Notice I don't say insemination. A turkey baster does the job with much less fuss. Sex indeed! Most of them are pathetic in bed. After the first flush of passion, I had to take Simon in hand. Quite literally. And show him what to do. Honestly. What are you staring at?" she snarls at the builders at the next table. "You could learn some useful lessons if you listened without that silly sniggering. Now. Becka. We'll have to organise you some credit cards, but in the meantime

274

here's some cash. I should think five thousand will see you through."

"You are joking? Are you seriously going to hand over five thousand pounds in cash in a greasy spoon in front of loads of people?"

"Of course not, you retarded cretin," she yells, snapping the handbag shut again. "Come outside and we'll sort it out in the car. In fact, I'll drop you off at the travel agent's on the way. Come on, for Christ's sake! Move it!"

We race to the car and with a roar and a two-fingered salute to a white van or two we're off.

"Amanda!" I scream. "Slow down!"

"Why?"

"Because you're scaring the shit out of me!"

"Oh, grow up. You know, I used to drive like a mouse waiting for a cataract operation. Now I have fun. Can you guess how much this car cost? Seventy six thousand pounds. No, I'm not joking. You get a lot of muscle for that. Yeah, yeah, fuck you too!"

I sink down into my leather bucket seat and put my sunglasses on with trembling hands. "Amanda, you can't cut people up like that. Those blokes looked pretty hardcore to me. Oh God. What? Are you using your mobile at sixty miles per hour in a 30 miles per hour zone?"

"What are you, my grandmother?"

"No, but you're terrifying me!"

"You used to drive like a fucking maniac!"

"Yeah, but a child could just walk out and... what are you doing now?"

"Getting the cash out for you, of course. We're nearly there."

"Where? Northern Pakistan? We've driven fast enough to make it in the time."

"No, the travel agent's. Here's the cash. Now get out. I'll see you at the airport."

275

"What airport?"

"Christ, don't you listen to a word I say? We're going to New York. Tonight. I'm flying out to film the new series of Sex and No Supermarkets. I need you as my runner. There's a team of twelve flying – oh for God's sake, just get into the travel agency and pay for the tickets. They know all about it. And be at Heathrow at six thirty at the latest. I'll see you by First Class check in."

"We're travelling First Class?"

"Only me. You lot are in Economy. Now fuck off. Leave the tickets at Check In and I'll see you at JFK."

She doesn't actually apply her stiletto-heeled, crocodile-skin, knee-length boots to my backside and push, but the effect is the same. I'm dumped on the pavement like a sack of potatoes, the Porsche is revved like an Apollo Mars mission launch engine and, in a cloud of the proverbial dust, Amanda is history.

What a cow.

Okay, so here I am, with five thousand quid in hand, standing outside a Mayfair travel agency with my whole entire future trembling in the balance. I start looking at posters idly. There's one for my immediate destination, New York, and I've always loved New York. There's also one for Barbados and that's somewhere I've always been interested in spending a month or two. Come to think of it, five grand would see me over to Australia, no make that New Zealand, much classier, and I could start a new life – there are rich men aplenty in grand hotels and millionaires from foreign climes always go mad for my posh voice and classic English rose (with thorns, mind you) look. And I've always trusted in my luck. Besides, Irene can email me my novel and I can work on it in the spare moments I have between going out to dinner and spending the day on some arsehole's yacht.

New York – it's not to be sneezed at, though. I could go there, put up with Amanda for a bit, and carve out a very

276

comfortable niche for myself. Amanda is, although I hate to admit it, a famous and wealthy media star these days, and just a little of her reflected glory – not to mention her contacts – could kick-start a whole new life for me. New York, New York!

Then my roving eye alights on a shabby little poster that's come off its blue tack and slid down the window, landing in a dusty corner and curling up at the edges. The sun hasn't quite faded the picture. Peering closer I see that it's an advert for British breaks, and the image is a tiny cottage with a dear little garden full of lavender and roses. Somebody I love lives in a cottage just like that. Could I pocket the pounds as a sort of peaceful pay off from Amanda for nicking my life, and head back to Much Jenner to find Bill and settle down to growing some serious roots in the middle of nowhere?

It's as I'm pondering these weighty matters that I notice a sturdy looking bloke in black trousers and a Rolling Stones sweatshirt in the window of the Café Nero opposite the travel agency. As soon as I catch his eye, he looks away but too late. It's Steve, Amanda's cameraman. Of course! It's a set up! I'd completely forgotten about the lunatic documentary Amanda's so fixated on. Naturally, Amanda is hoping that I scarper with the money. Great television. Then she can have a good cry for the cameras about her sister and the ultimate betrayal, while the credits roll. Not likely. I'd rather cut my nose to spite my face than let her get one over me. So I stick my nose - securely screwed onto my face - into the air and walk into the travel agency...

Then it's homeward ho! And don't spare the Steve. Poised on the threshold of the agency, I glance theatrically at my watch, toss my hair back over the shoulders and hail a cab. I sneak a glance at Café Nero. Yes, there's Steve, hiding behind his rucksack. I'm sure there's a camera concealed within. I slowly get into the cab, giving Steve all the time he needs, then tell the driver to head back to the flat. I keep a sharp eye out of the back, and sure enough, see a cab following mine. Steve, of course. On arrival, I make sure I leave plenty of time for Steve to film me paying, greeting the doorman and so on – it's quite fun, like being in a film. Well, I suppose I am in a film. Weird.

I make myself a vodka tonic – I'd prefer an energizing carrot, apple and ginger smoothie to be honest but needs must – and wander around, checking out the fabulous views over the Thames, the fantastic designer furniture and all that I used to hold so dear. Not that I'm complaining. I mean, it's all great and if Kate Moss phoned up and asked me to be her new best friend and come to a fashion show with her I wouldn't say no, I think, but it doesn't quite feel like home anymore.

I heave a heavy sigh, drain my drink with a shudder and go to inspect Amanda's – no, actually, my – wardrobe. I'll need something really glamorous where I'm going. It cannot be denied that I have put on a pound or two, but eventually I come across an old black linen Droopy and Browns suit that was always a bit loose on me. I pop it into one of the large, shiny shopping bags that Amanda has lying around along with smart shoes, my makeup bag, passport, a hairdryer and brush. Then I pick up my bag, look around one last time and set out for the airport, Steve hard on my heels.

The cab stops in the drop off area, and I literally throw the money at the man and race in. A backward glance shows that Steve is panicking, fumbling with change and juggling his gear. Now's my chance to lose him. I disappear into the ladies – the one place he can't follow. Now I take my time. I insert myself into the suit and carefully do my makeup and hair in an attempt to look as much like the old me as possible. I have my moments, but in the end, I make quite a good job of it.

Then I burst out of the ladies and set out in search of Steve. I find him, as predicted, at the bar. As I come in, I hear him talking frantically to another man in black trousers and a Glastonbury 99 t-shirt.

"Yeah, no mate. I've got no idea where she is. Give me the slip, didn't she? Could be anywhere. Thank Christ she got here early."

"You're bloody lucky Prize Bitch isn't here, mate."

"Too right, mate."

"But I am here," I snarl. "And I do appreciate my nickname."

Both men jump sky-high and leap round. "Yes," I say, stabbing a finger at their horrified faces. "I'm here, all right. Got here early to check that you were watching my sister like hawks. And what do I find? Slackers! Steve, you're pathetic. If it were down to you, the show would be flushed quicker than a tampon down the toilet. Now. My sister will be at the First Class check in desk. I told her to be there at six thirty at the latest, which means she'll be there a little early – now, in fact. I want you to get right over there and get filming.

"I'm excited to say that there may well be a little twist to the tale. I've got an idea that she's going to pretend to be me, just to cause trouble. Ridiculous, I know, but it'll make great television. Don't mess around, let her know you don't believe her and get her reaction on tape. I'll be lurking around and I'll come in on the scene when the moment's just right.

"Now concentrate, men, because this is where it'll get really exciting. She'll need to show her passport to get through security. But the fun thing is, that she'll have my passport – not her own. The name in the passport will be Rebecca Crisis. And of course, her name is Amanda! So the joke is, once you explain to passport control that she's attempting to impersonate me, she won't be able to fly! Great television, guys, great television."

279

"Yeah, great television!" they chortle, beer-bellies wobbling with glee.

"So – go to it! And one little tip, don't call me Prize Bitch again. Not if you don't want me to castrate you and consume your testicles with a glass of fine wine having simmered them in cream and a selection of garden herbs. Is that clear?"

"Yes Miss Crisis."

"Then off you go."

Really, I feel quite maternal as I see Amanda's team trotting off to First Class Check In. I feel as if I've given birth to the mother of all airport scenes. I'll be surprised if the terrorist squad aren't involved. Then, with a happy sigh, I turn away towards the taxi rank. I have things to do. And someone to see.

CHAPTER FOURTEEN

With almost five thousand in my handbag and a craving for passionate kisses as soon as technically possible, given the rules of time and space, I flag down a taxi wishing it had wings and could fly me to the countryside. I'm so happy that even the little Christmas tree air freshener above the 'Please Don't Smoke' sign doesn't make me foam at the mouth with rage. Come to think of it, I've quit smoking, anyway. I can't imagine why I ever wanted to poison myself like that. Drinking, too. And drugs. Who needs them? I'm high on life! Surfing on a wave of euphoria, I lean forward and inform the taxi driver, such a lovely man, that we are all free to feel good. And I'm so grateful that he is kind enough to provide customers, like me, with a nice smoke-free zone. He gives me a big, big smile in return and starts telling me all about his three-year-old. So I tell him all about Pumpkin. Why didn't anybody ever tell me before that if you share happiness, you get more happiness back? The journey passes in a happy dream. I'm on my way home to the man I love. All I need is a classical music soundtrack.

Who cares that the journey costs sixty quid? I tip the man twenty and remind him not to spend it all in one place. Then with his cries of joy echoing in my ears, I lug my bags up the little garden path and go to knock on the door, which is ajar and swings open at the slight pressure. I call, but nobody replies. He must be in. Still in bed perhaps? I'll creep up and surprise him.

I tiptoe into the sitting room and dump my bags in breathless silence – and then I see it. Dawn's purple sweater. It's lying on the floor by the sofa, partially concealed by a dropped cushion.

If you've ever heard of hair standing on end and cold shivers running up and down the spine, it's all true. It can happen. And more. My blood runs cold and my heart stops and my liver palpitates and all sorts of other horrid things unite to make me feel like fainting or fighting gorillas or something else very dramatic.

Up to now, all I have been thinking about is flinging myself into Bill's arms. But now a horrific vision fills my entire being. I left him completely gutted outside the offy last night, with Dawn. I'll bet that her idea of comforting him was to sneak home with him for the classic sympathy shag. That would be so like her. To get a man when he's down. But it's so like Bill, too, to give into her pressure.

If it's true, I have to find proof. I glance around. The cushions on the sofa are all squashed in a loathsome parody of sensuality. Oh God. Snogging on the sofa before going upstairs, clearly. I slip into the kitchen - there I find not one, but two used cups on the sideboard, one with a trace of mauve lipstick. Double – nay, triple - God! I know it. I just know it in my poor wounded, vengeful heart. They're in bed together, upstairs. In his bed. The bed I have never seen. Well, the pretty pair will live to regret their little lie-in.

All Much Jennerites have compost buckets, and grimly I grab Bill's from its position by the back door. The contents are already looking pretty nasty, but they could be worse. I add two pints of milk, a can of lager, a tub of organic yoghurt, nine eggs and some washing up liquid.

Bucket in hand, I silently creep up the stairs and gently open the first door I see. A bathroom. Then what is obviously a spare bedroom. Then a box room. The last door is pushed closed and I lurk outside it for a moment or two, until I have identified the rumbling noise within as Dawn snoring. Bill couldn't snore. Other than shagging Dawn, he's perfect. Then, with a gigantic cry of "Die, you cheating bastards!" I kick the door open and hurl the contents of my vat of doom over the bed.

Obviously my eyes are misted over with rage, but I am speedily aware of something rather peculiar. Something has sat up, indeed, but not a human being. It's a large object... it's a large round object... it's a grape. Actually, Bill still in his grape costume but without the cork over his head - and he's alone. Well, he has to be. There's only room for one giant grape even in a double bed.

"What? What's going on?" he groans, rubbing his face with his hand, then drawing it away and looking with astonishment at the disgusting mixture with which it is besmeared.

"Where is she then?" I cry.

"Who?"

I pounce to the built in cupboard and fling it open. A football, two cricket pads and a brilllantly patterned sweater fall on my head. I plunge to the floor and closely inspect the situation under the bed. A suitcase and a million dustballs meet my eye. I put my hands on the edge of the bed and look up into Bill's puzzled face, beautiful to me although covered with slops.

"Are you alone?" I falter.

"Of course I am. Are you back?"

"Of course I am."

"But what about London? What about your glamorous lifestyle?"

"Nothing without you."

283

"But you said that money mattered so much to you! And I've got so little."

"I don't want it."

"You don't?"

"No."

"Really?"

"Really."

"But what about this place? You've always said you've hated it."

"Well, for some strange reason, I now think it's a little paradise on earth."

"The people..."

"Charming. Look how they rallied around about Pepys."

"The shops..."

"Who needs designer clothes when you can stock up on organic parsnips?"

"The school..."

"The very place to send our five children."

"Becky!" He opens his arms for an embrace.

"Er – I'd love to, I mean, we ought to get started on those children as soon as possible... but you're a bit slimy, aren't you?"

"What is all this stuff?"

"Oh, that. Yes. Well. I slipped. And the bucket fell out of my hand."

"What bucket?"

"Your bucket. The bucket I was carrying."

"What on earth was in the bucket?"

"Well, to be honest with you, I was going to feed the pigs."

"But I haven't got any pigs. I've got four bantams, but no pigs."

"Oh yes, the bantams. That's right. I was going to feed them and I thought they deserved a special treat, but then, as I say, on my way to the bathroom to add some toothpaste so that they could have some fluoride for the better development of their... erm... beaks, I fell and the bucket with the hens' breakfast unfortunately fell on you. But anyway," I add hastily, "what happened to you last night? After I left, I mean."

"After I gathered together the broken pieces of my heart and found the strength to stagger on without throwing myself under a bus?"

"Yep."

"We got a few bottles of wine and I got completely pissed."

"You were meant to be protesting about the wine from that off-licence! I was there!"

"Well, I know. It's not good. I admit that we shouldn't have drunk it. Especially me, but I was depressed. We all got pissed and stuck it out until about three, then Susan was sick and we called it a night. Dawn got me home..."

"Hah!"

"Sorry?"

"Nothing. Go on."

"She made us a cup of coffee and then she asked to stay the night. In fact, she started trying to get me out of my grape costume. And I told her in no uncertain terms where to go."

"You did?"

"And then she told me that I could shove my grape costume where the sun don't shine. And I said that that was fine by me, because she was never going to get close to that general area in a thousand years."

"You should have said a million. A million zillion."

"You're right. I should have. And then I said that I loved you, and always had done."

"You said you loved me?"

"Like a steam train, and she stormed off into the night and I passed out on my bed. And while I have had better awakenings before, and I do have a terrible hangover, and the smell of... um... hens' breakfast in here is truly awful –

285

I'm happier than I've ever been. Becky, will you marry me?"

The perfect venue, a divine dress, soft breezes, a full moon and all the trimmings are probably incorporated in your dreams of the proposal scene that will fix your affections for ever. Here in the real world, I looked at my Bill, a giant grape in an untidy bedroom covered in kitchen waste, and it couldn't have been a more perfect moment.

"Yes," I said softly. "I will. But if you don't mind, we'll seal it with a kiss *after* you've had a long bath."

THE END

POSTSCRIPT

WELL HEELED TERRORIST GETS THE BOOT AT HEATHROW *by Garth Williams, the London Star's man at Europe's busiest airport*

The anti-terrorist squad was called in yesterday at Heathrow airport after a suspected militant was arrested by airport police following a tense scene at First Class Check In.

The suspect, a woman who appeared to be in her late twenties, attempted to board flight NY932 to New York without a ticket and using a stolen passport.

HIGH KICKS
Trouble began when friends of the genuine passport holder confronted the woman, described by bystanders as 'smartly dressed'. Security was called and she became hysterical, claiming that a 'sister' had 'stolen her identity'.

When she threatened airport staff and attempted to kick box her way through onlookers, police were called and an arrest was made.

The anti-terrorist squad was drafted in when an eagle-eyed airline representative voiced her concerns that the woman had intended to hold the aircraft hostage using her boots, which featured an exceptionally long stiletto heel, as weapons.

Witnesses reported that the suspect had threatened to 'burst the flight attendant's fakies' using the heels. The remark alerted hostess Cheryl Saunders to the possibility of a serious in-flight situation.

WHAT THE HEEL'S GOING ON

"I was very concerned," said Cheryl Saunders, 42. "I like high heels as much as the next woman, but those boots were unusual. I've never seen such high, sharp protuberances. I wouldn't want them in my cabin."

The suspect had to be sedated before being removed from the scene strapped to a stretcher, but no bystander was seriously hurt. She was later arrested and taken into custody. No bail has been granted.

TROUBLE AFOOT

Chief Inspector Alan Hayes commented: "I would warn members of the public to be vigilant. If you have any suspicions, make them known to persons in authority. I would commend Miss Saunders for her prompt action in identifying a stiletto heel as a potential deadly weapon.

"And for the future, I would advise female members of the public to travel in flat footwear."

Printed in Great Britain
by Amazon.co.uk, Ltd.,
Marston Gate.